Praise for
KATHLEEN EAGLE

"Kathleen Eagle is an author without peer."
—*New York Times* bestselling author Tami Hoag

"A compelling story...
This rich tale shows how love can unite very
different people in deeply satisfying relationships."
—*Sunday Chicago Times* on *The Night Remembers*

"Readers will enjoy Eagle's romantic tale about long-
postponed passion and long-kept family secrets."
—*Booklist* on *The Last True Cowboy*

"Kathleen Eagle is a national treasure."
—Bestselling author Susan Elizabeth Phillips

"Readers who liked *The Horse Whisperer* will love this
contemporary boots-and-saddle romance."
—*Publishers Weekly* on *The Last True Cowboy*

"Clean prose, a clear sense of time and place,
and realistic, multidimensional characters
[create] a poignant and unforgettable tale
that transcends the type."
—*Library Journal* on *What the Heart Knows*

"Filled with 100 years of Native American history,
this unique read weaves the magical world of love
with the realities of life, past and present. Ms. Eagle
is as comfortable in this century as she is in the last.
Her characters are as real as her talent! A timeless
tale from an unrestricted talent!"
—*Literary Times* on *Fire and Rain*

A VIEW *of the* RIVER

KATHLEEN EAGLE

MIRA®

ISBN 0-7783-2098-7

A VIEW OF THE RIVER

www.MIRABooks.com

Printed in U.S.A.

ACKNOWLEDGMENTS

This story was inspired by my visits to Linden Hill in Little Falls, Minnesota, which was built by lumber barons Weyerhaeuser and Musser in the late nineteenth century. The estate, donated to the community by the last Musser heir, is a beautiful conference and retreat center and was the setting for my younger son's Valentine's Day wedding. I am indebted to Linden Hill's gracious hostess and manager, Susan Haugen, for making that day and many more so special.

For Christopher and Micah,
in celebration of their marriage
and
to honor the memory of my favorite aunt,
Margaret Garner Lennon

Prologue

Rebecca was dressed for drowning.

Anyone who might intrude on her would be surprised to find her seated before the vanity mirror, all done up. Anyone who did not know her—and almost no one did—would assume that she had taken the odd notion to join the party, that she was ready to soon descend the paneled staircase, choose a partner among her sister's guests and dance the night away. But there was nothing so frivolous in her choice of layered crinoline and satin. A thick wool cape lay across the bed, and her winter boots stood nearby in testimony. Rebecca would soon be going out.

She could delay no longer. The advent of winter was too unpredictable in this godforsaken place. The cheerless season had already begun to press the day into a few gray hours, to squeeze Rebecca's mind, freeze her feet, grind her joints and bind her muscles. Soon she would be powerless to free herself.

But not yet.

Her heart pounded, pressured by the thrill of self-determination. She could still make a choice for herself, still act on it. She was, for this one night, in control of something. A small thing, her life, but something truly in her hands, at least for tonight.

Her sister's annual harvest party had started with a musical flourish, but Rebecca would not be missed. Nor would she be missed from her sister's house unless the baby woke up and managed to make his voice heard. Taking pen in hand, she imagined Rose's lithe fingers dancing over the piano keys, ivory on ivory, delighting her guests with her own clever arrangement of lively ragtime tunes.

Dearest Sister,

Be brief, she told herself as she dipped into the inkwell. A guest's poor attempt to sing might prompt Rose to decide to come looking for her. Rebecca had not sung in years—not since she had left the warmth and sunshine of New Orleans, where there had been something to sing about. No wonder

the new-sprung Mississippi rushed headlong past
this grand misfit of a house on its way to the South.

> Winter is coming. I feel my humor declin-
> ing by the hour. I am forbidden all company
> that gives me pleasure except yours. I cannot
> continue to live this way, but after giving a
> great deal of thought to the problem, I find
> myself at a complete loss for any other way to
> live. And so I am content to seek the alterna-
> tive. I have puzzled for some time over the
> questions of time and means. For a few hours
> I thought giving birth would kill me, but un-
> fortunately, it did not. A fat lot of pain wasted,
> if you ask me.

Rebecca smiled at the shadow she cast over the
paper. Slight and fair, she appeared to be the more
fragile of the two sisters, but she had a strong body.
Sadly, weakness prevailed in her mind and will.

> Only God knows why I am cursed with a child
> and he with me. It does not take a sane mind
> to breed, but a woman ought to have her wits
> about her for mothering, as you and I well
> know. I leave the whelp in your capable hands,
> sister, for he is the child you were meant to

have. If this was the purpose for my existence—and I can think of no other—then it is fulfilled. Please, may I be excused now?

A wave of nausea precluded her from signing any more than an *R*. With a clammy hand, she carefully placed the pen in the inkwell tray. She did not look forward to the act itself. She had to think past it. Better yet, she had to stop thinking and simply move along with her plan, taking her cue and her direction from the river. She would depend on the river to deliver her.

She opened the window, dropped her cape onto the roof below, pulled the back of her skirt between her legs and secured it to her waist. Cautiously, she climbed from sill to ledge to jutting roof. It would not be long before the cold air woke the baby, even though she had swaddled him in warm wool. With her last breath, she would will him to survive and live well.

At the edge of the second-story eave, she enlisted help from the Woman Tree, making a practiced descent along the forked trunk until her right foot found secure perch in the tree's crotch. Shifting her weight onto her left hip, she found the navel knot with the toe of her left boot, stretching her own birthing-battered crotch almost unbearably.

Like the tree, whose human features she and her sister had discovered together, she bore abuse with hushed horror.

Look, Rosie, doesn't this look like a woman standing on her head? Look at her from this angle. See? The roots look like a woman's hair spreading over the ground.

Her sister was dubious, as always. Rose had never been able to do a handstand the way Rebecca could, not even when they were girls, and she would never wear men's pants or tie her skirts up for fun. But Rebecca did. Rebecca was a woman like no other. Rose was a lady, like many others. For Rebecca's sake, Rose had relented and tipped her head. Yes, that could be a face at the base of the tree, the eyes there, and there the mouth, laughing or screaming, with no sound coming out.

And these gnarly bumps—one breast hanging a little lower than the other, the nice deep navel here. And look at the way she's spreading her legs for God! No, it isn't lewd or disgusting. Why wouldn't God make love to a tree?

Because trees are trees, and God is God.

And Rose has no imagination. Rock-a-bye baby, in the treetop. Look at her slim hips and her strong thighs, Rosie. If God felt like having an earthy, pas-

sionate, sexual experience, He would choose that tree. I'm sure of it.

The memory sent Rebecca fairly skipping through the wet grass. She avoided the garden paths, even though she knew she could not be seen from the brightly lit windows on this moonless night. The music had stopped. Guests were taking their places for dinner. Martin Bruner's business associates would find their place cards on the dining-room table, while Rose's book-club friends would dine on the River Porch. Sometime between dinner and the return to music and dancing, Rose would send a plate of food upstairs for her sister. By that time, food would no longer be necessary.

Cupid's Bench was Rebecca's favorite place in the gardens. Perched just above the rocky shoreline, the massive stone bench was her place to have her communion with the river. Night was the best time, when the lumber mills on the opposite shore were hardly visible. Summer voices had gone dormant, all but one. The baby's dreaded bleating came sooner than expected.

Rebecca found a large rock for every pocket in her cape, then sat down to put her boots on and partake of her last rites. The outward, visible sign—the river's soft gurgle and sweet eddy—assured her of inward, invisible grace. No more long winters. No more desperate, impossible liaisons. No uninvited child to tend. Rebecca would wrap herself in the river and ride its currents home.

Mary clutched one child in her arms and shouted the other's name. The baby bleated like a terrorized lamb. Mary's father had gone back into their burning cabin for little Trueblood, and neither of them had reappeared. "Help us," she pleaded, reaching for her neighbor as he hurried past her with a bucket of lake water in each hand. "They haven't come out yet!"

"Stay back, Mary!" Arlin shouted, sparing a glance that his tired, tearing eyes could ill afford. "Take the baby and run!"

"That's your uncle in there, Arlin. Can't you try the back door?"

Backpedaling, water sloshing over his boots, Arlin had the dazed look of a lost soul. "It's all going to burn!"

"Let the houses go," Mary pleaded. Surely the man could see that his efforts to douse the flames were useless. The loss of their homes was nothing new for the Ojibwe people, but the loss of a man's sense of what he had to do was unnerving to a woman of clear vision.

See to the children and the elders, you crazy man.

"Here, hold the baby," Mary persisted as she shoved her bundled daughter against her befuddled cousin's chest. "I'll get them out myself."

"Stay back," the big man ordered, backing away from the proffered howling baby. One bucket slipped from his hand and landed on its side in the dry grass. "Who are they to tell us we cannot live where we have always lived? We are so few, and they—" He flung the other bucket toward the house with a furious howl. "They have no right!" he shouted as he ran toward the back of Mary's house.

They were the white sheriff and his men, and they came to the village many times to deliver paper demands from this one and final notices from that one—the Minnesota governor, the army, the department in Washington—all strangers to the people of Chief Wadena's small village on the lake. This time the sheriff and his posse had brought guns instead of paper, and fire instead of words.

There were so few of them left on the wooded south shore of Mille Lacs, where earthen mounds and burial grounds stood witness to their timeless occupation. Most of the people had yielded to the whites' demand for their relocation, but Mary and her relatives had stayed. Wadena, one of their leaders, insisted that no response was warranted. Saying nothing, they would neither move nor be moved.

There was no stopping the white men from doing as they pleased, Wadena told his people, but surely they could take all they wanted without bothering to bodily lug fewer than a hundred Ojibwe holdouts all the way to the northwestern corner of the state.

It was not the Ojibwe themselves the whites had come to remove, but as much of their property as would fit into the wagons the sheriff's men had brought to the village. He had ordered the winter cabins dismantled, and while the people watched, the logs from some of the roofs had been pulled down and tossed in a pile. It was a strange bit of business. The Ojibwe didn't know what to think. They had not anticipated the torching, and when the first kerosene-drenched rags were set aflame, they stood momentarily dumbfounded, as though the white men had come to entertain them with fire.

But a sudden move from Wadena caused a flurry of activity. "Watch them!" the sheriff shouted as he clapped Wadena in irons. "You people stay away from any weapons!"

Arlin and a few others had gone for buckets and cook pots instead.

Now Arlin staggered forth just as Mary's home caved in on itself. But she gave a joyous squeal. A squirming, slippery prize, little Trueblood was unceremoniously dropped at his mother's feet by his exhausted deliverer, who retained his hold on a small coat sleeve.

The boy tried to shake him off. "He won't get up," Trueblood sobbed, clutching his grandfather's medicine bundle close to his chest. "Grandfather won't get up."

"'We will not be moved,' he said." Gulping several breaths, Arlin shook his head. "His legs were broken, Mary."

"Better than his spirit." Her teary gaze followed the smoke that carried her father into the purpling sky. "They cannot deny us that."

Chapter One

Little Falls, Minnesota, present day

Rochelle smelled grass burning somewhere in the cold night. And it was no ordinary Kentucky Blue.

The light was still on in Aunt Meg's bedroom window, even though she had sworn that she was too tired to eat or bathe or brush her teeth before going to bed. But it was just the two of them at Rosewood tonight, and somebody was burning something. It wasn't Rochelle. In her condition, Aunt Meg was liable to set her precious old mansion on fire. Hadn't she had enough *smokus pokus* for one day?

Rochelle hated to go back inside. She had just gotten comfortable on the stone bench overlooking the river, tucking herself in a blanket to keep the early-autumn chill at bay while she listened to the water lap against the rocks below. She loved this time of year in this place she would always call home. She particularly loved to wrap herself in the seclusion of this tranquil spot at the edge of the gardens and dream, especially after a day of being painfully nice to some very strange people and an evening of tallying the columns in all-too-familiar books. What a pleasure to count stars for a while instead of pennies!

The granddaughter of Minnesota lumber baron Martin Bruner, Aunt Meg didn't know how to be anything but wealthy. But the Bruner money no longer grew on trees, and Rochelle had all she could do to keep the two roofs of Rosewood over the old woman's head. The Bruner estate had been named for Great-grandmother Rose, Martin's *beloved* wife. *Dear* wife. *Precious* wife. During the years that had passed between her death and his, the terms of endearment had been applied with such consistency that even now the name *Rose* or the words *Martin's wife* were never spoken at Rosewood without one of his favorite qualifiers.

The rambling vestiges of Bruner family life on the upper Mississippi—a far cry from Mark Twain territory in almost every way imaginable—were all Aunt Meg had left, whether she realized it or not. From all indications—the variety of books shelved in every room in either house, the music, the letters from prestigious acquaintances—Margaret Bruner had been a woman of independent thought in her day, if not independent means. As near as Rochelle could tell, she had not spent money so much as she had donated it. She had given it away hand over fist, which was fine. It was her money.

But Rochelle would not allow the houses to go before Aunt Meg did. Now, as the threat of fire smelled more imminent than bankruptcy, Rochelle dragged herself off the bench, tossed a corner of the wool blanket over her shoulder and trudged up the gravel path toward the "new" house, the home Martin Bruner had purchased from his partner for his only son, Ernest, who had enlisted in the army against his father's wishes in 1941 and gone missing somewhere in France. Ernest's wife had then gone missing somewhere in Chicago. Family tradition, the old woman was wont to say without elaborating, but Rochelle imagined two poor little rich girls who would one day be her mother and aunt left to rattle around Rosewood with their grandfather and his household staff.

Aunt Meg had modernized the new house when she'd taken charge after her grandfather's death in the early 1950s, but she had not seen fit to change much since that time. Its dark green siding and *Father Knows Best* furnishings were right in style with the current retro craze. But for the main house, dear

Rose had known best. It remained white. Inside, Martin Bruner had kept every stick of dark wood, every scrap of Victorian wallpaper, every glass lampshade and every bit of embroidered linen, the way his precious wife had left it. The main house was perfect for the business Rochelle was now struggling to establish in what had become an out-of-the-way town after its single industry had dried up. And the new house was perfect for preserving two generations of girlish daydreams.

"Aunt Meg, is everything all right?"

"Some things are. Some aren't." The old woman turned from the window, lifting her chin to welcome the sound of Rochelle's voice even before she angled the wheelchair for a frank look. "I'm feeling restless. It's still too early in the season to turn the heat on, but the night's chill has a way of sinking into dry old bones. I feel old and cold, and that makes me restless."

"This is what you used to call good sleeping weather, isn't it? Are you burning something in here?" She'd lost track of the smell, but she scanned the room for other signs.

"After I caught hell for burning a few little candles the other night? I should say not."

"It was only because you fell asleep."

"Oh, yes, that's right. You said something about a warning label. Everything comes with a warning these days. Be afraid, they say. Be very afraid. But technically, they weren't burning unattended. I was only half asleep."

"And you only caught half a hell." Rochelle smiled as she claimed the window seat—her own special place in her aunt's bedroom ever since she could remember—putting them knee to knee and eye to eye. "I was outside, sitting by the river on Cupid's Bench, and I'm sure I smelled grass or incense—something was burning. If I didn't know you better, I'd swear you were up here smoking a joint."

"Do you smell anything now?"

Rochelle diffidently lifted one shoulder, easy with being quizzed. Looking after the woman she had looked up to all her life felt awkward at best. She wanted her old role back.

"It must have been from before," Meg said absently, turning her attention beyond the window, into the darkness.

"But they've been gone for hours." Worried about coming across as a cynic rather than a bemused skeptic, Rochelle had carefully avoided the odd group of women who had spent the weekend at Rosewood. She didn't want to make the Daughters of Earth feel uncomfortable. They were good for several weekend retreats a year.

"Some of them have been gone years," Meg mused. "Centuries. But I sense their presence more all the time—those who were here before our time."

"What are you saying, Aunt Meg? Be—"

"Afraid," the old woman chimed in, a sign that she was, in Rochelle's mind and much to her relief, back from beyond. Smiling at each other, they chanted in unison, "Be very afraid."

"But you're not," Rochelle said.

"Of course not. They've done no harm yet, and I don't expect them to start now. Do you?"

"Oh, Aunt Meg." Rochelle laughed and shook her head. "I don't know what to say to you on that score."

"Then don't say anything. I don't want you to start patronizing me in my dotage, dear girl. I never patronized you, did I?"

"You never treated me like a child, even when I was one."

"You've always been a worthy companion, no matter what your age. Age is nothing, Shelly. An open mind is ageless and boundless, you know. You've never been stingy with your views, and I've never been offended by them. So feel free to say what's on your mind. After all, to say a thing is or is not doesn't make it so."

"What about seeing it or not seeing it? Doesn't that make a difference?"

"I have a friend who is blind. She sees nothing through her eyes. Does that mean we're all invisible?"

"She can feel our physicality," Rochelle reasoned.

Dim lamp light softened Aunt Meg's crafty smile. "And you smelled their *scent*-sitivity."

"I smelled *something*," Rochelle admitted. "It was real, though, really in the air—right now, tonight. *In the moment,* as they say. Clear and present smell, and that's all I know for sure. Whether one of our weekend guests was still lurking in the bushes, I couldn't say, but I do know that I saw every one of them off with a very polite smile—even that crabby old Marilee."

"I'm sorry that woman turned out to be such a poop," Aunt Meg said with a sigh. "When she approached me about offering her program at Rosewood, she seemed pleasant enough, and the topic sounded interesting—finding your creative spirit."

"That's the way I worded the announcement, but I now stand corrected. Repeatedly. The title was The Road To Creativity—Getting Acquainted With Your Spirit Guides."

"She certainly turned out to be a sour soul, didn't she? Ariel's friends seemed to take her in stride, but I think Ariel's right. We need to purge the grounds of her bad vibes. Although, if you're smelling something burning, maybe the spirits have already taken care of it."

"Ariel!" Rochelle wagged an *aha* finger. "She must be burning some of her herbal delights."

"Oh, no, she went home earlier. I spoke with her on the phone a few minutes ago. We're going to have a ceremony as soon as she can arrange something."

A warning light flashed in Rochelle's mind. "What kind of a ceremony?"

"We'll see what Ariel can come up with," the old woman said with a shrug. "A cleansing ceremony. The road to the spirit guides runs right through Rosewood, and I don't want it littered with bad vibes."

"You made another donation to the Indians at Mille Lacs, didn't you?" Rochelle surmised.

"A very small one."

"Aunt Meg, you have to consult with me first," Rochelle pleaded. But her aunt looked away. She was a proud woman, unaccustomed to being on the receiving end of a consultation, and Rochelle wasn't taking well to the giving end. "Or at least tell me right away so I can—"

"Five thousand for a new display at the museum. That's all." She lifted her hand, gnarled fingers splayed. "Five thousand. And it's all tax deductible."

Rochelle nodded. No use scolding the woman. After sisters Margaret and Selena had inherited the Bruner fortune, each one had practiced her own method of relieving herself of the burden of wealth. Rochelle's mother had spent hers on old wine, new clothes, young men and unreliable advice. She had been the proverbial prodigal daughter. Rochelle always believed that the woman had lived and died exactly the way she chose.

Aunt Meg, on the other hand, had given much of hers away. She had supported fledgling artists, talented prodigies and gifted scholars, particularly those whose eligibility for funds was tacitly undermined by their gender or race or some other fact of life that should not have put them at a disadvantage. But Margaret Bruner understood that it did. She invested in the "underfunded," as she called them—both people and programs—with her mind and her money. She would not say *heart,* which sounded too much like charity.

When she had divested herself down to the two old Victorian mansions, their contents and the grounds, her own heart revealed its frailty. She claimed to be experiencing her mother's "spells," and her doctors agreed that she was in trouble. The summer Rochelle had planned to spend taking care of her had turned into more than a year spent devising ways to stall off selling the property and thereby save her aunt's peace of mind. She had agreed to take charge of the bookkeeping in return for Aunt Meg's consent to a business experiment, "just for fun." Rochelle's claim that teaching in Minneapolis had become increasingly difficult and proportionately less fulfilling was true—talk about underfunding... No, she could not talk about it, not with Aunt Meg. Any more donations and she would be out in the street.

She was also unwilling to admit that she didn't intend to give up entirely on her career as a teacher and become a full-time innkeeper. If Rochelle could get the business started, she hoped that Ariel might be able to keep it running. In fact, the promise of keeping Ariel on the payroll was the best part of Rochelle's pitch. While Aunt Meg couldn't imagine doing without her housekeeper and personal assistant, she already suspected that Ariel had cut her own wages. If she found out that she had nothing left to give away, Aunt Meg might well decide that her job was done and that it was time to join her invisible grass-burning friends in the next life.

But Rochelle was not ready for that to happen.

"Do we have any bookings for the first week in November?" Aunt Meg couched her surprising question in a casual tone. She rarely asked about bookings. It was understood that hosting guests in her home for money was fundamentally distasteful to her, and so they spoke little of the details of the business or the necessity to make it work.

"They normally taper off around then."

In fact, they had no bookings for November. Or December.

"What about the writers' retreat we talked about? It's so peaceful here. You promised me that we'd be hosting artists and writers and musicians if we opened our home for these so-called retreats. So far it's been bankers, salesmen and Ariel's interesting but half-a-bubble-off-plumb friends."

"So you're not really buying into that stuff?"

"I'm not buying into *their* stuff, Shelly. I have my own ideas, my own *stuff*. Look around you, dear." Her sweeping gesture directed her niece's attention to a fraction of the book collection she housed at Rosewood. "There's a lifetime of study on these bookshelves. My lifetime, and my studies. I didn't suddenly notice this aging face in the mirror one day and start hatching reassuring notions about the spirit world."

"I know that, Aunt Meg." She also knew that the woman had read every book on the premises and loved nothing more than a lively discussion of any idea they might contain. "And we do have the Midwest Ghost Photography Association booked again for next spring, which should lift your spirits."

"Indeed." Aunt Meg smiled, leaving Rochelle to wonder what her knowing look was all about.

Sometimes it was better to wonder than to ask. All too often the *knowing* was really an invitation to one of those lively discussions, which could be exhausting. Rochelle couldn't remember a time when she hadn't longed to impress Margaret Bruner with an original thought about some enduring question. She continued to come up short, probably because her curiosity only stretched so far. Beyond earth, flower, river or bird in the bush, Rochelle was on shaky ground. And like most Midwesterners, she didn't much like shaky ground.

"Don't you think our ghosts would appeal to writers?" her aunt persisted.

"I'm working on it, Aunt Meg. It seems that writers would rather retreat to places like Hawaii or southern California. Minnesota isn't top on the re- treat list."

"Not even in the fall?"

The disappointment in her aunt's voice was enough to send Rochelle out on a writer hunt. "Maybe if we—"

"I'm sure a painter would be enchanted by the way the spiritual presence in the garden enhances the fall colors. Your great-grandmother was a wonderful painter, you know. What do they call those photographs with the showers of colored lights?"

Trick photography, Rochelle thought, but she said, "Orbs?"

"The orbs are the circles—those wonderful white bubbles. But the colorful shower of tiny lights that shows up in some of the pictures taken in the garden would surely inspire a lovely watercolor."

"And we could call it The Thousand Points of Light in Rosewood's Bushes."

"Oh, Shelly, we used to have wonderful parties here when I was a girl," Aunt Meg enthused without so much as a chuckle for Rochelle's show of wit. "I would invite people I'd met in New York. Van played the grand piano in the music room. Chloe Finch read her poetry on the river porch. Oh, there were some whispers about town when Marian Adams visited. In those days, you know, people raised a fuss when I entertained people of color, but I didn't give a fig for that kind of attitude. And, oh, that woman had the voice of an angel."

"You were a generous patron of the arts, Aunt Meg."

"As I see it, that's our job. What did I do to deserve all this money? I was born a Bruner. My only gift is in recognizing the gifts of others. Grandfather didn't always approve, but he indulged me. And when he died, well..."

"You went all out."

"Those are the people we must bring to these retreats of yours, Shelly. I want you to enjoy the company of gifted people." She patted Rochelle's knee. "Not that you aren't gifted yourself, my dear, but mixing with interesting and talented people helps us develop our gifts. I've gained far more than I could ever give, and so will you."

"You had a reason for asking about the first week in November?"

"Oh, yes." She took a pale blue envelope from the pocket of her robe. "I have a letter from your sister."

"Crystal wrote you a *letter?*"

"She's getting married again."

"Really." That her older sister would remarry was no surprise, but it was the kind of news Rochelle would expect to be the first to hear in gushing detail. "And she *wrote* to tell you about it?"

"I'm sure the letter was meant for both of us. She must not have our phone number."

"It's easy enough to find."

"She's thinking of having the wedding here."

"That would be quite a switch from the first wedding." Rochelle didn't want to dampen Aunt Meg's enthusiasm before Crystal did, but she needed to get real from the outset. "Did you tell her what the rates are?"

The old woman raised her brow. "Do I detect an unseemly bite to that remark?"

Rochelle smiled affectionately. "Unlike some people, I still have all my teeth."

"Ouch. Another bite."

"Is she still in California? The last time I tried to call her, the number was no longer in service."

"The letter came from Chicago." Aunt Meg checked the postmark to make sure. "Yes, Chicago. Interesting." She reached for Rochelle's hand. "I know what it's like, Shelly. Crystal is so much like her mother. Selena had no use for family ties. If it hadn't been for you, I might have lost track of her, too." They exchanged hand squeezes. "But wouldn't it be lovely to have a family wedding here? There was only one other."

"Not my mother's."

"Oh, no, that one was held at the Plaza. No, you've seen the pictures of your grandparents' wedding. Mother's dress was so beautiful." She brightened. "We should find it, Shelly. Maybe it would fit Crystal."

"Even if it did, don't you think it might bode ill? That marriage was relatively short. Your parents both died so young."

"Don't tell me that my skeptical Shelly has a superstitious streak."

"Of course not. Crystal wouldn't wear it, anyway. She'll go for a designer dress, and she'll look fabulous in it. But this would hardly be the place to show it off, so I can't see…" With no reaction from her aunt, Rochelle puzzled over the situations. "Have you spoken to her lately?"

"I can't remember when I last heard from her. And when your memory gets to be as bad as mine, you'll be relieved of the burden of keeping score." Aunt Meg offered a sympathetic smile. "I'm not being judgmental, Shelly. It's just that I went through all this with my sister. You are who you are, and—"

"She is who she is, I know. It's fine with me. I just can't believe she'll go through with it, and I don't want us to be disappointed. She'll have us all psyched for November, and then she'll decide on Paris in the spring."

"But she's marrying a Minnesota boy, and he has family close by. As for Crystal, we're the only family she has besides little Garth, and I haven't seen him since he was a tot. She knows I don't get out much anymore."

Rochelle let the assumption pass unanswered. The call she hadn't been able to complete had been her dutiful attempt to let Crystal know that Aunt Meg was in the hospital. She'd hoped her sister would come. She'd imagined a happy reunion, the delight in seeing how much her nephew had grown, the sweet surprise for a sick woman.

"It would be fun to have a wedding here," Rochelle allowed softly.

"I've always hoped we'd have yours in the gardens."

Rochelle laughed reflexively, the way she always did when the subject of men, marriage or maiden aunts came up. "Let's practice on Crystal's. Did she give us a phone number?"

"Read the letter," Meg urged, pressing the envelope into her hand. "We can probably find out from the address."

"I'll take care of that. You need your rest now. You have a big day ahead of you tomorrow."

"I do," Meg remembered happily. She was to be the grand marshal of the town's Labor Day parade. "And then Ariel's group will be coming back. They're all set to partake in a thorough purification of Rosewood whenever I get it organized."

"If you go chasing the spirits out of their haunts, we'll have nothing to draw the creative retreaters to our chilly climes."

"It's not the spirits' side we're purifying. It's ours.

I think I'll ask Birch Trueblood to take charge of the ceremony. You remember him, don't you?"

Rochelle stiffened. Her aunt knew perfectly well what she remembered about Birch Trueblood. She'd made a fool of herself every time she ran into the Ojibwe medicine man. As a teenager and beyond, she had followed Margaret Bruner around in her quest to show her interest in and appreciation for the small band of American Indians who, through generations of challenge, had managed to hang on to a tiny piece of the Mille Lacs shoreline.

The twinkle in Aunt Meg's eyes drew Rochelle's obligatory groan. Oh, yes, she certainly remembered the way Birch's easy smile made her insides turn somersaults.

Oh, this was perfect. With Sinclair Lewis's birthplace just down the road, wasn't purification from the Native American Elmer Gantry just what she needed?

Chapter Two

"Daddy?"

The small voice wasn't much of a fog cutter. It took some persistent shoulder shaking to raise Birch Trueblood from the underworld of his dreams. Recoiling, he squinted at the little face, unable to make sense of it in the context of murky water and cloying trees.

"It's time to get up, Daddy. You said to get you up early and not take no for an answer."

Robin. His baby girl. Without her, how would he make sense of anything else in his life? He rested his arm over his eyes and groaned. "When did I say that?"

"Yesterday at four o'clock, and again at seven-thirty."

"Can I see some proof?" The smell of the coffee she made him every morning wasn't enough to justify *early.* Not this early. Not today. Which was, what? Saturday? Sunday?

"You can if you just look. I'm your proof, standing right here, looking at my watch."

She knew it, too. How did a person get to be so sure of herself in nine short years?

Robin was a chip off the old block. Fortunately, it was the maternal block. Staff Sergeant Deanna Trueblood would be proud.

Unfortunately, the maternal block had been hard-headed about her duty to Uncle Sam. Every family needed a warrior, she'd told her little girl before she'd shipped out for her eagerly anticipated overseas tour. It had been more than two years since those words had spoiled her farewell kiss, leaving a bad taste in her husband's mouth. Little had he known that taste would be the last he would have of her.

But he still had Robin. Birch Trueblood was running low on reasons to look forward to getting up in the morning, but he still had his little girl. And she had become the keeper of reasons. He moved his arm on command, and there stood his little trouper, bathed, combed, dressed and ready to get her dad's show on the road.

He smiled. "You look like you're ready to boogie."

"Teenagers boogie." She reached for the mug of steaming coffee she'd set on the nightstand. "I don't like teenagers. I've decided I'm going to skip over being a dumb teenager."

"That'll sure save me a few headaches."

"I'm going to dance in the parade, though. And I'm not going to put my jingle dress on until we get there, because it'll get all wrinkled. So let's get moving."

"You can just leave that," he said with a nod toward the coffee.

But she was backing away. "I'm putting it by the bathroom sink."

"You're a coldhearted kid sometimes."

"We should leave in half an hour. You promised Egg McMuffins, which means we have to get to Little Falls before ten. After that you can only get hamburgers and stuff."

The thought of eggs of any kind agitated Birch's gut. He had polished off his stash of Cutty Sark late last night—had to wait until his small female conscience had finally given up on silently but surely reading his mind and gone to bed—and he was feeling it this morning. He'd successfully sworn off his closet habit for the past few months, but the end of summer had a way of doing him in. Quiet house, cool night air, a lonely loon calling for company out on the lake—Birch hadn't even checked to see that Robin was asleep first. He'd pushed aside the ten-pound sack of flour he would never use and unearthed the bottle, still wrapped in its brown bag.

He had to get up. He had plenty of things to look forward to, he told himself. But looking in the mirror was not one of them. One of these days he was going to be greeted by a face that looked as bad as Birch felt, at which point the jig would be up and the gig over. His paying clients were mostly women, and in recent years, he had been making a sweet living.

It had not always been so. The pipe and the medicine bundle had come to him through his father, but with few instructions. Ceremonies were learned, not taught. You paid attention to the way they were done, the songs that were sung, the words that were said, and you made them your own. But you didn't own them, and they were not for sale. In Indian country, ceremonies were not done for pay, although gifts of goods were always welcome. Not the best way to make a living, nor was it meant to be. It had once been a way of life.

But times had changed, and Birch Trueblood had changed with them. He lived in two worlds—only two existed, after all: Indian and non-Indian—and the rules for one didn't necessarily apply in the other. Outside Indian country, people had little time for a way of life beyond the making-a-living part.

They commonly treated both religion and medicine as businesses rather than gifts. But they were hungry for something they thought Birch could provide, even if they had no idea what it might be.

Who was he to deny them? He understood their expectations better than they did. He had a role to play, a persona to portray. He was attractive in every way—a mentor, a mystic, a man who could create extraordinary connections. Fees were never discussed, and gifts of cash were never refused.

Birch stroked his chin, assessed the need for a shave and decided he could go another day, wondering when his lean, brown face had gone from chiseled to craggy. Not that it mattered. However you cut it, rocky was rocky. He slugged down a tumblerful of water to help set his head straight, then washed what needed washing, brushed what needed brushing and dressed what needed dressing. With his bases covered, he was ready to face the non-Indian devotees of Indian spirituality.

Like most small Midwestern towns, Little Falls was big on holiday parades. The official end of summer vacation, Labor Day marked the beginning of what many considered to be the queen of seasons in Minnesota. The kids would be back in school; the countryside would soon be dressed in autumn jewel tones; and Jack Frost would put the mosquitoes on the run. The stage would be set for hunting season, which vied with ice-fishing season for the title of king. To every season there was a parade somewhere in Minnesota, where windchills built character.

But this Labor Day the weather was warm and fine. For her part in the celebration, Margaret Bruner was decked out like a queen in a royal-blue Chanel suit that fit her almost as well as it had when she'd bought it during one of her frequent trips to New York more than half a century ago. She'd rejected Rochelle's offer of a shopping trip for a new outfit on the grounds that her size hadn't changed since she'd "developed a woman's bust" and she had a closet full of classics.

True enough, Rochelle had to admit. Rosewood was replete with classics for a classic, right down to the car. Since Aunt Meg had never bothered to learn to drive, she had given the car to Fred Doyle, her chauffeur of more than thirty years. Fred had started a limousine service with it, but she still called on "Mr. Doyle" to "bring the Packard around" whenever she needed a ride, which had recently been so seldom that Mr. Doyle behaved more like a nervous suitor than a driver as he stood in the driveway waiting for his passenger.

Rochelle nodded toward the front window and smiled. "Did you call for a brand-new car, Aunt Meg?"

"I called for the Packard. Don't tell me Mr. Doyle sent—" The push of a button had Meg's wheels rolling her toward the window.

"It's Mr. Doyle, all right, but that has to be the shiniest car in town. I can't believe it was made in 1949. Be sure to mention how good it looks."

"It looks the way it has always looked." But the old woman's face softened as she peered through the curtain sheers, words of protest dissolving on her tongue. She would have her car, her driver and her style, and this would still be her day.

"Miss Bruner, your car's here," Ariel announced, hurrying in from the kitchen to help get the wheelchair down the back ramp. "Will you be needing a light wrap?"

"No, but I might need a little assistance. I shall be using the front door today."

"But the steps…" Rochelle warned. As sure and determined as her aunt's mind was, her body was fragile, and this was no time for anything to go wrong and spoil her day.

"We can handle them," said Ariel.

Rochelle opened the front door so that Aunt Meg could ride through to the front porch, but Meg turned the power chair off in the foyer. "I'll have my pocketbook and my cane, please. And a strong woman on each arm."

The sidewalk along the parade route was filling up with viewers as Ariel hurried Rochelle along, block after block, until they reached the intersection of Main and Rosewood. "This is perfect," she announced as the marching band struck up its first tune. Rochelle remembered tootling her flute down the same street wearing the same gold-trimmed uniform the musicians paraded in today. The jacket had made her look like a football player. She'd longed to wear the cute little skirt and sweater the cheerleaders sported, leading the parade with the Little Falls High School banner. It was a wish she'd kept to herself when Aunt Meg had said, "I'm so proud that you're a flutist and not a *flirtist.*"

It was all in the lips.

The parade was not long, but there was no shortage of costumes and color. The Shriners in their fezzes and the Quarter Horse drill team in their cowboy hats were both outdone by the Arabian Horse Club, dressed in Bedouin finery. The fire department paraded its original truck. A pony cart full of children represented the town's zoo. There were school floats on flatbed trailers, children riding beribboned bicycles and noisy go-carts, clowns wielding "pooper scoopers," Brownies and Cub Scouts, all marching to the tune of "I've Been Working on the Railroad," and celebrating the value of labor and the joy of getting a day off.

Rochelle smiled when she glimpsed the majestic Packard, glinting in the midmorning sun as proudly as any parade horse. Was it just her, she wondered, or did anyone else see the irony in their choice for Labor Day grand marshal being a woman who had never collected a paycheck in her life?

There was no need for announcement, introduction or sign. Cheers rolled down the street following a car as unique to its passenger as any royal carriage. "Miss Margaret! You go, girl!"

Mr. Doyle stopped the limousine in the middle of the intersection. Aunt Meg leaned out the back window and waved to Rochelle and Ariel, who couldn't hear what she was yelling at them over the cheers and the mighty strains of Dinah blowing her horn, but they nodded and waved back.

Suddenly the band stopped playing. From somewhere in the crowd a steady drumbeat sounded, and a voice single rose, followed by a chorus, chanting in Ojibwe. Dancers costumed in jingly buckskin dresses and bell-trimmed leggings slipped through the crowd and flowed into the street. Like bright water tinkling through a sieve, they surrounded the stately old Packard. The drummers sang a solemn tune as the troupe performed a traditional circle dance.

"It's an honor song," Ariel whispered to Rochelle. "I knew the Mille Lacs dancers were planning this as a surprise for her, and I had to practically sit on my hands to keep it a secret."

"Sit on your hands?"

"Well, you know what I mean." Ariel elbowed Rochelle and nodded toward the car. "She's going to cry. I knew it. I stuck an extra hankie in her bag."

"I don't think I've ever seen her cry." Her mother had been a big bawler, but not Aunt Meg, and the sight of her tears made Rochelle's throat tingle.

"I knew this would get her going. She's just feeling the love. " Ariel leaned against Rochelle. "Don't look now, but there's a surprise in store for you, too, Miss Shelly."

Rochelle followed Ariel's gaze.

"I *said* don't look."

It was too late, but it didn't matter. She'd had the feeling before actually spotting him a few yards away. The old face-flushing, bone-melting, Birch-Trueblood-is-in-the-house feeling made more than her throat tingle. *Still,* after all these years.

"It's okay. He's looking right at me, trying to figure out why I look familiar. He doesn't have a clue."

But he was smiling. Sort of. He rarely parted his lips when he smiled, hardly parted them when he spoke. Ah, but when he kissed…

"Rochelle," he said as he offered a handshake.

Okay, one clue.

She was staring. He'd changed. Leaner, harder, more angular, more arresting. There were traces of gray in his black hair and care lines around his dark eyes.

Care lines, for God's sake. Try wrinkles, Rochelle.

"Birch Trueblood," he reminded her. "It's been a long time."

"Ten years, at least." If she was hearing herself right, she sounded electrified. "It's so good…" Zapped with his heat, the hand he'd caught and released flopped up and down like a fish, a vague gesture toward the dancers. "This is such a wonderful treat."

"If you're here for the weekend, it gets better."

"I'm here as long as my aunt needs me," she volunteered. "We've started a business at Rosewood, and I'm…" *Slow down, silly. He didn't ask.* "I meant the dancers. A wonderful treat for Aunt Meg."

His eyes smiled. "And I meant it gets better.

Since I'm doing a ceremony for you, we've decided to accept Ariel's offer of free lodging. We're staying at Rosewood."

"All of you?"

"My daughter and me." He nodded, directing her attention to the performers. "That's Robin, the one with the flowers. Isn't she somethin' else?"

"She certainly is." Certainly a pretty child. Certainly Birch Trueblood's daughter. Certainly an indication that he was taken, which was certainly too bad.

After a word from his passenger, Mr. Doyle emerged and opened the back door. Birch's daughter did a jingly spin and then reached inside to present the bouquet.

"Oh, how sweet," Ariel said.

"Is your wife here, too?" The question was out before it was fully formed in Rochelle's mind. What *was* fully formed was the memory of a young Indian woman with long, lush hair and flashing eyes. "I remember...you must have married that lovely—"

"She's dead."

Rochelle pressed her hand to her chest. "I'm so sorry."

More like surprised. It wasn't sorrow that had shifted her heartbeat into high gear, and she hoped to God he couldn't tell, because she truly meant to feel nothing but sorrow. "The last time I saw you, you two were—"

"On the outs, as I remember. She'd kicked me out and told me not to come back until I was ready to sign on the line."

"Fish or cook bait, huh?" Ariel, the unabashed eavesdropper, put in.

"Something like that." He gave Ariel a second glance and an iffy chuckle, in case there'd been a joke there somewhere. "Anyway, she got what she wanted, for better or worse. That little girl is the better."

"And the worse must have been…illness?" Rochelle persisted.

"She was killed. Wrong place, wrong time. Yeah, that day was the worst, but…" He caught himself, as though he'd just remembered what day it was now, and he smiled a different smile. A public smile to hide a private thought. "But it's the Bruner ghosts we're worried about now. Right, Ariel?"

"Personally, I think what we have at Rosewood goes back much further than that," Ariel said earnestly. "It's such a strong spiritual presence. You'll feel it right away, Mr. Trueblood, someone with your sensitivity." She flashed Rochelle an indulgent grin. "Shelly's our skeptic."

"Every family should have one," Birch said as the drummers picked up the dance's pace.

"It's not that I don't respect your beliefs and practices," Rochelle protested, lifting her voice. "I'm just not sure that we need to be ghost busting at Rosewood. But I won't be getting in your way."

Birch laughed. "I'm not a ghost buster. I met one once. Quite a character. He wanted me to make him a blood brother."

"And did you?"

"We've updated our policy on blood. It's more blessed to give than to receive. When I put it that way, he passed on my offer."

"Smart man."

"Thank you." He turned his smile on Ariel. "You promised bed and breakfast this weekend. Does that mean breakfast in bed?"

"Most of our guests prefer breakfast on the River Porch," Rochelle said, distracted by the activity in the street. Mr. Doyle had just helped Aunt Meg out of the car.

"But we'll be more than happy to take yours up to your room," Ariel quickly offered. "I can just imagine how draining it must be for you, filling everyone else's well, so to speak."

"Which is why coffee will do me just fine. My daughter's the morning person. She loves breakfast.

If you can persuade her to let me sleep in, I'll burn some special grass for you tonight. Canadian Gold."

"You're talking about sweetgrass," Rochelle supposed absently as she watched her aunt—with a little help from her chauffeur—move to join the dancers.

"Our neighbors to the north had a succulent crop this year."

"I'm sure the spirits will be pleased."

"You don't have to worry about Robin," Ariel promised. "She'll be surrounded by morning people. We'll make sure you get your rest. We really appreciate your willingness to clear the air at Rosewood, so to speak."

"Margaret Bruner has been a good friend to us," he said. "I hope we can clear her path."

"What path?" Rochelle turned a scowl on the man. "You're here to clear the air. Aunt Meg doesn't fly."

"But look at her dance." Ariel waved at the old woman, who had begun to bounce slightly at the knee, like a piston in desperate need of oil. She smiled and raised her cane, then waved it back and forth the way a woman in the troupe used her dance feather. "Way to go!"

"*Hoka!*" Birch shouted.

Rochelle turned away from them, feeling foolish

for taking offense. But his comment seemed oddly threatening, even to a skeptic.

She felt his breath on her neck. "Wherever her journey takes her."

Wherever her journey takes her.

Birch Trueblood could save the "mystical Indian" routine. He was hardly dealing with an impressionable schoolgirl anymore. Rochelle made a habit of mentally lecturing herself in the bright fluorescent light of the playroom while she plied her hobby of restoring the collection of dolls the Bruner girls had amassed over the course of a century. Somebody had to. With a small composition finger in one hand and a bit of sandpaper in the other, she carefully buffed a repair she'd made earlier. If worse came to worst, the dolls could bring in some needed cash.

And if push came to shove, maybe she could talk herself out of saying or doing something clichéd and embarrassing, at least for the next twenty-four hours.

And didn't Birch recall that he'd already tipped his hand to her, years ago? Didn't he remember laughing at her or himself—she'd never been sure which—when he'd told her that he had inherited a sleeve full of tricks from his father, "the tribal magician." He wanted to be a musician, not a magician. Not tribal but *real*. His word. His dream. His guitar, his voice, his song. He didn't talk about it often, he'd said, and he didn't know why he was telling her.

Maybe it was just the blues and the beer talking, but she'd been enchanted, and she'd made a fool of herself by hanging on his every word, not to mention his lips when he'd favored her with one of those blindsiding firsts that made it hard to breathe and impossible to think. She'd been kissed before that night, but never by a man. Here was something completely new, at once wonderful and awful. Here was magic and reality—dreamy levitation and hard lesson—braided together in one cherished memory. Unlike a boy's desperate advances, a man's kiss might well leave her wanting more than he was willing to give.

I'm sorry, Rochelle. I shouldn't have done that.

But *she* hadn't been sorry. She'd felt foolish, but not sorry. Chalk it up to experience, Rochelle told herself. A defining moment and, yes, mystical. Certainly unforgettable. She'd always wondered what might have happened if he hadn't been in love with someone else. Maybe she'd dodged a bullet. An arrow? Some sort of piercing. Surely he'd been tempted, too. She laughed out loud. Maybe if she'd gotten more than a kiss out of him that night, maybe if she'd been sexier or he'd been hornier...

Maybe she wouldn't be playing with dolls in the basement of her maiden aunt's house.

God help her, her self-talk had gone from sensible to self-pity.

Thunk!

Startled, Rochelle spun around in her swivel chair. Robin Trueblood was sitting at the bottom of the oak stairs in her stocking feet, looking equally surprised.

"Don't worry. I'm okay," the girl said quickly, as she reached for the handrail to pull herself up. "I only slipped down the last three steps. I didn't mean to scare you."

"It's okay." Rochelle smiled, glad for the company. She had already discovered that Robin was well-mannered but hardly shy. "Come on in. I guess the idea of appeasing the spirits has me a little jumpy."

"I saw that there was a light on down here, so I peeked in the window and I could see your head, so I just came in. I took off my shoes at the door and everything. I wanted to see what you were doing."

"Has your dad started his ceremony yet?"

"Yeah, they're all sitting outside in the dark." Robin dropped her jacket over the slim arm of a brown Swedish modern sofa as she approached Rochelle's worktable. "Are you playing with dolls?"

"I'm repairing this one. Her hand broke."

Robin's glance paid quick deference to the wounded specimen before taking in the array of dolls surrounding them on shelves, tables, play furniture, even the floor. "Are these all yours?"

"Sort of." Rochelle went back to buffing blond, blue-eyed Patsy's new finger. "Some of them were my mother's and my aunt's, from when they were little girls, but Aunt Meg says they're mine now. I think they really belong to the house. My great-grandmother started collecting them more than a hundred years ago."

"This is a lot of dolls." Robin was drawn to a breakfront cabinet that contained a rare complete set of Dionne quintuplet baby dolls. "Who plays with them?"

"Nobody, really. They're more for looking at now."

"Because they're so old?"

"That's right."

The child turned, curious. "Are there any that were yours when you were a kid?"

"Actually…" Rochelle chuckled as she remembered watching the trashman claim a box full of naked, decapitated Barbie dolls off the curb. Taking the heads off had made it easier to change their clothes, but when the heads wouldn't stay on anymore, out they went. "No, there aren't. I didn't take very good care of my toys. When they got broken, my mother threw them away."

"But you could have fixed them."

"I didn't know how then, and I guess I didn't care that much. When I was your age, I kept wanting new things to play with. I wanted everything I saw on TV. Do you like dolls?"

"I like these. They're different from the ones you see in the stores with the bug eyes and the big huge lips."

Suddenly a haunting song rose outside, somewhere in the dark. Rochelle didn't understand the words, but she recognized the voice and the solemn tone. It was hard to think cynically in the presence of a song that sounded so strong, forthright and faithful.

Robin came around to Rochelle's side and poked Patsy's tin eye open with her finger. "Are you afraid of ghosts?"

"You want to know the truth?" Rochelle slipped her arm around the little girl's shoulders. She knew a frightened child when she saw one, and she responded instinctively to the artlessness in that upturned face. "I don't really believe in ghosts. I can't prove that they don't exist, but I've never come across any proof that they do. So I'm not really worried about them." She gave a gentle squeeze. "How about you?"

"I'm not scared for myself, but sometimes I worry about my dad. He's around them all the time."

"Then I'm sure he knows how to handle himself. You know, like somebody who works with wild animals."

"See, that's what I mean," Robin said eagerly. "It's like, you can never really trust a bear or a cougar. You never know what they might do. They're not like us. They're…they're wild."

Rochelle nodded. The comparison with a natural threat was a help. "What do you think a ghost might do to him?"

"Kill him, maybe." Robin hung her head, adding quietly, "My mother got killed in the army."

"But not by ghosts."

"I'm not sure what it was. My dad said she was in a dangerous place where there was fighting and shooting going on. But she told me she was a communications specialist, and that meant she would send messages and stuff. I don't think she was a fighter so much. But I know for sure she really liked being a soldier, because she used to say stuff about her job and Daddy's job and how he wasn't so…"

Robin slid Rochelle a wary glance. "I just know she got killed by something in the army."

"I met her once."

The child looked at her, wide-eyed, eager for details, and Rochelle saw Robin's mother in those dark eyes, those generous lips. This was no ghost; it was a dead woman's living legacy.

"She was a very beautiful woman, Robin. It's a brave thing to do, being a soldier, and she had to be very smart to be a communications specialist. I'm sure you miss her a lot, and I know that must be hard. But I'm also pretty sure your dad's going to be fine. Rosewood isn't a dangerous place at all."

"It's really big. You have to be really rich to have two big houses. Do you have one house for you and one for Miss Margaret?"

"Both houses belong to Miss Margaret. Her grandfather and her grandfather's partner built them a very long time ago. Back then there were two families, so they needed two houses."

"What happened to the other family?"

"They sold out to my great-grandfather and moved to a place where there were more trees for them to cut down. They made lumber. Boards to build houses and barns and such. But after a while, they started running low on trees."

"Where we live we have lots of trees."

"It's been almost a hundred years. They grew back." She didn't know why she felt the need to confess to a nine-year-old, but there it was, her customary unbidden candor. "My great-grandfather and his partner got their trees from Mille Lacs."

"Oh." Robin frowned. "I've seen some pictures in the museum."

"I've seen them, too." Clear-cutting at its best or worst, depending upon your perspective. She'd written a poem about it when she was in college. She'd expected Aunt Meg to be impressed with the clever title—The Rape of the Lake—and the lyrical apology that followed, but her role model for the New Woman had only congratulated her on the excellent grade she'd received.

"Your great-grandfather did all that?"

"Not all. A lot of it."

"Miss Margaret helped us build our museum."

"Yes, she did. She's helped a lot of people. She's done a lot of good with the money she got from her grandfather. There isn't much left." Quickly she added, "But please don't tell her that I told you that."

"Is she poor now?"

"Oh, no. She'll do just fine. I just have to figure out a way for these old houses to earn their keep."

"Is that why you're having the purification tonight?"

"It's as good a reason as any, I guess."

Robin pondered the problem for a moment. "Maybe you could have a haunted house for Halloween. We had one last year to earn money for our class to take a trip. People paid to go though it and get scared."

"You can do that in your school? Halloween stuff is a big taboo at my school. We can only do pumpkins." She reached for the Wizard of Oz Scarecrow doll, who was awaiting new face paint. "Even this guy might be questionable."

"It wasn't in school. It was after school. We had it in a scary old boathouse, with scary music and spiderwebs and Dracula popping out of his coffin. We made over two hundred dollars."

"Wow, that must have been some haunted house."

"If you want me to, I could help you set it up. We could hang bats and ghosts all around, and make witches and monsters out of some of these dolls."

Rochelle smiled. "You know what, I'm going to keep that in mind. That's a very generous offer. But, Robin, I don't think you have to worry about your dad. He sounds like a very powerful force against any ghost that might be lurking in the gardens."

"He is strong and powerful, but he gets sad a lot."

"For your mom?"

"I think so." She tipped her head, listening for a moment like an eager puppy. "I can hear his feelings. Can't you? Sometimes when he sings like that, I think she might hear him, and if she does, she might come for him."

"Have you told him this?"

"I haven't told anybody." She grabbed Rochelle's hand. "I promise not to tell Miss Margaret that you said her money's all gone, but you have to promise not to tell my dad what I just said. Okay?"

"I promise not to tell him, but I think you should tell him yourself, Robin. I think he'd tell you that ghosts can't really take people away." *Except, perhaps, in their minds.*

"When people die, the spirits come to get them."

"Maybe *after* they die," Rochelle allowed. "But if you ask me, your dad is going to be around for a good long time, honey. He's young and strong and…" She smiled, remembering his blood-brother comment. "Well, he's careful."

"I know." Robin turned to examine the storybook dolls lined up on the worktable. "I'll bet people would pay you to fix their dolls. You know, so you and Miss Margaret wouldn't have to be poor."

"We're not—" *Poor* was a relative term, Rochelle reminded herself. "You know, that's another good idea. You've given me two very good ideas. But... okay, here's one more secret I want you to keep for me. Don't tell your father that, um...you know, anything about us maybe being poor. Because we're not. I took a leave of absence from my teaching job to help out here, so I'm not in any danger of being poor."

"Me, neither. But Miss Margaret is, right? Her car is really old."

"Yes, but it's actually worth a lot of money." Rochelle chuckled, wagging her head. "And it's not really hers anymore. She gave it away."

"We had a giveaway for my mom. A year after she died we had a giveaway to honor her. We gave away a lot of blankets and stuff."

"I've been to Indian giveaways before. It's a wonderful tradition."

"Miss Margaret cried when we honored her today."

"It was a beautiful surprise. You made her so happy, she couldn't help crying."

"Miss Margaret doesn't need to give my dad anything. You tell her, okay? People always give him stuff, but he wouldn't want her to. Because, you know, we don't want her to get poor. She's a great lady. That's what our chairman said when he told us we were going to dance for her in the parade."

"We'll let him sleep in tomorrow morning and take him breakfast in bed. Would he like that?"

"Oh, yes, he'd *really* like that. But do it late. He hates getting up in the morning."

Birch plugged the drain in the claw-foot bathtub with its chained-up rubber stopper and flipped the faucet handle. He had been looking forward to a long, hot soak all evening—so much so that he'd been tempted to cut back on the singing and shorten the ceremony by half a braid of sweetgrass. But he guessed he just wasn't that kind of a guy. He gave himself a mental pat on the back as he pulled his shirt over his head. He'd given the ladies of Rosewood the full treatment, earning himself a warm bed and a hearty breakfast, not to mention a nice, hot bath. Not only that—he moved from lighted bathroom to darkened bedroom—he deserved a drink and a little music along with it. He was pretty sure the funny-looking brown box on the fireplace mantel was a radio.

But it didn't work. Even more disappointing, the pint he could have sworn he'd tucked into the side pocket of his duffel bag wasn't there. Unless he wanted to sip on mouthwash, he would have to depend on the hot water to unwind his brain and untie his knots. In the dark, he felt around the ruffles surrounding the windows, looking for a cord or a shade, and he noticed a light on in the other house.

He felt a little slighted. Rochelle LeClair had shown no interest in his ceremony. She had said as much, but he'd expected her to show up, anyway. No longer did she wear her girlish interests all over her face, and she hadn't let her mouth give her away the way she once did, but the vibes were still there, and he'd expected her to show. He'd been looking for her the whole time he was singing and smudging, smoking the spirits out of every nook and cranny on the place. Maybe she'd been watching him from behind a tree or a curtain. Had to be. He wasn't one to misread a woman's signals.

She'd always been kind of sweet and shy. A kid the first time he'd met her, a young woman the next, she'd been visibly drawn by the Trueblood magnetism. He remembered thinking, *Wipe that look off your face, rich girl, before it buys you more trouble than you can afford.* But he'd played around with her some, either because he'd been feeling sorry for himself or just because he could. He couldn't remember which.

It was a little vexing that she hadn't given him his due this time. Things were different now, and she was just as tempting as ever. Maybe he was losing his appeal.

He stripped off his boots and his jeans, and stole a glance at himself in an old freestanding mirror as he reached for the towels, folded and stacked at the foot of the bed.

Same ol' Trueblood.

And then some.

Something extra, *somebody* extra. Someone standing behind him in the shadows.

He smiled, mostly to himself—*You doubted?*—and turned to welcome his overdue visitor.

It was a wooden coat tree.

He moved in for a closer look at the imposter. Befuddled, he pulled a heavy wool coat off its hook and dropped it onto the floor, leaving a skinny wooden pole to mock his conceit.

He breathed. Then he chuckled and turned away. How long had it been since he'd gotten laid? Obviously he was the one who was overdue.

He tried to move away, but the mirror beckoned. He risked a second glance. Wrapped in the dark coat, the unmistakably human image was back, reflected even more clearly than before. It was definitely a woman. She had smoky eyes, honey-colored hair and tissue-paper skin. She looked familiar, but he couldn't say he knew her.

In fact, he couldn't say anything at all. His mouth was suddenly stuffed to the gills with his own swollen tongue. His lips felt icy. If he could only release his breath, he knew it would form a cold mist. He shivered uncontrollably inside, but he saw no movement in the mirror. Just a man in a towel staring at a woman in a coat who simply stood there, waiting.

For what? If she wanted sex, she wasn't getting it from him right now. Something had suddenly struck him dumb and chilled him boneless. It seemed like an eternity before he could tear his gaze from the mirror and his bare, frozen feet from the floor, but finally he turned around.

She was gone. The coat lay on the floor where he'd dropped it, at the base of the pole that stood as rigid as his own.

Goddamn. He had to look down to make sure what he thought he felt was real. Sure enough, he had a spectacular boner. Where had that come from? He felt a little embarrassed by it, and then stupid over the embarrassment, and then angry over the stupidity.

What the hell was going on?

"Is there someone here?"

At least his tongue had shrunk back to normal. As for the other…

"Is this how you women get your excitement around here?" he asked, finding his cool in a sarcastic tone as he reached for the light switch. Nothing was out of place except the coat. He checked the closet on the opposite side of the room and found nothing but his own clothes and a white bathrobe that he hadn't noticed before. He checked the bathroom. It was steamy, the tub full of billowing water. Who had turned off the faucet? Had he? He did a double take in the mirror, making sure his face was the only one he saw. It had lost a little color and maybe some of his faculties, but it was Birch Trueblood.

Old houses were famous for having secret doors and passages, weren't they? But if he was being watched, he wasn't about to make a fool of himself by tapping around on the walls.

"Okay, you got me. Whatever the trick is, I'm impressed." He stepped back, flashing his palms in surrender, along with everything else he had to offer. "Are you? Do I pass muster? Because there's more where that came from."

Which made no sense, but in the absence of an answer, he felt like he had to keep talking while he pulled on his jeans. This kind of silence was not golden. "You can't keep a good man down with, uh…whatever."

Damn, he needed a drink. He crept downstairs to

see what the kitchen had to offer, but he came up empty.

He'd been had by the Rosewood ladies. What he ought to do was forget the whole thing, pretend it never happened. Take his bath. Crawl into that frilly bed upstairs and get some sleep.

But there was that light on in the other house. He lifted a lacy kitchen curtain and took another look. Across the dark way—if he wasn't mistaken, dreaming, or completely unscrewed—that was a female silhouette behind the drawn shade.

Birch smiled. "All right, lady, you asked for it."

Chapter Three

Birch let himself in the front door.

The light upstairs had been turned off, but the steps leading down from the foyer offered a lighted path to a seriously retro basement—wood paneling, funky fifties lamps, blond end tables—and a surprisingly sexy lady putting her toys away. She was dressed in a pink version of his own ice-fishing underwear, but unlike his, her bottoms didn't sag for comfort. The little rooster tail of reddish-brown hair clipped up on the back of her head bobbed flirtatiously as she danced on tiptoe, trying to steady a baby doll on a high shelf. Strangely enough—and this place was getting stranger by the minute—she looked blessedly real.

Damn. Nice ass.

"What does a guy have to do to get a drink around here? Whatever it is—"

"Shh!" She jumped to give the doll a final push and landed facing him, finger to lips.

Damn. Sweet move.

He noticed a glass of something that looked like it had a kick to it sitting on her desk. "—I'm willing," he whispered with a wink and a prayer. *Make it interesting, honey. You're doing just fine so far.*

She snatched a plaid blanket off the back of a chair. "Did you try the refrigerator?"

"I tried every door in the kitchen over there. I should have guessed you'd have your personal stash…." He helped himself to a sip from her glass. "A little heavy on the fruit."

"Apple juice. How do you take yours?"

"Fermented."

"We aren't licensed to serve it that way," she said as she twirled the blanket over her head and around her shoulders.

Blanket. Black cloak. Who did Peeping Shelly think she was fooling with the modesty act?

"Are you having trouble sleeping?" she asked, all innocence. "If your bed doesn't suit you, you can certainly try a different one."

He cocked her a knowing smile. "Which one would you suggest?"

"I've already suggested the one I like best."

"Yeah, the one conveniently located near—"

"Near the room we like to put the children in,

with the big rocking horse and the children's books. I thought Robin would like it, but she—"

"She likes it fine. She skipped the purification ceremony and turned in early."

She looked surprised. "You checked on her?"

He avoided the question with a shrug and a gesture. "What are you doing down here? Playing with dolls?"

"Restoring them. It's a hobby. This is a family collection." Pink slippers flapping against her heels, she pardoned herself past him, either bored with their conversation or looking for something to pump it up.

Her demeanor in that outfit amused him—the lady in the clown suit—and he was so intent on watching her every move that he didn't see the wrinkle in the program until the pink suit met the brown sofa, where his daughter lay sleeping.

"I was going to move her upstairs, but I hate to wake her," she whispered.

"I'll bunk in over there." He nodded toward another sad-looking basement sofa.

"That one will kill your back. Do you want to carry her upstairs? We'll put her in the little room next to Aunt Meg's." When he hesitated, she added, "Then we'll see what's in the wine cellar."

No more hesitation. He smiled. "Are you buying?"

"It's already bought and paid for, long ago. It's a little creepy back there, but I think that's what gives the wine its character."

He lifted his little girl into his arms.

"Daddy?"

His kiss soothed her heavy eyelids. He followed Rochelle's lead up the stairs, though the shadowy living room and down a dimly lighted hall. Robin barely stirred as he settled her into the small bed, while their hostess installed a night-light in a plug near the door.

"Do you think she'll get scared if she wakes up in there?" she whispered to him in the hallway.

"Nah, she'll be fine. Robin's a pretty big girl."

She motioned him back the way they'd come— a promising direction. Basement, cellar, wine, woman, all good. But he'd had enough song.

"Did she come over here bothering you?" Not that he cared, under the circumstances, but it seemed like a civilized question for a guy whose kid had been snooping around somebody else's house.

"I was glad to have some company. She noticed me through the window and came in to visit. Does she play with dolls?"

"She has a couple, so I'm sure she does. She's still a little girl when it comes to toys." As was Rochelle, if the shelves full of old kid junk that lined the maze

of twists and turns in her basement were any indication.

"You don't know which toys she likes to play
with?"

"She's pretty good with a basketball. Skates.
Video games." He bristled when she flashed him
what struck him as a patronizing smile. "Hey, I'm
doing the best I can, all right?"

"I'm sorry. That sounded like a loaded question,
and I didn't mean it to be."

"Was she complaining to you about not having
any dolls? Because if she sounded like she was hint-
ing around, she's in big trouble."

"Oh, no, it was nothing like that. She helped me
do some re-stringing." Rochelle stopped in front of
a closed door, deep in the bowels of the basement.
The blanket slipped off her shoulder as she stood on
tiptoe and felt around on the ledge above the door.
"It's here somewhere."

"Can I—" he caught the skeleton key midfall
and presented it with a smile when she turned "—help
you?"

"Maybe I still need to stand on a chair." She motioned for him to do the honors.

"I don't think I've ever seen a real wine cellar."

The door creaked on its hinges. The air smelled
dank and musty, and when the light came on at the

tug of a string, he could see why. Cinder blocks and wooden wine racks were all that separated the room from an old-fashioned root cellar. He couldn't even tell how big it was; the room ran out of light before it ran out of wine racks.

"Cozy," he said. "Do you slip in here often?"

"Not since the time a girlfriend and I tried enough of the stuff to find out that it tasted slightly better going down than it did coming up."

"Is this Miss Margaret's stash, then?"

"I think most of it even predates her. From what little I know about wine, I'd say this stuff has either increased in value or turned to vinegar." She took a flashlight and a corkscrew off a shelf, and handed him the flashlight. "Choose your poison."

"I generally put my trust in the brothers." He pulled out a few bottles at random and tried to read the labels. "I'm not seeing any Christian or Gallo here. How about…" He rolled the bottle in his hand, adjusting to the light. "Saint somebody—must be church wine. *Rouge.* That means red, right? Red is a good color."

Smiling, she opened the bottle, took a glass from a rack, dusted it off with the corner of her blanket and poured him enough wine for a taste. "Swallow or spit?"

"Savor and swallow. Very sexy. Try it," he suggested, offering her the glass.

She sipped and pulled him a sour face. "You call that sexy?"

"Yeah, like, full-bodied."

"So you like 'em tart," she muttered, pulling out several bottles before settling on something else *rouge.* "I like mine on the sweeter side. Let's go up to the kitchen and find something to go along with this. I think there's some Brie, maybe some Camembert. I just got some French bread."

"Bread." None too sorry to get out of this hole, he held the door for her. "Now you're talking my language."

Rochelle tucked the bottle under her arm and clutched the blanket around her. What was it with these Truebloods? Didn't they believe in knocking? With Robin asleep on the good couch, she'd been all set to spend the night on the back-killer. She'd already decided which sweater she was going to wear tomorrow with her new slacks, and how she and Robin would cut some flowers from the garden for the dining-room table and fix up the breakfast tray with a pretty bud vase.

But instead, here she was fixing up a late-night, not-on-the-diet snack in her late-night, not-for-public-display comfy clothes. Without a single protest, she was hauling out food and utensils.

"Do you want to slice up the bread while I get dressed?"

"Nope." He laughed at the surprised look she gave him as he took the bread knife from her hand. "I'll do the cutting, but I'm not letting you out of my sight, funny girl. Besides, there's nothing wrong with what you're wearing now. You look cute."

"I should put on a robe," she said, but without much conviction. Her robe looked even frumpier than her thermal undies. Worse, his proximity was doing funny things to her insides, raising goose bumps on her skin and making her keenly aware that she wore no undies under her undies.

"You been playing with your dolls all evening?" he asked as he started slicing.

"Only when Robin came down. Otherwise, I was *working* on my dolls."

"Nothing better to do?"

"I didn't think it would be appropriate for me to participate in the…" What to call it? She didn't want to sound sarcastic, but she wasn't one to disguise her doubts with political correctness. She gave him a basket for the bread. "Evening activities."

"Which ones? The smudging or the charade?"

"I didn't say it was a charade. I just don't happen to be a believer, and I don't want to offend anyone by not being, you know, fully—"

"That's not what I'm talking about." He looked her in the eye with some expectancy. "Look, what I do has nothing to do with haunted houses or goblins or devils or any of that stuff. I don't buy into any of that, either. So if you want to mock me or whatever, that's…that's not gonna cut it."

"By not participating in your ceremonies?"

"No, by…" He gave a dry chuckle and turned away. "Okay, never mind. I'll forget it if you will. Since we seem to be birds of a feather, let's talk about something else." He looked up from loading the bread into the basket and smiled. "Night owls."

"Only since I moved back here. When I was teaching in the Cities, it was early to bed, early to rise. I still haven't gotten used to the quiet here." His dark eyes drilled right through her. Small talk clearly wasn't his strong suit. She glanced out the kitchen window, into the dark backyard overlooking the river. "But imagine what it must have been like when the lumber mill was running full tilt and they were floating the logs down the river. I'm sure it wasn't so quiet here then."

"The good ol' days, huh?" Reaching across her over the sink, he brushed the bread crumbs from his hands. "Did the laborers get to go to the Labor Day parade back then? I'm pretty sure the Indian dancers didn't."

"I don't know whether they had a parade then, or whether it was even a holiday."

"There wouldn't have been enough Indians around to make a good show even if they were welcome. They'd all been moved up north."

"Except your band. They were courageous people, and I know my family had a hand in testing their mettle."

"A hand?"

"I mean…" She stared at his hands, low and loose on his hips, tanned skin on blue denim, taking cool exception. "More than a hand. I know that, in order to get access to the timber, there were things that were done, things that were really unfair."

Things that were done.

Nothing like owning up. Why was she never short on stupid things to say to this man? What kind of response would she come up with when he came back with some form of, *Gee, you think?*

But instead he said, "It's a lot quieter up at Mille Lacs these days, too. Quieter than it was back then when the trees were falling." He shrugged. "Or so they say. There's some question about whether a tree makes a sound if only Indians hear it fall."

"All I can say is that there's no more Mississippi River Lumber Company, and the Bruner name ends with Aunt Meg."

"But not the family."

"Not quite." She brightened. "Oh, and guess what. My sister's getting married."

"That's nice." He smiled. "Guess what. I didn't know you had a sister. I thought it was just you and Miss Margaret rattling around down here with your cats and your ghosts."

"I have no cats and no ghosts, more's the pity, but I do have a sister."

"More's the pity," he echoed with a chuckle. "The way you talk was always such a kick. All kind of nose-in-the-air and twinkle-in-the-eyes."

"You'd really like my sister."

There was genuine warmth in his soft smile. "Does she talk like you?"

"She doesn't do anything like me, but she's nevertheless very attractive. She has a magnetic personality, just as you—" she glanced away, too late to catch herself "—do. Attractive, you know. You'd really like her."

"I really like *you.* You've got spunk, but you're not always out there with it, like some women."

She laughed. "This is a *compliment?*"

"Absolutely. From me to you." He winked at her. "Magnetic personality, huh? That's a new one."

"I find that hard to believe, but you're welcome to add my endorsement to your resumé. That's also a compliment." She'd been winked at, of all things, and she could feel herself blushing. Red was not always a good color. She noticed a blue tin on the counter next to the coffee and tea canisters. "Oh, how about some French chocolate?"

"This is turning into a party."

"Let's invite Aunt Meg."

"Let's not. Your aunt, my daughter—let's let them sleep. We'll have a quiet little party, just us two." She glanced toward the window again as he cupped his hand around the back of her neck. "A picnic, maybe, like the time you came to the pow-wow with your aunt, and I gave you a ride to the store, and then we parked by the lake and ate the fruit you'd bought."

"I was hoping you'd forgotten all about that," she whispered, feeling nervous, then feeling ridiculous for feeling nervous. "I was such a silly goose back then."

Which clearly hadn't changed.

"Silly goose?" He chuckled. "That's not what I remember. You were soft and sweet, and I came this close to getting myself into some serious hot water."

Half relieved, half grieved that he'd removed his hand from her tingling nape, she risked a glance at the tiny space between his thumb and forefinger and shook her head. "I don't think so. You had everything under control except your girlfriend, and you must have patched that up soon afterward. Did her seeing us together move the two of you closer to the altar?"

"Deanna doesn't operate that way. *Didn't*," he amended quickly. "She always had a mind of her own, and you never knew what she'd latch onto next. She kept things interesting."

"And you?"

"I kept a roof over our heads." He shrugged. "Whenever she felt like being under it."

"It must have been difficult, with her military career."

"It wasn't full-time. Or wasn't supposed to be. She was in the Guards." Suddenly impatient with the preparations, he grabbed his chosen wine and took a drink from the bottle. Then he smacked his lips and took up the bread basket. "What do you say we take our wine-and-cheese party down by the river and talk over old times? Anything but Guards and ghosts."

"Let me get some glasses."

"What for? Tonight I say we drink from the bottle, eat with our hands and relive our youth." He gestured with the bottle. "Hey, you're way ahead of me. You've got a basement full of toys."

He had her laughing, then kept teasing as she

filled his arms with food and his hands with bottles, made an adjustment with the blanket on her shoulders and opened the kitchen door for him.

"What are *you* carrying?" he demanded.

"Oh, yes." She grabbed the tin of chocolates, closed the door behind him and took the lead down the path toward the river.

"Hey, Walks Fast Woman, what's the big hurry? If your packhorse stumbles in the dark, you'll lose all your wine and cheese."

"*Our* wine and cheese, so don't stumble."

"Where're we—oops!" His misstep was too controlled to be accidental, but he had her jumping to his rescue. He laughed. "Close one. Is that a bench?"

"That's Cupid's Bench." She didn't know where the name had originated, but the huge stone bench had undoubtedly been a favorite resting place for generations of Bruners. Since childhood, it had been hers. It wasn't one of her secret places— everyone knew about Cupid's Bench—but it *was* her favorite place. Tucked into the rocky riverbank, it had a tall, sheltering back and curved, comforting arms. Beneath a stand of old oak trees, the carved stone was cool in the summer, but it could be a cozy place to sit in any season, as long as you came prepared.

And they had. "Seriously, watch your step here," she warned as she reached the old flagstone steps. "Let me take some of that."

"This looks like a cold bench," he said as they piled their picnic in one corner. "I hope your blanket's big enough for two."

"But you have a jacket on."

He took it off. Wordlessly, he coaxed her to surrender the blanket to him. Then he draped his flannel shirt jacket across her shoulders, tossed the blanket over the bench and gestured with a flourish. "The bench is made, madam."

"Thank you, sir. Are you sure you're going to be warm enough?"

"Absolutely." He took a seat and patted the blanketed space next to him. "Plant it here and pass the bottle."

They snacked on bread and cheese while she spoke of the landmarks silhouetted against the night sky on the opposite bank of the river. The old lumber mill still dominated the view. The dam, which was just upriver, produced the purling, gurgling current that lapped the rocks below the bench, and the water twinkled—magically, it would seem, since so few lights were visible.

"And that's the Treaty Table." Rochelle pointed below to a thick slab of slate.

"You guys signed a treaty with somebody?" he asked around a mouthful of bread.

"I always thought it was *you* guys. The Ojibwe and the Dakota. I was hoping you could tell me more about it."

"We signed a treaty in your backyard?"

"Before it was our backyard."

"Whose backyard was it?"

"Old Man River's, I guess. Seriously, this is supposed to be the site where the two tribes agreed to a peace treaty way back when. Do you know what they agreed to?"

"The Ojibwe kicked the Lakota out, but they said they'd let the Dakota stay around if they'd keep the loggers out of their country."

"Really?"

"Clearly we made a bad bargain. The loggers got rich off our trees, anyway, and the Dakota got the best casino sites." He tipped the bottle to his mouth, glancing askance as he drank. He swallowed, stared, finally laughed. "I have no idea what they might have agreed to. Sounds like non-Indian lore to me." He gestured with the bottle. "Now it's your turn to own up. That room I'm staying in—where's the hidden door?"

"Hidden door?"

"Come on, Rochelle. It's a neat little trick, and

you really had me goin', at least for half a minute, so it's only fair for you to let me in on the secret. Especially since you enjoyed quite an eyeful."

"What are you talking about?"

"The woman in the mirror. That was you, right?"

"What woman?" She had him grinning. "Seriously, what mirror?"

"You say *seriously* like you mean it."

"I do. If I did something funny, it was purely by accident. I'm hardly ever funny on purpose. Not that I wouldn't like to be, but—"

"Okay, I'll respect the family secret. The Truebloods like to guard theirs, too. I just don't want you thinking I fell for it for more than thirty seconds."

"Fell for what? Any joke I'm involved in is undoubtedly on me. I swear to you, Birch, I do not know what you're talking about."

"Right." He bobbed his head in mock acceptance. "You're talking to a professional here, lady. And I gotta say, you're good."

"Professional what? Is something wrong with your accommodations?"

"Not at all, honey, not at all." He chuckled. "How's your wine?"

"It does chase the chill away, doesn't it?"

He reached behind her for the corner of the blanket, draped it around her shoulder, then wrapped the other side around himself. She leaned against his side, just enough to let him know that his arm was welcome around her.

She drew a deep breath. "I can still smell the sweetgrass. That's what you burned out here, isn't it?"

"Mostly, yeah. Funny the smell is still so strong. There was a breeze earlier. Maybe it's the spirits."

"'The ones who were here before,'" she quoted her aunt. "Between you and Ariel, I think Aunt Meg is thoroughly hooked."

"I swear, I don't know what you're talking about, Rochelle," he aped.

"Do you believe in what you do?"

"I used to."

"You don't anymore?"

"You gotta do what you gotta do, right? It's not the *what*. It's the *way*. My way is…" He sighed. "I get calls to do ceremonies for all kinds of retreats, people from all over the world in places where no Indian has lived in two, three hundred years. And I do them. I take the money they offer, and I say 'I accept this as a gift.' And they tell me that people in this day and age are hungry for traditional wisdom, and they're grateful that I'm keeping faith with the old ways and sharing them, and they're glad to help out. It's like a full-time job now. Professional holy man."

"Is that what you put on your resumé?"

"I don't have a resumé."

"You used to work construction, didn't you?"

He nodded.

"And you were a musician, too. I remember you telling me that you were a pipe carrier, but that wasn't your job."

"If whatever pays the bills is a job, then it was. And this is now." He glanced at her. "If it's what these people want, why shouldn't I be the one to bring it to them? And why shouldn't I get paid for it?"

"As long as you believe in what you're doing."

"I do what I do because it was given to me to do it. I'm the man. Grandson of Trueblood, son of Tiny Trueblood."

"*Tiny* Trueblood?"

"No reflection on any of the man's physical attributes, mind you. From what I've been told, many a woman claimed him to be a lotta man. My mom finally wrestled him to the ground and made him settle down, but she had the advantage of youth. He was twenty-seven years her senior. He didn't get married until he was fifty-three."

"And he was a holy man?"

"Yeah, but we don't use that term like, you know, his *holiness*. I've taken no vows of chastity, and I won't be shedding any tears of shame on TV. I don't preach, and I don't evangelize. All I do is pray with people in the way my father and grandfather were taught. I guess you could say I know the drill." He shook his head. "But it's not really that, either, because it's not an institution. It's traditional."

"And you're a believer."

"I'm…yeah." He sang it out. "I'm a belieeever."

"But you said you didn't believe in ghosts and goblins, so I'm not sure I understand what these ceremonies people ask you to do are all about."

"They're more about the living than they are about the dead. You know, your aunt loves to get me into these deep, philosophical discussions. It looks to me like she's trying to piece her God together using all her books and her studies, trying to come up with some new world order kind of an afterlife. I try to tell her that, myself, I don't get the ghosts knocking on the door at night and the saints appearing on the wing in the morning. It adds up to a black-and-white afterlife, and I just don't see it."

"But I don't—"

"But, you know what?" He gave her shoulders a quick squeeze. "We said we weren't gonna talk about ghosts."

"You brought it up," she reminded. "The woman in the mirror."

"She was no more a ghost than you are, sweet Shelly," he teased, touching his thumb to her lips. "Still soft and sweet, but now you've added a little mischief to the mix. I like that."

She smiled. His touch coaxed her to accept any credit he offered. "Better than philosophy?"

"Much better. Mischief is down-to-earth. Challenging." He leaned away, challenging her himself with a raised eyebrow. "I'll figure it out, though. Just give me a little time."

"Take all the time you need." How much more before he got around to kissing her? "I'd even give you a clue if I had one."

"I'd rather have the time."

"Would you like to stay another night?"

"Can't. School starts this week. But I'll take the rest of this night if that's okay with you."

"Be my..." A nervous laugh betrayed her. "But you are, aren't you?" she whispered. "You are my guest."

"I feel very much at home here, but we'd be more comfortable..." He drew her with him as he moved to the end of the bench, turned to lean back against the arm and positioned her between his legs, with his chest as her backrest, the blanket enveloping them. "Okay?"

"Okay."

"Indians like to do their courting under a blanket."

"Do they?" she said, afraid to speak too loud or breathe too deep as he crossed his arms over her breasts. Oh, God, how they ached.

"Do you have a man, Rochelle?"

"Of my very own?" She gave another jittery laugh.

"In your life." He swept her hair back with his nose and feathered kisses up the side of her neck, shoulder to earlobe. "Is there a number you call, a name you whisper? Someone who touches you in special ways?" His questions felt warm and sweet in her ear.

"I'm currently…unattached."

He gave a low chuckle. "You say that like you're filling out a form."

"Check all that apply. Maybe that's the way to simplify all this."

"All what? What can I do for you, Rochelle?"

"A kiss would be nice."

She turned her face to him, and he shifted to oblige, his arms brushing over her breasts in a way that was meant to tantalize. His kiss was open and unhurried, his tongue speculative. It was better than nice.

"Simple enough?" he whispered against her lips.

Her slight nod invited more kisses, each one warmer, wetter and deeper than its predecessor. He tucked his hands beneath her shirt and stroked her belly. She shivered.

"Cold?"

Was that it? She couldn't say. Against the night sky, the beauty of the dark silhouette that was his face made her mouth go dry. She reached back, slid her fingers into his thick hair, pulled his head down and hunted up another kiss. He tasted like sugar and smelled like spice.

He drew a slow breath and walked his fingers rib to rib, seeking her breasts. She knew where he was going, and she held her breath until he got there. Her nipples were already taut, waiting. He toyed with them until she sighed and shivered again.

"Aren't you getting warmer?"

"You are," she whispered.

He made a funny sound—pleased, amused, aroused—she had no idea. Ideas drifted beyond her reach. On a deep breath, she lifted her chest, pressed her breasts into his palms—*do them harder*—and she whimpered when his sorcerous fingers abandoned one aching nipple and slowly traveled southward.

"Relax," he whispered. "Let me take care of you."

"I shouldn't."

Stroking fingertips ducked under the elastic at her waist and headed for the deep end. She took a breath and lowered her tummy level.

"Your body tells me otherwise."

She sighed. "Yes, well…"

"Talk to the hand, Rochelle."

"Oh…"

"Oh, yeah. Found a warm place." He held her mons and her breast like precious fruit, not to be bruised by the seeker's rough hands in the picking and the peeling and the search for the juiciest part.

She nearly died when he found it, finessed it, made a sweet, sweet sting.

Nuzzling her temple, he poured warm breath into her ear. "And a hot button," he whispered.

"Birch…"

"Say it again, just like that."

She said it again twice before he covered her mouth and filled it with his rolling tongue. And then, with a plucking thumb and a plunging finger, he rocked her world.

Chapter Four

Rochelle loved the smell of bacon in the morning.

She loved hearing that sizzle when she walked in the front door of the main house, loved the rattle of the plates and the promising scent of strong coffee. She especially loved knowing that all those homey sounds and smells were traveling up Rosewood's beautiful old staircase, a cheery wake-up call for her guest on the second floor. She smiled at the thought of his senses being pleasantly surprised this morning—and the memory of the way he had surprised her senses oh-so-pleasantly last night.

The mirror above the console in the dark foyer brought her up short. There she was, smiling at no one but herself. She liked the look. She pulled a purple aster from the little bunch of flowers she'd picked on her way over and tucked it behind her ear. She like that look, too.

But it was too much. Too obvious. The aster was

back with the bunch by the time Rochelle waltzed into the kitchen.

"Aren't we looking bright-eyed and bushy haired this morning?" Ariel chirped, glancing up from pushing the bacon around in the iron skillet with a fork. She blew at a wisp of brown hair, grinning as it parachuted back over her eye. "Are we having fun yet?"

Rochelle worked at getting her game face back on.

"Who's we? What are you getting at? And good morning to you, too, Ariel."

"I was just wondering how your heart is handling this weekend with Birch Trueblood as a guest. Pitty-pitty pat-pat-pat?" She demonstrated, tapping on her chest with a flat hand.

"He's a guest in my house, not my heart." Rochelle tried to snatch a piece of bacon off the paper towel in the middle of the huge old gas range, but it was too hot to handle. *Much like herself.* She chuckled as she divided the asters and the baby's breath among the bud vases Ariel had put out. "Aunt Meg's house, I mean. *Our* house, *our* B&B."

"Would you like to deliver B-two up to your guest's B-one?" A clanging egg timer punctuated the elbowing Ariel delivered to Rochelle's side. "Be-*fore* it's time for lunch." She spooned coddled eggs onto whole-grain toast, giggling like a fourth-grader. With her long, straight ponytail, chubby little Ariel almost fit the part. "I'm a poet, and I know it," she said merrily. "I may not exactly cut the cheese as far as business matters are concerned, but I'm good with a turn of phrase."

"Mustard, Ariel."

"Why would anyone want mustard with eggs?"

"The expression is…" Rochelle shook her head and laughed. She had to stop trying to get Ariel to talk like everyone else. "You're right. Mustard makes no sense to me, either."

"But if he's a mustard guy, take him some mustard. Men really like it when a woman remembers their preferences, especially when it comes to food. The way to a man's heart is through his mouth."

"What makes you think I'm looking for an anatomical path to this man's heart?"

"I'm told you've had a crush on him since you were sixteen years old."

"When I was sixteen, maybe, but not since."

"Ah, but you haven't met anyone since who could measure up to his snuff and ring your bells."

"Ariel, you are truly one of a kind."

"I just call 'em like I see 'em, sweetie, and I see that you spiffed up a little bit extra this morning."

She touched the soft curl in Rochelle's hair. "This is your dress-up do."

"Oh, it is not," she lied. "Where's Robin?"

"The little girl? I haven't seen her. She must be sleeping in, too."

"I put her to bed in the room next to Aunt Meg last night after she fell asleep on the couch. She came downstairs looking for company while the rest of you were out ghost busting."

"We weren't ghost busting," Ariel insisted. "Purification is a lot like cleaning the house. It's perfectly—"

"It's a bit too creepy for bringing a little girl along, if you ask me. Especially at night. Can't you purify the place in the light of day? I mean, if it's like cleaning…" She started loading up the plate Ariel had set out on a wicker breakfast tray. "I thought she'd be hanging out with you in the kitchen, but maybe she's outside. I should go look for her."

"You should not. I'll take care of Robin while you do her father."

"Ariel, Ariel, Ariel," Rochelle scolded, laughing.

It didn't take much to make her laugh this morning. The idea of somebody *doing* somebody should have embarrassed her after what had happened last night. It had been just like that—him doing her without doing *it*. An adolescent kind of intimacy, really.

But he'd held her late into the night, and they'd whispered secrets and wished on stars, and the only thing she'd felt bad about was saying good-night after he'd walked her back to the house.

She added coffee, orange juice, tiny crystal salt-and-pepper shakers, and flowers to the breakfast tray. "I'll be right back."

"No need to hurry, missy."

Ariel was surprisingly right about most things, including the fact that any reason Rochelle might have had for hurrying upstairs had disappeared. The door to the Lady Slipper room—Rochelle had named the rooms herself—stood open. The bed was made, and the closet was empty.

She set the breakfast tray on the bed and knocked on the bathroom door, softly calling his name before she tried the doorknob. The only evidence of his stay was the scent of wild sage and the dampness she discovered when she laid her hand atop a pile of neatly folded towels.

"Don't bother with another tray," Rochelle announced on her way into the kitchen. "They're gone."

"They can't be." Ariel finished off a piece of bacon and licked her fingers, wide-eyed all the while. "I've been here since six, and I didn't hear anyone leave."

"They're definitely gone." Rochelle set the breakfast tray on the butcher-block island in the center of the kitchen. "Birch seemed to think I tried to play some kind of trick on him. Something about a hidden door in his room and a woman in the mirror." She turned, fist on her hip. "You wouldn't happen to know anything about that, would you, Ariel?"

"I haven't run across any hidden doors." She squinted, puzzling. "He actually saw someone in the mirror? Which mirror? The one in Lady Slipper?"

"I guess. I thought he was teasing. He does it so deadpan, it's impossible to tell."

"Does what so deadpan?"

"Teases. You know, the way he can get you going."

"Get who going? I have a feeling I'm missing out on something."

"Not that you'd notice, Ariel."

"Would that be *Ariel, Ariel, Ariel?* Or just a simple Ariel? Just because a person doesn't get teased doesn't mean she doesn't notice. I can still get going, you know. I'm not dead in the pan yet."

"I meant deadpan, like, you know…" All expression evaporated as Rochelle passed her fingers in front of her face to illustrate.

"I know what deadpan means. It's not letting your feelings show."

"Well, more like—"

"If you think your feelings aren't showing, you've got another think coming, missy." Ariel hiked herself up on a kitchen stool and claimed another strip of crisp bacon. "Did he say what this woman looked like?"

"He thought it was me, so I guess…" Rochelle shook her head. She refused to stray into Ariel's woo-woo world. "But it wasn't me, and there was no one else here, so she didn't look like anything, and I'm sure he was teasing."

"A reflection in the mirror of a woman who's not there," Ariel mused. "Isn't that interesting? That he would be the one."

Rochelle rolled her eyes.

"You look a lot like your great-grandmother, missy. Even more like your great-aunt."

"You keep saying that, but I don't see it." She glanced out the window and across the river. The mill's towering chimneys served no purpose but to stand in silent testimony to days gone by. "I look at the pictures, and I wonder what I have in common with those people. You know, besides this house and all its dusty antiques. I'm not really proud of the way my family made its fortune, Ariel."

"How about the way your aunt unloaded her share of what was left?"

She turned away from the window. "Better than the way my mother squandered hers."

"It's not wise to dis those who have passed on."

"I'm not dissing her. I'm telling it like it is. She spent her inheritance. She made no apologies for herself, and neither do I."

"I'm sure that everything Miss Margaret has left will be yours."

"All I'm worried about is keeping this place from falling down around her ears. The guy from the gas company says we should upgrade the boilers in both houses. 'A plague on both your houses,'" she quipped as she took up a fork and dramatized with a gesture. "A boil on the butt of your boiler."

"Boiler?" Ariel scowled. "If I know my Shakespeare, I'm pretty sure he said *humanity*. Wasn't it Hamlet's uncle who was a boil on the butt of humanity?"

"Oh, yeah." The eggs were probably cold by now, but Rochelle punctured the yolks, anyway. Rosewood couldn't afford waste. "Something like that."

"I haven't seen the play in ages, but that part with the ghost was, like, he wanted Hamlet to just squeeze that nasty boil, like…"

"Yuck!" Rochelle's fork clattered on the plate. "So much for breakfast."

"Sorry." Ariel laid claim to what would have been

Birch's orange juice. "Do you think the spirits we have here are walking around suffering?"

"No idea."

"Do you think they're actually seeking revenge? Would they still care?"

"If they do, and if they're 'the ones who were here before,' as Aunt Meg calls them, then, okay, maybe Rosewood is in for serious trouble. The Indian people who lived here were cheated at every turn, and my family got rich off the land that should have been *their* families' inheritance. Which makes me wonder why they've waited so long." She laughed and shook her head. "Nope, can't go there. All that stuff will just have to be water over the town dam, because there isn't a damn thing I can do about it now."

"It's simply too much for our mortal minds to grapple with, isn't it? I'm of the opinion that it takes more than one lifetime for a soul to come full circle."

"It's an interesting theory." Rochelle nibbled on a piece of dry toast. "Sort of comforting. If I think about it long enough, maybe I can make it work for me. Or maybe I'll just work myself into a headache. I don't do ghosts, but guilt is a whole different territory."

"What you need is some lavender and bergamot oil, along with a bit of sage. Just the thing for disappointment and depression."

"Who's disappointed? Ariel, I am *not* depressed."

But Ariel was already rattling the little bottles she kept on the shelf above the spices, searching for her prescribed combination.

"Why should I be depressed? Or disappointed, for Pete's sake?" Rochelle continued to protest even as she allowed Ariel to herd her into the sunny sitting room off the kitchen and seat her on the chaise. "With our weekend guests leaving early, we should be able to get the place cleaned up in time to have the afternoon for ourselves."

There would be no fighting it. The essence of Ariel's herb garden had been uncorked. Rochelle slipped off her shoes and drew a deep breath as she sank back against a pillow. "Mmm, what's that?"

"It's called Peace and Quiet. My own recipe. Close your eyes and breathe."

"School's starting Tuesday. Maybe that's why I feel a little depressed."

"Do you plan to go back to it?"

"I thought so, but the inn-keeping business is…" Her toes twitched at the initial touch of oily fingers. "I feel funny letting you massage my feet with that, Ariel. I can't return the favor because I'm no…good at…mmm, right there, if you mmm-must."

There was the curve of her blessed arches, fallen as they were.

"I'm of the opinion that we do unto others as they would do unto us."

"As we would *have* others—"

"No, I said it right," Ariel said softly. "As they would do unto us if they had our special knack for doing unto someone."

"It just seems funny."

Funny wasn't the word, as Rochelle well knew, but letting on that it felt good would be too embarrassing, especially after last night—so good, so otherworldly, so *not* funny—but she couldn't let herself think about it right now. Too confusing. Because he was gone, had just up and left without another word. And because thinking led to words, and you couldn't put something like that into words. Words would ruin it. Make it sound embarrassing and worldly. And funny.

"Sometimes," Ariel was saying, "when they relax and let it be done unto them a few times, they start to get more comfortable with the *doing* part."

"Mmm, I've lost you."

"Take a deep breath and your nose will find me."

"My nose is finding your Peace and Quiet."

"That's what I said."

"Ouch!" Rochelle's flashlight clattered to the floor as she felt the top of her head and rubbed hard.

"Oooosh. Eeee. Oooo." She had cracked her skull on the, "Stupid slanted ceiling of this stuuuupid… owww…closet!"

The cursing wasn't doing anything for the growing lump, but the rubbing helped. At least it was moving the spots around in front of her eyes. Either that or the friction was setting her hair on fire.

She sucked a breath through her teeth and cautiously backed out of the wedge of a closet in the Lady Slipper room. For all her trouble, the flashlight revealed nothing so much as a mouse hole that anyone could crawl through. But she'd found another glass inkwell and a button hook.

Rosewood had no secret passages, but between the two houses there were plenty of nooks, closets and cubbyholes full of the kind of old stuff that would make a garage-sale junkie slaver over the prospect of being first in line. Rochelle had been sorting through the Bruner family treasures for the better part of a year, but she had barely scratched the surface of the carefully preserved trove. She enjoyed dusting off her favorite finds and putting them on display all over the house.

She took a special interest in the clothes, like the velvet-trimmed cloak she'd hung on the coat tree in this room. The matching bonnet adorned a foam head on the shelf in the closet, along with a pair of ladies' high-button boots that Rochelle might have been able to wear when she was about six. She wasn't sure where she'd gotten her big, flat feet, but it wasn't from her Bruner ancestry.

A close watch on the classifieds had finally netted her a petite mannequin for Rose Bruner's elegant, satin wedding gown. She'd set it up in the sitting room adjoining the Rose Boudoir. A snappy Edwardian-vintage caped suit and a beaded black flapper dress hung on padded hangers in the wardrobe. From room to room she had found ways to display everything from Martin Bruner's top hat to a newborn's delicately embroidered layette. Her plan for a display of "unmentionables" was on hold until she figured out how some of the garments she'd discovered were worn. She wondered how long it had taken her great-grandmother to dress for one of the illustrious soirees Rochelle had read about in some of Rose's letters.

Strange finds redoubled her curiosity about the family members who had come before Aunt Meg, whose adventures had always fascinated her. But who were the others in the black-and-white photographs she'd always studied in silence? What were their thoughts when the camera clicked, and had they acted on them the instant they left those poses behind for the times they would not know and the family they would never see?

Her grandfather, who had returned from a battle-field in Italy in a flag-draped casket, had posed in happier days with his beautiful bride. Why was her likeness nowhere else to be found? Her great-grand-mother, whose expression for the camera had gradually changed from demure to dour, and that fine-featured great-aunt whom Rochelle was supposed to favor—they had known these rooms as well as Rochelle did, worn these clothes, which they had stored in these closets. They could not have known that Rochelle LeClair was the future of their blood, but did they know her now? Was that why she had this nagging need to know them?

Aunt Meg wasn't much help. She loved to tell stories about the places she'd been and the people she'd met, but she hardly spoke of what had become of their forebears. Rochelle's questions were met with an elliptical comment or some obscure remembrance. As food for her imagination, it served like a tray of sweets.

The one ancestor Rochelle was sure she had pegged was Martin Bruner, the lumber baron. His methods for acquiring the family fortune had been crafty, expedient, effective, undoubtedly respected and even considered admirable in his day. *Go for it, Mr. Bruner.* For the good of the country and its growing population, put the land and its resources to use. Move the Indians out of the way of progress. Surely they could do their hunting, fishing, squatting in their primitive lodges, smoking and telling tales of times long gone somewhere else. Anywhere else, really. The more isolated from good Christian white folk, the better.

Aunt Meg had once said that if her grandfather hadn't made use of the Mille Lacs forest, someone else would have. It had seemed an odd thing for her to say, given the past thirty years the woman had spent paying them back. Not that she'd ever called it that. Other than the occasional odd statement—to which Rochelle deferred without comment, sensing that none had been invited— they spoke as little of the right or wrong of the family business as they did of their ancestors. If Rochelle had any problems with it, she would have to find her own answers, just as Aunt Meg had clearly done.

But if the sins of the fathers were to be visited on the children, shouldn't the children learn the truth about them? How could she atone without knowing the whole story?

Rochelle's quick laugh sounded dull and flat within the confines of the closet. Atonement was a word and surely a concept for some other time and place. She was, as Ariel had said, the family skeptic. She was interested in family history, willing to acknowledge the wrongs that had been done, but how would that change anything? Her answers would have to be down-to-earth, tangible, realistic—and personal. Living, breathing answers, firmly planted in the present. Nothing else made any sense.

Could Birch Trueblood be her answer? Lonely, attractive, maybe even *attracted*—perhaps a man like that could be her cause.

No, not a man *like* that. *That* man. Now *that* was personal. Ariel was right about her crush, her torch, her long-standing enchantment with the way he parted seas of people, believers and skeptics alike. He created an air of anticipation whenever he came on the scene. *The holy man is here. Don't mess with him. He acts like he's got connections. Who knows what kind, but why take a chance?*

Rochelle wondered how many people had been privy to his doubts. She fancied being a rarity in his life, a person he could *personally* trust. He struck her as a loner, and she particularly liked that image. Not only did he have room in his life for a friend, but he had a big empty room, a crying need. Not like the one he'd created in her last night for whatever reason—maybe simply to prove that he could—but the kind of need that a man like Birch might not easily recognize. That was probably why he'd left without saying goodbye. He didn't know what to make of his feelings for her.

Excellent hypothesis. She decided to stop the reverie right there. If she took it much further, it was bound to turn on her.

She couldn't help burying her nose in the sheets as she stripped the bed. Pure, unadulterated fabric softener. At least the towels had been adulterated. She would put them in the washing machine with her pink pajamas and have her own little ceremony in the laundry room.

A familiar noise drew her to the window in time to catch Aunt Meg sneaking down the garden path in her motorized wheelchair. Rochelle had asked her not to go outside alone after the time she'd gotten stuck in the mud and overexerted herself trying to get out. But her aunt was not one to accept even the most sensible suggestion when it threatened her independence.

And she'd forgotten to wear a hat.

By the time Rochelle reached the edge of the garden, Aunt Meg had parked her chair behind the hydrangeas overlooking the river. She was talking to herself. It was a new twist in the old woman's increasingly worrisome habits. Rochelle allowed her boot heels to announce her approach before she could hear what was being said. She didn't want to know.

"Aunt Meg, are you out here?"

"Busted," came the reply.

"I know what a daredevil you are, but it's too late in the year for a swim."

"I know what I'm doing, missy. The ground is dry, and I've got my parking brake on."

"You promised me you wouldn't—" Rochelle swept an armful of snowball blooms aside and stifled a gasp. The wheelchair was parked on the Treaty Table. It wouldn't have to roll far to dump its passenger into the drink.

"I did not promise." Meg adjusted her lap robe. "You took my reticence for submission and stretched that to a promise. Submission is never more than incidental. It is not a permanent commitment."

"I could have sworn you said you wouldn't come out here alone anymore." She tried to be discreet about checking the lock on the wheels as she bent to buss her aunt's softly etched cheek and cap her gray head with a low-brimmed tribute to the Minnesota Timberwolves.

"I'm never alone out here." Meg pointed to the slate promontory. "Stop fretting and sit."

"You have a guardian angel? That would give me some comfort." *Unless the nosy sprite had been hanging around the garden late last night.*

"I've got friends in high places." She chuckled. "And low ones, too. Here, there, everywhere you look."

"It's all about staying in touch with your roots, right? Friendly ties and fond memories."

"Not always," Meg admitted. "But you can't pick and choose. Roots are roots, and family is family."

"And guests are guests until they go home, which is what ours have done. The Truebloods left without breakfast or a by-your-leave."

"I had coffee with Birch before they left."

Rochelle gave a double take as she seated herself beside Aunt Meg's locked wheel.

"Yes, it was early. We greeted the sunrise together. It's a wonderful little ceremony. I wonder why we don't have ceremonies like that?"

"To each her own. When I was teaching, I greeted the morning by kicking the alarm clock and cursing the woman upstairs for flushing the toilet in the middle of my shower."

"That isn't a ceremony, Shelly. That's a rut."

"Pardon me for being an ordinary working slob."

"It's nothing to do with working and everything to do with being. You're no longer teaching. Besides cursing the woman upstairs, how has your morning ritual changed?"

Rochelle squinted into the sun, grinning. "Who says it's changed at all?"

"You see? It's all about being. It's about attitude. And you'd better change your 'tude and be nice to your old aunt, lest you find yourself totally dissed." Aunt Meg came back with an old woman's eerie grin. "Disinherited, that is."

"Well, aren't you feeling hip? I take it this morning's ceremony was performed in the vernacular."

"It's not a performance. Ritual is a performance. Ceremony is something else. Ritual bores me, but ceremony…" Meg pulled at the brim of her cap and smiled. "Humor me, Shelly."

"I am."

"Birch said to tell you that it was good seeing you again."

With a look, Rochelle demanded details.

"Wrong word. He didn't say *good*. He said it was *a pleasure*, and that I must be sure to tell you that for him. I think he was a little hurt."

"By what?"

"Your lack of interest. You were the only one here who didn't participate."

"Robin didn't participate," Rochelle averred. "I'm not sure she's all that comfortable with what her father does. That whole ghost thing seemed to make her a little nervous, and I know she was glad to have a human being to hang out with while everyone else was busy seeking the company of spirits."

"I still think Birch was a little hurt. Not offended, mind you, but I think he wanted you to take part. He's not very good at hiding how much he misses his wife."

"Which has exactly nothing to do with me, but speaking of wives…" A change of subject was in order. "Do you really think we should block out a whole week for Crystal's wedding?"

"She's *your* sister." A second thought shifted Aunt Meg's spin. "I mean, she's your *sister.* We should kill the fatted calf and put on the dog. Or is it the other way around?"

"You've been hanging around Ariel too long."

"Dear Ariel." The years dropped away from Meg's face with her smile. "No matter how she explains it, she always does just the right thing."

"And she won't stand for us killing any calf, fatted or otherwise."

"Wait until you see what she comes up with instead. Even for the simplest tea or afternoon card game, Ariel comes up with the most glorious ideas when it's time to entertain." She snatched her cap off by the bill and waved it toward the river. "Whoopie! Time to kill the fatted tofu!"

"Careful. Let's not be ejecting prematurely." Rochelle grabbed the arm of the wheelchair. "How disappointed would Ariel be if she gave a party and nobody came? Because the chances of Crystal actually going though with her plans are probably no better than—"

"Let's not make any bets," Meg warned. "It's bad luck. We'll take her at her word and enjoy the preparations. You'll call her today?"

"My sister?" Rochelle sighed. "All right. We don't have much time."

"Whatever time we have is all we need. You have so many beautiful things on display now that I feel as though we're almost ready for Grandmother's house to come alive again."

Aunt Meg's excitement came as a surprise. She'd balked at Rochelle's initial suggestion to turn the main house into a bed-and-breakfast, but she'd finally agreed that its pristine turn-of-the-century state suited Rochelle's plan. And if the plan would bring Rochelle back home, then innkeepers they would be.

"Why did you close the main house up and move back into the new one?"

"It was easier. Grandfather kept the main house exactly the way Grandmother had left it. Whenever I wanted anything modern, it went into the new house. After he died, I saw little reason to make changes. I turned to other activities, endeavors of my own." She gazed across the glistening water to the west bank of the river. "My grandparents were part of a different era, and I needed to step away from it even as I kept its shell intact. I needed to be able to see it through another window."

"You're talking about your concern for the Indian communities," Rochelle inferred.

"My *concern*," Aunt Meg echoed. "That's a good word for it. There's always been that measure of reserve. Grandmother insisted that women in our position must maintain our dignity. *Women*." She gave a wry smile. "I was only a girl in pigtails at the time. But I've often wondered whether dignity is a genetic disorder. Perhaps it keeps the blood a degree or two cooler than normal."

"You almost lost the Bruner cool at the end of the parade, right there in the middle of the street."

"I did, didn't I? Did you think I'd get wild and crazy and dance up a storm?"

"For a minute there—"

"I saw myself joining in and becoming a real part of it all. I saw it in my head. I felt completely warm and welcome, and my heart was so full. In my mind I became the cripple at the tent revival, throwing crutches aside and crying buckets of joy for all the world to see." She squeezed Rochelle's hand. "Wouldn't that have been a sight?"

"I saw you, Aunt Meg. I knew how you felt."

"I envy you, dear girl. By becoming a teacher, you've taken *concern* another step. You've become so involved that you've worn yourself out emotionally."

"And you think that's a *good* thing?"

"You have a difficult job, Shelly. You give until you have nothing left, which makes it hard to recharge. But that's exactly what you're doing now."

"I thought I was taking care of you."

"Is that what you thought?" The old woman eyed her for a moment. "Have you found anything interesting in the attic lately?"

Caught, like a mouse in a box. Nothing scented, nothing nibbled, but she blushed for her snooping.

"I'm just trying to organize some of that stuff. There are so many papers, Aunt Meg. If we ever had a fire…"

"Dry bones are the most vulnerable tinder."

"Papers," Rochelle insisted. An intriguing skeleton or an infamous ancestor would be too much to hope for. "Did no one ever think of tossing a letter or a bill?"

"I remember a time after Grandmother died when Grandfather took a notion to sort through the business records and put together some sort of history. He lost interest in the project, and when I offered to help, he told me to stay out of that stuff. He said that he was going to get rid of it, but he didn't like going up there. I offered to hire someone to clean it all out, but he wouldn't hear of it."

"Maybe it was difficult for him—" Rochelle raised an eyebrow "—emotionally."

"You didn't inherit your soft side from him, missy. He was not an emotional man. Nor was he superstitious, but there were parts of the house that disturbed him."

"Maybe I'll be able to get to know him a little bit if I can figure out what was so disturbing. I've been trying to come up with some kind of order, trying to make chronological sense of the business papers and some personhood sense of the personal papers."

"Careful not to rub one against another, Shelly. Dry bones, dry bones, them dr-y-y bones," Meg crooned.

"Oh, for Pete's sake, don't go spooky on me." She squinted into the sun again, trying to get a look at her aunt's face. "What happened to Rose's sister?"

"I don't know much about her. She died quite young, and Grandmother would never talk about her. I think it was one of those matters of dignity."

"It was too emotional for her?"

"Grandmother wouldn't even admit to that much. I learned that if I pressed the issue, she would simply leave the room. Being in Grandmother's presence was a privilege for me, so I didn't press."

"But you were curious."

"Not enough to make me go digging. Since you're not spooky, I'll leave the digging to you."

"I'm not afraid to discover old secrets."

"That's because you didn't experience the privilege of Grandmother's company or the emptiness when she was gone. I wish you could have known her. But since you didn't, you're free to go digging." She smiled in the shade of her billed cap. "I mean that in a positive way. You're a step removed. You'll be looking through an added window, you see. Objectivity makes one feel marvelously safe."

"At least I can organize things. Until I know exactly what's there, I can't seem to bring myself to throw any of it away, which must be another genetic disorder. If I find anything interesting, I'll let you know."

"I've pursued answers to every question I've ever had, all the world's mysteries. Every secret except two, and you've hit upon one of them. What really happened to my grandmother's sister?"

"What's the other one?"

"When you hit it, did you feel resistance?" the old woman mused. "I felt it in myself. For the first time I faced a question I wasn't sure I wanted answered. Did you feel that resistance, Shelly?"

"No."

"Good," she whispered.

"What's the other question, Aunt Meg?"

Margaret Bruner went quite still for a moment. Then she turned her attention upriver. "The other one concerns my grandfather and the Ojibwe."

"What about them?"

"Exactly." She nodded and stared northward. "What about them?"

Chapter Five

Ariel Sweet believed in signs.

It was a sign when someone who had dropped out of a person's life suddenly dropped back in. Birch Trueblood's brief stay at Rosewood was a clear sign, as was his abrupt departure. Ariel felt a new charge in Rosewood's atmosphere.

She wasn't one to predict specifics—leave that to those spendy phone-in fortune-tellers—but she could hardly stand keeping her thoughts about it all to herself while she tossed letter after bill after order after inventory into the plastic bins Rochelle had designated for sorting out a century's worth of the stuff. Had she known what she was getting herself into with the project, Ariel might have thought twice about offering to help. But at the risk of tampering with good instincts, she rarely gave a second thought. And she was dying to get a handle on those delicious signs.

So far Rochelle was playing it close to the breast. She was taking Birch's behavior personally, of course, which put her in the dark, along with everyone else who had not learned to use the third eye. Without that third eye, who could possibly see the forest for the twists and turns of the garden path? With the third eye closed, a person had to find it dark and scary deep down inside the vulnerable self. And smart people were the most vulnerable. How was a person like Rochelle—too smart for her own britches, dear as she was—supposed to find her way when she had no sense of signs?

Fortunately, Ariel was attuned to these things, which was probably why she had been drawn to Rosewood in the first place. She wasn't one to let logic or reason limit her keen sense of what was true. She was needed here.

But at the moment, Rochelle would have her believe that she was actually interested in the Bruner paper trail, which was bound to lead her up the wrong tree.

"Look at this," Rochelle insisted, waving another bill under Ariel's nose. "Ladies' dresses shipped from the Charles William Stores of New York in 1915. They cost between ten and twelve dollars apiece. I wonder if any of the dresses are still around. Wouldn't it be fun to match them to the bill?"

"By *fun* we mean…"

"Taffeta and French serge," she read off the bill. "What's French serge?"

"Something you make cheap dresses out of?"

"This probably wasn't that cheap." Another yellowed paper was eagerly proffered. "Look, Ariel, here's one for custom-tailored suits."

"For Mr. Bruner?"

"No, women's suits. This outfit—*costume*, it says—took six and a half yards of whipcord for jacket, waistcoat and flared skirt with loose box plaits. Do you think that means *pleats?*"

Ariel offered no opinion.

Rochelle puzzled a moment longer. "I'll bet we can find some of these."

"Probably. Unlike his granddaughter, Mr. Bruner obviously wasn't one for giving stuff away."

"But the upside is that there's still so much history here. I feel like we should try to make some sense of it."

Ariel plunged both hands into the carton she'd been picking through. "All right, then, let's feel our way—"

"I mean, as time permits, what with the wedding in the works. Have you heard that Crystal wants Aunt Meg to give her away?"

"I think that's nice."

"Nobody gave her away to her first husband," Rochelle recalled with a chuckle. "She said it was an archaic tradition. Prefeminist."

"Oh, well, you know what they say. What goes around, comes back."

"Maybe, but Crystal hasn't shown much interest in coming back *here* until now."

"Let it be, Rochelle. Let the time and your sister come. It'll be good for everyone."

"It's been almost three years. Three years ago Christmas." She shoved another box aside and smiled. "You're right, Ariel. Oh me of little faith."

"Would I say that?" She reached across the box, but Rochelle moved her arm before Ariel could deliver the friendly touch she intended. She'd spotted the spine of a ledger in the next box. Oh, endless forest! Ariel smiled indulgently. "You're our rock, Rochelle. And Crystal, well, she was aptly named."

"Aren't crystals rocks? What do you call that?" She pointed to Ariel's quartz pendant.

"Your sister is more like crystal glassware. Pretty, but handle with care."

"The way we'd all like to be…" A loose page in the ledger had claimed her attention. "Well, what do you know?"

"A few things." Ariel craned her neck to get a look at the news on the paper. "What about you?"

"That Martin Bruner was more generous than I thought. He supported a school up in…oh, my God, look at this." She read aloud. "'Young Trueblood is an apt student, but his mother refuses to allow him to be baptized and given a Christian name. This sets a bad example, so I hope you will speak with the family. I find it odd since their other children have been baptized. God bless you for your generous support. Sister Madeline.'" She looked up in amazement. "It's dated December, 1921."

"My, my." Ariel smiled. Her instincts hadn't failed her.

"Do you think this would interest Birch?"

"He might be able to expand on the story, hmm?"

"He might take offense. He might think I'm suggesting that giving financial support to an Indian school and taking an interest in his…" Rochelle frowned. "Isn't that weird? Young Trueblood. I can't imagine what Birch would think."

"What do *you* think?"

"I just think that…" She reread the letter, repeating only the name, and shook her head. "I just think it's too weird. Birch's great-grandfather. Of course, the world was a whole lot smaller back then."

"Size doesn't matter, missy. It's the connection, the energy, the…" Words, words, words. She punched her fist into her palm. "Zap! The heat-seeking arrow that will not be deflected by dimensional limitation."

"Arrow?"

"Whatever. Nothing is ever over just because one person's finished. Because—" she punched and punched again "—it's that life force that just keeps—"

Rochelle was laughing at her.

"How can you doubt when the proof is right there in your hand? Birch's ancestor and your ancestor, right there in black-and-white. I can feel the energy without even touching the paper." No call to admit that these dull, dry papers were the last place Ariel had expected to find any energy.

But she hadn't found it, had she? No, the letter—the energy in the letter—had found its way to Rochelle's hand. Exactly the kind of sign that would speak to someone like Rochelle.

Oh, the haunting titillation!

"The next time Birch Trueblood comes to Rosewood, we must keep him here awhile. I think he ought to spend lots of time in the bedrooms," Ariel said.

Rochelle challenged her with a dubious glance.

"Think of the generations of dreams up there," Ariel explained. "Their dreams echo in ours."

"Seriously?"

"Seriously sometimes," she mused, enthralled with possibilities. "Sometimes sadly, sometimes humorously, sometimes…"

Ariel didn't mind Rochelle's laughter, because it wasn't meant to make her feel silly. She enjoyed the ideas, even though she couldn't buy them, and she laughed with love in her eyes.

"Okay, where do *you* think dreams come from?"

"The sandman," Rochelle said merrily.

"Seriously?"

"And don't try to confuse me with any more theories of relativity. I prefer lyric and melody, and three part-harmony and—"

"As I was saying, we must find a way to keep Mr. Birch Trueblood around the house a little longer."

"Mmm." Rochelle added the ledger to the stack of items she'd chosen for a closer look and pulled a satin letter box from the same carton. "Elderberry wine might do it."

"We don't want him to fall off the rocker, Rochelle. We just want him to hang around long enough to get a true sense of everything here. He has such a sensitive nature."

"Right."

"He simply hasn't realized its full potential. Not unlike Rochelle of little faith."

"You mean I still have room to grow?" she wondered absently as she pulled on the end of a satin ribbon inside the letter box.

"There's always that. Some people buy their clothes a size too small, thinking they're going to lose a few inches. Me, I leave a little extra room. It's like my mother used to say—you know you're gonna grow."

"Look at this, Ariel." She named each lovely old card as she handed it over for inspection. "Here's a party invitation. Another one. Another one. And a wedding. Oh, look, here's Aunt Meg's birth announcement! Margaret Elizabeth, born September 22, 1931. And my mother, eight years later." Rochelle looked up, enchanted. "All beautifully handwritten."

"They must have hired a calligrapher."

"And kept a copy of everything in this box. How far back do they go?" She reclaimed the wedding announcement. "The marriage of Rose Analise Richard to Martin Karl Bruner on the first of June in the year of our Lord eighteen hundred ninety-six. They were married in Louisiana."

"Rose's people came from there."

"I knew that, but…" She looked through the rest of the cards. "I don't see a birth announcement for my grandfather. He was their only child. You would expect to find an announcement written on silk in gold leaf. When was he born?"

"You'll have to ask your aunt. I believe he was in his early thirties when he was killed in World War II."

"Here's an invitation to his wedding in 1930. They certainly wasted no time having their first child." She examined both sides of the elegant card. "Very pretty. Do you think we could do something like this for Crystal? How's your penmanship?"

"I'm in charge of food. You're the crafty one. Do we know how many guests they're inviting?"

"No number so far. I offered to take care of invitations, but so far, no list. 'Just a small group.' That's all she says."

"If she sticks to that, no problem. If she's willing to be flexible with the menu, we'll be flexible with her guest list."

"Or lack thereof." With Ariel's help she began putting the old cards back in the box. "I do have some ideas for the table. I'm thinking fall colors with Victorian details, like lace and ribbons and old buttons. I found a whole jar of old buttons in the sewing room."

"You know what would be fun? We could dress in period clothing. There's so much stuff up there, Rochelle. I know we could find something for everyone."

"Crystal would never go for that." But the idea was too good to dismiss. "Would she?"

"She's going for Rosewood," Ariel reminded her.

"And we've been sorting through all those trunks and closets anyway."

"If she doesn't go for it, fine."

"But we'll set the table our way, and we'll get the catering and the music lined up."

"She might not give us any more direction than what we have now."

"And she might not even show up."

"Then we'll make sure nothing's lost if she backs out. But she won't. We're going to have a family wedding at Rosewood." Ariel smiled wistfully. "I can just see it."

"Guess what, Ariel." Rochelle closed the letter box, clutched it to her breast and smiled back. "My little faith is growing. I can just *feel* it."

Birch had a stubborn kid on his hands, but there was no way he was giving in to her. He had a funeral to attend to, and since it involved some shirttail relations, Robin was going along. She'd never complained before, but lately she'd been giving him the third degree about his ceremonies. Were spirits the same as ghosts? Could spirits make people do things? If a ghost touched you in the dark, would it feel cold or slimy or prickly? Did ghosts pop out of dead bodies?

And why couldn't they just visit their cousins after the grandma got buried?

"Because that's not the way we do things," he told her as he watched her buckle herself into the back seat of the car. "You can stay outside if you want to. Other kids will be there, and you can play."

"I'll stay with you."

"Lookin' out for the old man, are you?"

"Somebody has to," she primly reminded him. "And you're not old. I mean you are, but you don't look it."

"Don't worry, Tweety bird." He couldn't resist taking a glance at himself in the rearview mirror to confirm before giving her the reflection of a smile. "I don't plan to live so long that you really do end up taking care of me."

"Daddy, don't talk like that. You *are too* going to live long enough."

"You wanna be spooning baby food past your old dad's toothless gums someday?" he asked as he switched the car's gears.

"Didn't you feed me my baby food before I had any teeth?"

"Yeah, I did. You got that stuff all over me, too. All over your face, the walls, the floor. What if you have to clean up after me the same way I did for you?"

"I do, anyway, sometimes."

"Yeah, right." He shrugged. "Okay, maybe sometimes. But I'm a guy. Guys are messy."

"Like babies."

"And senile old men."

"I don't care. Anyway, you don't even have any fillings, so how can you get toothless?"

"That's right, in'it? I'm the one with the good teeth." He flashed them in the mirror for her. "Look, Mom, no cavities."

Old advertising trivia was wasted on her. She thought he was ragging on her again about her baby teeth being rotten, which was his fault for letting her have too much junk. But her second set was coming in nicely.

What should he say to break the silence? It wasn't as easy to coax her over a pout as it used to be, which worried him. His kid's behavior was becoming less kid and more female.

She was sitting back there, staring out the window, probably thinking up some new problem to dump in his lap. Pretty soon he would be apologizing for something he'd said that her female ears had twisted around until it hurt, or trying to figure out how to buy her something she wanted that he couldn't afford, or how to fix some gadget that only a woman could find a way to break. Or he'd be telling her she couldn't go somewhere, and the words *you can't stop me* would come out of her mouth and hit him in the gut.

"Daddy, what's senile?"

"Something I'm not gonna get."

"What is it?"

"It's like a little bit crazy. Sometimes when people get old, they lose their minds a little bit. You know, they forget things. They don't know what they're doing half the time." He glanced in the mirror and smiled. *Pretty soon, maybe, but not today.* "Don't look at me like that. I'm not that bad."

"You forgot my school conferences last year."

"Once." He punctuated the claim with a finger. "One time."

"You only went to one."

"You're a straight-A student, for crissake. I got nothing to worry about." And neither did she, not today. "I'm not senile."

"You shouldn't cuss."

"Sorry. Bad habit."

They buried it for the moment in silence.

"Daddy?" She gave him pause to tune in. "When people die of old age, how old are they?"

"A lot older than me."

"A hundred?"

"Sometimes. You never know. I met a woman at

a ceremony up at Red Lake a few weeks ago, and she was sharp and spry. Had long white braids, bright eyes. I couldn't believe she was a hundred and three years old." He slowed the car at a four-way stop. It was an intersection between two remote roads that barely rated two lanes each, never mind four stop signs, but he stopped, anyway. He had his baby on board.

He glanced in the mirror again and couldn't help smiling. She would give him hell if he didn't stop.

"Damn few Indians ever live that long."

"Why not?"

"Lotta reasons, I guess." He turned onto the road less graveled. "But all that's changing, Tweety bird. You're gonna live to be a hundred and three, bouncing lots of great-grandbabies on your knee." He caught her doubting glance in the mirror. "Okay, me, too. A *hell* of an old man. You want it, you got it."

"You shouldn't cuss."

He sighed. "I guess I wasn't cut out for raising girls."

"You only have one. That's not too much." Her sigh echoed his. "I guess you can cuss if you want, but just don't do it when you're talking to the spirits. You don't want to get them mad."

"I don't really talk to spirits. I mean, not like

some weird guy who, uh…" Who what? Channeled some poor widow's husband? "I do traditional ceremonies. It's like when you dance."

"Do you dance with ghosts?"

"No." Better men than him had tried that and gotten themselves shot. "I don't dance much at all anymore."

"Is Mama a ghost now?"

"I don't…" Wrong response. He had to know something. "She's in a good place, Tweety bird. The best place you can imagine, that's where she is."

"But if she comes around, do you chase her away?"

"No. I mean, she doesn't…" But she knew better. She'd seen him put the bits of fruit and meat in the dish, and smudge it and himself, the way he'd been taught to do. "I feed her spirit."

"Why is her spirit hungry if she's in such a good place?"

"Why do you ask so many hard questions?"

"I just wanna know."

"You worry too much already, Robin." Birch shook his head. "And here I am, taking you to a funeral."

"It's okay, Daddy. I'm not scared. You're a holy man."

"Yeah." He glanced up and thanked her with a

soft smile. She was a little beauty, sitting up so tall, all alone in the big back seat. "Did you come up with an idea for your Halloween costume yet?"

"I want to be Glenda, the good witch."

"There's no such thing as a good witch. How did you come up with that?"

"Rochelle has Wizard of Oz dolls, and Glenda is the good witch. She's beautiful. Not ugly like the bad witch."

"Rochelle, huh?" She tossed the name out like they were neighbors. "Why don't you be the little girl with the black braids? What's her name?"

"Dorothy. She has a dog. I can't be her because you won't let me have a dog."

He groaned.

"Well, you won't. Besides, Glenda wears a crown and a beautiful white dress. Auntie Regina said she'd make it for me. And she's making me a new jingle dress. Mine's getting too small."

"You're getting too big," he scolded. "I wish you'd slow down. Pretty soon you'll be a teenager, and I'll be fighting off the boys."

"You don't have to worry. I hate boys. They act stupid."

"And don't you forget it." He was beginning to feel bad about the long ride. There were no straight roads in the North Country. They wound around lake after lake, and he knew that an hour in the car felt like ten to a kid. "Why don't you take a little nap?"

"I'm not tired. Besides, when we talk, I don't get carsick so easy."

"Sooo, you've got your Halloween costume all planned, huh? How about Thanksgiving? You wanna be a Pilgrim or an Indian?"

"I'm always an Indian, Daddy." Her laugh was the sweetest of all sweet sounds. "We don't need costumes for that."

"You've got that right, Tweety bird."

After a while, Robin fell asleep. Her head rested against the car door. He wished he could stop the car and tuck a pillow between her face and the window, but he didn't want to wake her. She was some chatterbox. Car time was the worst. The questions, the questions, the questions. His pitiful answers satisfied neither of them. How long would it be before his bright, beautiful daughter realized what a fraud he was? He could probably keep up the image indefinitely for everyone else, but Robin would figure him out one day. He was about as holy as shit.

Her mention of Rochelle rang in his ears. A starry night, a little wine, and what the hell was he doing, acting like a fourteen-year-old with a hard-on? What he'd needed was an unholy fuck, but he'd gone long and stopped short. Sweet Rochelle had him pegged, and, bless her, she wasn't looking for *holy*. If all she wanted was a slow hand, a deep voice and a hard cock, he was her man. They could play all kinds of tricks on each other, and no one would ever feel cheated. It would all be good.

So why had he left her house in such a killing hurry?

He'd thought about it a lot since Labor Day weekend, and he still didn't know the answer.

So what else was new?

He was sure of two things about that weekend. The woman was sweet, but that whole sprawling place by the river gave him the creeps. It was no good going back there.

By dusk they'd reached the home of the young man who would bury his mother tomorrow. A good time for Birch's entrance. A good turnout, judging by the number of vehicles in the yard. At least a few of them were bound to be permanent fixtures, being dead themselves. But that was okay. It was welcoming yard art, the kind that said *We won't throw you out, either.*

Who could tell when a dead pony might decide to run again?

He turned, rested his chin on the curl of his fist on the back of the car seat, gave himself over to the beauty of a sleeping child. He knew what Rochelle thought about him having Robin around the ceremonies, but Robin wasn't like Rochelle. She wasn't white. She was Ojibwe and Lakota. Maybe he ought to be leaving her home when he was doing the New Age stuff, but in Indian Country, the kids were included. They were seen and they were heard. If you couldn't see and hear them, something was wrong. Maybe they were hiding from something bad, or maybe there was sickness. Or, worst of all, maybe the children were all gone. Maybe they had been taken away, sent to foster homes or missions or boarding schools. If children weren't seen or heard in Indian Country, then times were bad.

Birch greeted everyone in the common area of the home—living room, dining area, kitchen—with a handshake. His daughter followed, encouraged to do the same. They made their way to the open casket, where a leathery, gray-headed woman with a cold, rubbery face lay at peace for the first time in many years.

"Was she the hundred-year-old lady?" Robin asked quietly.

"She was probably about half that."

"She looks a hundred."

A familiar voice cut in from behind them. "That's the way you look after you pack a hundred years' worth of parties into fifty-five."

"Jesus, Regina." Birch turned, eyes twinkling. Regina was more like a sister to him than an aunt, his father's baby sister. "Show some respect."

"I'm like Robin," the short, round-faced woman with sparkling obsidian eyes said. "I tell it like it is."

"You're not afraid her spirit might come after you?" Robin whispered.

"That's what your dad's here for, my girl—appeasing the spirits and singing her into the next world." Regina gave the deceased woman a leery once-over. "If they'll take her."

Birch tried hard not to smile. "If she gets there first, they might not take you."

"They'd better take her. I hate to think of her hangin' around here."

He laid a hand on Regina's shoulder and steered them clear of the corpse's rightful space. "Robin says you're making her a Halloween costume."

Regina brightened. "She brought over some library books and showed me a picture. It's a fancy one, but I think I can copy it pretty good."

"Wizard of Oz? I tried to talk her into the little girl outfit instead of the fancy witch, but then she started working on me for a dog."

"She had some books about dolls, too. Said she helped Margaret Bruner's niece fix some old dolls."

"We had a purification ceremony at that mansion

of theirs." Birch took a foam cup from an upended stack and slid it under the spigot on the three-gallon coffeemaker.

"Now, that's a place where I wouldn't wanna run into any spirits. Miss Margaret is a good woman, but she comes from a long line of thieves. I doubt if Martin Bruner has finished paying for his sins yet."

"Which means what?" He glanced at Robin and nodded in the direction of an enamel basin piled high with fresh fry bread.

"Who knows? White men's souls go the white man's way, I guess. Purgatory." Regina's gaze followed Robin's progress toward the food. "There's all kinds of stories about him coming around the girls up here," she confided.

"Ojibwe girls?"

"That's what they say. One in particular." She raised her brow. "You never heard this?"

"You're wasting your time trying to get me stirred up over hundred-year-old grievances, Regina. Bad times and bad blood don't interest me. My wife was the warrior, not me."

"Your ancestors—"

"Are dead and gone. I don't know about you, but I have to get along with those people. I've got a kid to support." He sipped his coffee and came up chuckling. "The ol' moccasin telegraph is amazing, isn't it? Once a story starts circulating, it keeps going round and round forever."

"That's what you call *oral tradition*."

"I call it old news."

"And maybe it doesn't affect you." She shrugged. "But maybe it will. You never know. These stories become part of the tradition for a reason. Sometimes it takes generations for them to come full circle."

"And do what? Bite us in the ass?"

"Who knows? That far back, maybe it doesn't matter. But maybe it does."

"*Maybe it will. Maybe it does.* What you're sayin' is maybe some of us are related to old man Bruner?" He laughed. "Maybe you ought to look for a job in television, Regina. You could write soap operas."

"We're all related," she said, quoting the traditional belief as she helped herself to the traditional funeral potato salad.

"That's right. My mom used to say that every family tree has its share of rotten branches, so it's best not to go climbin' up there."

"Strange thing for a Lakota to say. They love to tell how they're closely related to this one and that one. Sitting Bull, Crazy Horse, Red Cloud. How many kids did those guys have, anyway?"

"Cousins. *Tona* cousins. Plenty. Like I said, you could write the first Indian soap opera for TV. They'll be waiting on the edge of their seats for the next installment." He finished his coffee. "I've gotta do my part, then take Robin home. She's a little jumpy about funerals lately."

"It's the season. Fall and winter." And then she sang, "Oh, it's dyin' time again."

Birch wagged his head. "Woman, you're something else."

"When my time comes, I want Edna Rice to make the potato salad. This is good." She gave him the "Indian nod"—pooched lips and a jerk of the chin. "And I want you to sing for me."

"You'll outlive us all, Regina. Your only vice is gossiping." He squeezed her shoulder. "Thanks for the Halloween costume. I'll pay you for it. She never picks anything simple."

"That's all right. She's a good girl. I want to do for her the way her mother's sister would."

"Her mother, who threw her own life away halfway across the world in bum-fuck wherever."

"I know it's hard, but you can't let Robin hear you talk like that."

He nodded.

"You're mad at her for dying."

"The *hell* I am."

"It's hell, and you are. But it's time to move on, my brother."

"I am," he insisted. "I already have. Hell, it's been *years*."

"Two? Going on three?"

"Something like that. Forget what I said, Regina. She died for her country, okay? That's what I'm telling her daughter. 'Your mom was a good soldier, but don't even *think* of following in her path.' How does that sound?"

"Like you're mad at her for dying, but you'll get over it. That's part of the journey. I know it's a rough road. Especially for a man who's trying to travel with a moccasin on one foot and a white man's shoe on the other."

"I'm my father's son."

"You said a mouthful there." She filled her own with a plastic fork full of creamy potato salad. "From the stories they tell, he didn't carry your burden so easy, either," Regina said, swallowing after chewing twice. "And that was before being Indian got so popular. Back then, most white people didn't hardly know we were still around."

"Robin really wants a dog. I don't like having animals in the house." Now *there* was a burden. "Maybe I should get her a puppy, huh? A small one. Give her something to look out for besides me."

"They stink up the house, you ask me."

"Yeah, but if it makes her happy…"

"Trueblood." The dead woman's brother approached him and leaned close. "Some of the elders are getting tired. We're ready for you."

Chapter Six

Crystal blew into Rosewood's stately drive on a brisk autumn tailwind. If the rattle underpinning the roar of its engine was any indication, her little red car needed the boost.

Rochelle heard the car before she could actually see who was in it, but she had the feeling it was her sister. It had been exactly one week since she'd gotten the call saying, "We'll see you in a week." And here she was. Amazing. Only four days to go, and the November first wedding was apparently still on. She wouldn't let herself get too excited until she saw faces and heard assuring words, but the car was the right color, and rattle and roar made for a fine drumroll. She hurried out the front door and skipped down the steps, eager to make sure they came directly to the new house.

There were surprises in the old house that she wanted to show Crystal later. She and Ariel had taken every one of the house's five chandeliers apart, washed every glass bauble and bead in vinegar, and polished each piece to glittering effect. They had done up all the ruffles and flourishes in the rooms downstairs, and added frothy new touches of color—the rich purples, reds and golds of fall in Minnesota. The windows and doors, chairs and railings, were all artfully draped and swagged and tacitly approved by the women in the paintings and photographs that hung on Rosewood's walls. And they hadn't even started with the flowers.

But Rochelle would save wedding details for later. For now there were greetings to be exchanged and tension to be relieved with an embarrassment of fussing over how much ten-year-old Garth had grown. And where was the groom?

"Never mind him." Crystal squeezed Rochelle's shoulders and offered an oversize grin. "What about my little sister? Tell me all about your latest escapades."

"Escapades?"

"Oh, please, Shelly, tell me you've been gallivanting. Tell me you have an exciting man in your life, and you've been saving the news until you could tell me in person."

"Gallivanting?"

Was this English as a second language, for Pete's

sake? Flummoxed by her sister's paralyzing expectations, Rochelle didn't know quite what to do with the arm Crystal had pinned to her side. Withdraw, or take a little initiative, slip it around her sister's tiny waist and return the big squeeze?

Nothing had changed. The ball was always in Crystal's court.

"Haven't you learned how to do that yet?"

"Is it the latest dance? I haven't learned any new steps since you went away to college."

"That figures. Wasn't that about the time you moved here?" Crystal started to drop her keys into her purse, but on second thought she tossed them to her towheaded son. "Think fast, Garth." She laughed when he missed the catch. "You'll have to work on that some more, sweetie. Just get your own stuff so you have something to amuse yourself while we girls catch up".

Without missing a beat, Crystal pulled her wallet out and flipped it open to a fuzzy photograph. "So this is Tracy. He's almost forty, divorced, usually pretty quiet, and just very sweet. His family is well connected up here. His mother knows everyone in Brainerd and Aitken."

Side by side, they climbed the porch steps. "We mailed out the invitations to all the names you gave us. I hope we didn't miss any," Rochelle said.

"Oh, no, we're intentionally keeping it small. Vera—Vera is Tracy's mother—Vera just wants to get to know my little family. She knows the Bruner name, of course, but she's never been inside the gate at Rosewood."

"I'm so glad you decided to come." Rochelle opened the porch door for Crystal. "Aunt Meg is getting pretty frail."

"That's what Vera said. You know, that that's what she'd heard." She gave a dramatic sigh. "It's sort of like you don't see the sights in your own backyard until people come to visit. You lose track of what's going on with your family until you run into someone from your hometown."

"Crystal, I tried to get in touch with you when she was in the hospital, but I didn't know you'd moved. And you know about her surgery."

"The surgery, yes. I expected her to bounce right back from that. She's the strongest woman I know."

They entered the house together, towhead in silent tow. Ariel greeted them in the foyer, and they headed for the living room, now a bunch of four.

"When will we actually meet Tracy?" Rochelle asked.

"He had some work to finish up, and then he plans a rendezvous with his family. He'll be here for the rehearsal dinner."

"Rehearsal dinner?" She glanced at Ariel. "Rehearsal dinner."

"Absolutely," Ariel enthused. "Every wedding party has a rehearsal dinner."

"I'm here to tell you not to plan some elaborate party," Crystal instructed. "A simple sit-down for twenty people. Thirty, max. Time for everyone to get to know each other."

"We only sent out ten invitations for the wedding, and I thought it would just be family the night before the wedding," Rochelle said. "Call it a rehearsal dinner if you want to, but we weren't planning anything—"

"Elaborate, my point exactly. You can always add a few, can't you? I have no idea how many relatives Vera might bring along," Crystal warned as she sank back on the sofa with a deep sigh. "She's thrilled with the whole idea of a wedding at the Bruner estate. Don't worry, Shelly, we'll work out the details. But right now, I'm exhausted." She sat up suddenly. "Shouldn't someone check on Aunt Meg? I'm dying to see her."

"She's been looking forward to seeing you, too."
For years.

"How bad off is she?"

On cue, two big wheels and a blanket appeared in the hall. "Not so bad off that she doesn't feel her ears burning."

"That's why you need to stay out of the kitchen," Ariel said with a laugh. "If you can't stand red ears. Right, Garth?" She waved the boy in from the opposite direction. "My heavens, you've gotten big since we last saw you."

"Ears?" He plunked a duffel bag next to the sofa his mother was just vacating.

"And everything else," Ariel said. "You were just a little squirt. Barely walking."

"It hasn't been that long," Crystal tossed over her shoulder before ratcheting up the decibels. "Aunt Margaret, you look wonderful. I'm sure that wheelchair is just for backup."

"No, actually this time I'm the one who's barely walking, but the ears are still in fine working order." The old woman took Crystal's embrace sitting down. "And what about you, young man? How about a hug for your auntie?" The boy hung back, but she beckoned and left him no choice. "I know it's rough. I was never much of a hugger, either. And I'll bet you've been given strict orders to humor the old lady who lives in the big house."

"Who lives in the other house?" Garth asked as he suffered Aunt Meg's greeting, bobbing in and out of her hug like a cold water bather.

"All our ghosts," she said ominously.

Garth shivered. "What ghosts?"

"Aunt Meg, please," Rochelle scolded. "There are no ghosts, Garth. There's no such thing."

"Skeletons, then. The closets are full of them." She shook a bony finger. "You can't deny the existence of skeletons."

"Of course not," Crystal put in. "Have you been decorating for Halloween, Aunt Margaret?"

"Not this year. We've been too busy with wedding plans."

"When did we ever put up Halloween decorations here?" Ariel said. "Here at Rosewood, we do *autumn*. We do *harvest*. We do not do old cronies on broomsticks."

"Crones," Rochelle translated for her sister's benefit. "I hope you like fall colors. That's what we've chosen for the wedding."

"As long as I can have my wedding at Rosemond, that's all that matters. From now on I want us to be close."

"I'd like that," Rochelle said, and she meant it. So far. "What's your wedding dress like?"

"Can you believe I got the perfect dress right off the rack? Ivory satin, very simple lines, long sleeves. I wasn't even looking at the time. It just jumped out at me. It reminded me of Rosewood."

"How long have you been——" Rochelle noticed

Crystal's bare left hand…no big honking ring? "—engaged?"

"It's my second time around, Shelly. I don't need all the hoopla. All I want is family. Tracy's family, my family, our roots firmly planted right here in this wonderful old place."

"And you shall have all that, my dear."

"Thank you, Aunt Margaret. I can't tell you how much it means to me to hear you say that. I really need my…" Crystal perched on the arm of the over-stuffed chair Rochelle had claimed. "My family. I know I've been remiss in too many ways to count, but I want to make up for that. You know how it is when you get a little older."

"Older than what?"

"Older than a kid like Shelly," Crystal said with a laugh. "That would be you and me, wouldn't it, Aunt Margaret?"

"Speak for yourself, woman. I'm happily heading into second childhood."

"Then, speaking for the older generation, I'm realizing more every day how quickly time passes and how important it is to share as much of it as you can with your family. *Real* family. Blood relatives, if you will."

"Of course, we will." Aunt Meg glanced at Rochelle. *I will if you will.*

Crystal didn't notice. She was deep into thoughts of her mother.

"It's hard when you have a little one," Crystal said. "Your whole life revolves around him. You become so preoccupied with your own little world that you forget. You lose touch. It's all so…"

Aunt Meg shook her finger. "It's all your fault, young man."

"What is?"

"She's teasing you again, sweetie. It's your mother's very own fault and no one else's."

"It doesn't matter, Crystal," the old woman said. "You're here now, and we're going to have your wedding here. It'll be like old times, and I do mean *old* times. Rosewood has seen some glorious parties, especially in the old house. My grandmother was famous for her parties."

"That's exactly what I was hoping for, Aunt Margaret. I want family history to repeat itself. I want to make that connection. I want my son to know his heritage."

"We'll see how much of that we can squeeze in. Are you planning a wedding trip?"

"We're thinking about going somewhere during Christmas vacation. I don't want Garth to miss too much school. But we're free for Thanksgiving."

"What are we doing for Thanksgiving, ladies?"

Aunt Meg glanced from Rochelle to Ariel and back again. "Personally, I would love to see every chair at the table filled with family and friends."

"As small as our family is, we'd have to enlist quite a few friends to fill all the chairs at Rosewood," Crystal said.

"Rosewood hospitality doesn't stand on ceremony, does it, Shelly? Around our table, everyone is family. Can we use that as a motto for the inn?"

"Ooo, I like it!" Rochelle illustrated with an air sketch. "We're looking down at a round table, rose in the middle, words around the edge. *Around this table, everyone is family.*"

"I must say, I'm surprised to hear about this new enterprise," Crystal said. "Aren't you worried about letting perfect strangers stay here?"

"Would that include your future in-laws?" Rochelle wondered.

"No, but that's different. They'll be my—"

"And from what I've heard, your last in-laws weren't exactly perfect."

Crystal rolled a cold stare down her nose. "What I'm saying, Shelly, is that we have some very valuable property here."

"And we've been polishing silver and ironing table linens like chain-busters," Ariel contributed cheerfully.

With a laugh, Aunt Meg took up the cause. "Wait until you see all the trimmings your sister has planned."

"She's always been a great detail person. I did tell you that prime rib is Tracy's favorite, didn't I?"

"It would help if we had a firm number of guests," Rochelle grumbled.

"It can't be too hard to allow for a few extra," Crystal said with a shrug.

"Yeah, but prime rib for question mark plus X-tra equals an expensive formula."

"Didn't I tell you your aunt was just like you, Garth?" Crystal rubbed the top of Rochelle's head with her knuckles. "Another algebra equation. Nerd squared."

Crystal seemed pleased with the wedding preparations. Her comments fell short of the profusion of compliments Rochelle had imagined, but she hadn't started moving things around. So far, so good.

But when Rochelle tried to get away the next morning for a few errands, Crystal jumped at the chance to turn simple errands into major shopping. She put in a plug for Minneapolis, but the thirty-mile drive to St. Cloud was more than enough for Rochelle with Crystal in the car.

Not that she wasn't interested in her sister's life, but the stories always seemed to revolve around names and places and connections that meant nothing to Rochelle. They made her dizzy. She was the little sister all over again, dreading the question at the end of the conversation when her lack of social sophistication would be exposed. *Try to keep up, Shelly. You mean you don't even know who he is? I told you, his father owns, like, half the state.*

So get to the interesting part, Rochelle wanted to say. Where was the personality? The point? The punch line? Rochelle didn't get it. Sadly, she didn't get Crystal. She couldn't keep up, and she'd stopped trying long ago.

"This town has grown," Crystal mused as they passed a sign pointing the way to the university. "I'll bet the real estate market is hot."

"Suburban Minneapolis is threatening to sprawl this far west, if you can believe it." Rochelle smiled as she stopped for a traffic light. "And even if you can't."

"Oh, I can believe it. I'm actually thinking of getting into real estate."

"Buying, or selling?"

"Both. And maybe getting a license. You know, just for something different." A left turn after the light sparked Crystal's interest. "Are we going any-where near a Dayton's? I haven't been to a Dayton's in forever."

"And you can never go to one again." Rochelle smiled. She was one up on the shopping queen. "Where have you been? Dayton's is gone forever. They turned into Marshall Field's."

"How sad."

"It's the way of the world. They barely get the new signs up and they start looking for another buyer. Pretty soon all your favorite stores will have the same name."

"Oh, my God, and the same selection," Crystal said in mock horror. Then she frowned. "That can't happen. Can it?"

"You're the one who's interested in buying and selling. You tell me."

"Houses."

"It's all of a piece, it seems to me. Out with the old, in with the new." She pulled into a strip-mall parking lot for a quick stop at a garden center. "We'll save groceries for last. I have to pick up the tulip bulbs and—"

"Tulip bulbs? Doesn't the gardener take care of things like that?"

Rochelle laughed. "It's been a while since there was a real gardener at Rosewood. I switched maintenance services this year, too. Found a much better rate."

"Even when you were a kid you noticed the little details. Never the big picture. Always the cozy stuff." Crystal lifted her sunglasses for an unshaded look at the name of the store. No, it still wasn't Dayton's. Or Field's. "Myself, I haven't been able to get into gardening."

Rochelle opened the car door and swung her legs out. "You coming?"

"Tulip bulbs, huh?" Crystal emerged reluctantly. "I've been renting since we moved to Chicago—so much easier to let the owner do the dirty work—but even before that, when I was married to the name we shall not speak..." She doubled her stride to catch up as the store's automatic doors parted for Rochelle. "Isn't it late for planting flowers?"

"They'll be wedding favors." This was the fun part. Rochelle's territory. "I'm going to do them up in vintage hankies. As long as people get them in the ground before it freezes, they'll be a lovely remembrance when they bloom in the spring."

"Nice idea."

Rochelle gave her name to a clerk at the service counter. "I had to special-order them to get your color—that deep blue-red," she told Crystal.

"You're not referring to my eyes, now, are you?"

Rochelle laughed. "There was one dress I remember in particular. It had little cap sleeves and a mandarin collar. Long, with a deep slit up the side."

The light went on in Crystal's memory closet. "Oh, yes, Mama picked that one out. Were you with us? You weren't, were you?"

Rochelle shrugged. She wouldn't have wanted to go, anyway, painful as those marathon shopping trips with her mother and sister could be. They would always promise to bring her something, and it was always something she'd liked. They were excellent shoppers.

"That was when we lived in…"

"Baltimore."

"Baltimore," Crystal echoed. "I loved Baltimore. Mama knew so many influential people, and there was always something going on there."

Which was the very reason Rochelle had hated Baltimore.

"I wore that dress for some sort of naval cadet party," Crystal recalled as she fanned the pages of a plant catalog she found lying on the counter.

"And you weren't even old enough to go," Rochelle said, laughing. "Mama lied to get you invited."

"She didn't have to lie. One of her friends was in charge."

"Her friend lied, then." Which meant that Mama had lied, too. A white lie, which was the kind that didn't hurt anyone, according to Mama. And it was the kind of detail that stuck in Rochelle's mind. That and the image of Mama fussing over Crystal's makeup, getting it just right for party, and of Rochelle herself fastening her bracelet. "I remember how pretty you looked in that dress. Like Jennifer Jones in *Love Is a Many Splendored Thing*."

"Did I?" Crystal was pleased. "Is that good? That's an old movie, right? You're such a trivial expert."

Without comment, Rochelle chose to assume that her sister meant *trivia*.

She checked on the flower order and grabbed the latest copy of *Martha Stewart Weddings* magazine on her way to paying for the bulbs. She was still open for more ideas. This could be the first of many elegant events at Rosewood.

"What are you going to wear?" Crystal asked when they were back in the car.

"For the wedding? I have a nice blue suit that should be—"

"Suit? No, that won't do. You're my only attendant."

"But I'm also hostess, waitress and probably barmaid."

"You have to be joking, although I can never tell for sure. No, you're my very best and most important maid of honor, and it's up to you to supply the color."

"Your bouquet will do that," Rochelle promised. "Since you told me to pick anything, I went with bloodred roses."

"Sounds deadly."

"Not at all. Blood is life, and you absolutely come alive when you wear that shade of red."

"Then that's exactly the color we'll find for you. With the right makeup, you'll be positively vitalized. And poor me." Crystal struck a demure pose, fingers tip to tip beneath her chin. "I'll be the white wallflower."

"Like you've ever been a wallflower, Crystal."

"True. And we'll have none at my wedding." She pointed to the road. "We're going to find you a bloody dress!"

If Rochelle had had her way, they would have settled for the first red dress she tried on. It fit fine. The color was a little garish, but the fabric was sturdy, the style suitably simple—long-sleeved jacket over a simple shirtwaist dress. It was only the first of several possibilities that Crystal rejected, subjecting Rochelle to more changing, more scrutiny, more three-way mirrors.

Four dresses into the chore, Rochelle escaped to

the ladies' room. Her stomach hurt. She locked the stall door, grabbed the top for support and rested her face in the crook of her arm. God, she felt queasy. All she needed was for her stomach to start acting up. Damn nerves. More precisely *the damn nerve.* Crystal had it in spades. The nerve to use words like "dowdy" and "frumpish" when Rochelle stood in front of the mirror.

But this was about family, the only family she had. A wedding was a much better reason for a reunion than a funeral.

Fastidious about lining the toilet seat, Rochelle gasped when her bottom hit bare plastic. The toilet paper had fallen in. *She was doomed.* There would be a funeral in the family after all. The obituary would note that sitting on a public toilet without protection was the humiliating cause of Rochelle Le-Clair's untimely demise. She was preceded in death by her mother, who had, on more than one occasion, absolutely told her so.

The next dress would be the one, no matter how it looked on her. Take it and go, she told herself as she closed the door behind her. Her stomach was beginning to turn on itself like the agitator in a washing machine. Crystal was conferring with the saleswoman in the size-twelve section. In a store like this, wouldn't Rochelle be an upscale ten?

Crystal noticed her and shooed her along. "We put another one in the dressing room for you, honey. Try that on."

Rochelle complied immediately. *Get it on and get it done.* Why was it so much more fun to dress dolls than people?

Because that's what dolls are for, Rochelle told herself. They don't have anything better to do. But you do. You have a million details awaiting your attention, and here you are...

Here you are. That's your tussie-mussie head that just popped though the neckline. That's your face in the mirror, Rochelle.

But rosier than usual. *Rochelle*-ier.

Either the fatal fever was already setting in, or the color of the dress actually did flatter her. She left the dressing room feeling smiley, eager for the three-way mirror.

"Now, that's more like it," her sister said.

"This one really accentuates the waistline," the clerk said.

"It does," Crystal crooned. "I'm jealous, Shelly. I didn't even know you had a waistline. I knew you had boobs. Mama gave me the legs and saved the rack for you."

"I feel so blessed."

And surprisingly sassy. Hands on her hips, she

pirouetted on tiptoe, imagining high heels, relishing the caress of soft fabric and shamelessly admiring her rear view.

"You should. Men like a nice trophy rack. It reminds them of their favorite part of any sport—being in the hunt."

"Poor Tracy. Out of the hunt with nothing to hang on his wall." Rochelle flashed her sister a grin in the mirror. "Pretty difficult to have a pair of legs stuffed and mounted."

"I'm no man's wall hanging, sweetie." Crystal turned to the saleswoman. "Our hunt is over. She'll take this one, along with some really good control-top panty hose. How much do you weigh, Shelly? They go by weight."

Rochelle shot her a sharp glance and imagined a shattered Crystal. "I have panty hose."

"Go change." *Shoo-shoo,* Crystal gestured. "Let me treat you to a really good pair with a firm hold. It's all in the spandex. And you'll need shoes."

"I have shoes. Black or…black. Take your pick of flats or pumps."

"You can only wear black shoes if you buy underwear to match."

"Black?"

"A little flash of black lace when you kick up the heels of your black pumps on the dance floor."

"What dance floor?"

Crystal turned to the salesclerk. "Can you believe we're sisters?"

Rochelle's stomach threatened to start protesting again when she checked the tag on the sleeve. Four hundred dollars. She'd never paid that much for one dress. But she caught another glimpse of herself in the dressing-room mirror.

Here you are.

She lifted her chin. She lifted her chest. She looked herself in the eye, and she smiled. *And you look good.* She smoothed the soft fabric over her hip, her tummy. *Even without the spandex.*

On the way home, she glimpsed that same look in the rearview mirror. Knowing, daring, color-in-the-cheeks confident. She glanced at her sister, for whom knowing and daring had always been par for any course she had chosen to play. But what about now, with a few tough courses under her belt?

Go ahead, say it. You're helping her with her second wedding. What's that all about? Is it different this time? Because it should be. Come on, Rochelle, she's your sister. Ask her.

And without the slightest preamble.

"Do you love him?"

"Who? Tracy?"

Rochelle arched an eyebrow, challenging her sister for an immediate *Yes, of course. Absolutely.* But the ready answer didn't come and that, surprisingly, disappointed her.

Crystal smiled wistfully. "I think he'll be a decent husband, and I really love the idea of having a decent husband."

"But are you head-over-heels crazy in love with him?"

"Is that what you're waiting for?" She chuckled. "Honey, if you didn't get that fever when you were a teenager, it ain't gonna happen."

"Killjoy," Rochelle said. "How about the first time?"

"Haven't you had that yet?"

"No, I mean *you.* The first time you got married."

"To the one who shall remain nameless?" Crystal wagged a finger. "Now there was a real killjoy."

"But did you love him to begin with?"

"You're going to like Tracy," Crystal said, "once you get to know him. He's a private person, so you sort of have to draw him out. He's a lot like you. He lets me do most of the talking." She stared at the road for a moment before adding, "Maybe that's it. I'm marrying my sister."

Rochelle glanced askance in disbelief. Then they both laughed.

"Do you like your dress?" Crystal asked.

"I like that it doesn't scream *bridesmaid.* I could actually wear it in real life."

"And just what is 'real life' in Little Falls? New Year's Eve at the VFW?"

"Or…" Rochelle pointed to a Quonset building on the otherwise rural road and the sign that boasted *LIVE NUDE GIRLS.*

"Out here?" Crystal laughed. "What are they doing all the way out here?"

"Entertaining live, underdressed men, like this guy." One of several stickers on the rusty bumper ahead of them read *Real Men Don't Wear Couture.*

On cue, the car's turn signal blinked for the Quonset building.

"No way!" Crystal hooted, rubbernecking as they passed. "Mirrored sunglasses, can you believe it? Underdressed and incognito. Oh, and get this— *Real Men Don't Do Fruit!* A little defensive of our manhood, are we?"

"No raspberries, Crystal. We don't want him coming after us."

"He's too busy thinking about that banana in his pocket. Oh!" Giggling, Crystal smacked her own cheek. "Hush my mouth. What will my baby sister think?"

"She'll wonder what real life is like in Chicago."

"We go to the meat market, sweetie. But you'd

be proud of me. I keep my little melons under wraps."

The next building they passed had a neon cross above the door and a portable sign in the parking lot saying *Come As You Are.* "Perfect!" Crystal said, laughing again.

"Is that how you met Tracy?"

"At church? Or were you thinking *meat market?*"

"I'm just asking," Rochelle protested with a smile.

"You won't believe this, but his mother introduced us. I met Vera at the nail salon. Come to find out she was from Minnesota, too. They own a lodge up in Brainerd. She was pretty excited to find out I was a Bruner. She actually recognized the name."

"That surprises you?"

"I don't run into too many people who know that Martin Bruner built the lumber industry in this area. They recognize names like Weyerhauser and Leavitt, but I haven't been able to buy too many status points with *Bruner.*"

"It's obviously the wrong currency where you're shopping."

"All right, touché. I didn't mean to poke fun at your social opportunities up here in God's country."

"No, I'm serious, Crystal. Forget the lumber business. You're missing out on some meaningful bragging rights. Aunt Meg has made the Bruner name synonymous with other endeavors, like supporting the arts."

"The arts? I thought Indians were her favorite charity. I meant to tell her that Tracy has some Indian ancestry. Back several generations, but still...

"You must have mentioned it to somebody. Either she told me, or Ariel did."

"I thought she'd find it interesting. She's been giving money to them hand over fist for years."

"How do you know?"

"She's my aunt, too, Shelly. She's an influential person, and her activities are still news."

"In Chicago?"

"I have connections. And it's my business to know, just as much as—"

"She's influential up here in God's country, Crystal. I doubt if Aunt Meg's support for the museum in Mille Lacs has made the *Chicago Tribune*."

"Okay, well, shoot me for coming late to the party. I'm here now."

Crystal shifted in her seat, angling toward her sister. "Speaking of Ariel and Aunt Meg and, you know, making connections... Don't take this the wrong way, Shelly, but just how close are they?"

"That's an interesting question. What would be the wrong way to take it?"

Rochelle slowed the car, easing over the bridge into Little Falls, working on a straight face. "Ariel has worked for Aunt Meg for at least fifteen years, and you can be sure it's not for the money."

"That's what I thought."

"Ariel takes care of her like she would her own mother."

"Which is not what I thought."

"For the pleasure of her company. Aunt Meg is…" Rochelle gave in. "All right, tell me, what *did* you think?"

"When I see Ariel fussing over every step the woman takes…" Crystal shrugged dramatically. "Okay, the word *gold digger* comes to mind."

"Gold digger?" Rochelle laughed. "That's two words, and they're way off the mark, sister. The Rosewood mine done petered out long ago."

"What do you mean?"

"I'm hoping the B and B will keep the Bruner estate afloat a while longer, just for Aunt Meg's sake."

"Meaning she hasn't much…longer?"

"*Money,* Crystal. She hasn't much left."

"How would you ever know that, Shelly? That woman is as shrewd as they come. Mama inherited and spent a shitload of money from their grandfather. Aunt Margaret got an equal shitload, and she wasn't the kind to flush it down the river."

"True enough."

"Face it, honey, it's *time* she's really short on. I know it's hard, but…" Crystal lifted her hand as though she would touch Rochelle's shoulder, but she didn't extend herself far enough for anything but an air pat. "You said it yourself. She's fragile. And that makes her vulnerable to people like…well, to outsiders."

"Outsiders?" *Be still my tongue.* If she said another word, it would ruin the day. She wouldn't ask who Crystal considered to be an insider and whether she could imagine what it must be like for a woman like their aunt to be stuck inside in the winter of a lifetime of seasons she'd enjoyed without regard for *inside* and *outside.*

"Shelly, have you talked with her about her will?"

She has a will of her own. Yes, I should ask her about that, Rochelle thought. *I want one, too, just like hers. Where can I get one?*

Where does a woman get the nerve to be a warrior?

"She has an attorney for that," Rochelle said quietly as she turned the car onto Rosewood Drive, the estate's private road.

"We're the last of the Bruners. You, me, and don't forget Garth."

The two old houses presiding over the curve of

the horseshoe drive reminded Rochelle that their aunt was the last real Bruner, but they beckoned her, anyway. *Do something about this.* In defiance of Rochelle's neat little guest parking signs, an SUV was parked halfway between the two porches.

"Would this be the groom?"

"That's Tracy's truck," Crystal said as they passed.

For the sake of the groceries, Rochelle parked near the kitchen door. From there she could see the gardens, the river and a woman pointing a camera up at the white house. She lowered the camera and waved.

Rochelle waved back. "And this would be?"

"Vera! Welcome!" Crystal grinned. "My future mother-in-law."

Chapter Seven

No American tradition seemed more distasteful to Birch Trueblood than Halloween. It wasn't the silly celebration of ghosts and goblins that turned him off so much as the door-to-door solicitation of sweets. If his kid wanted a candy bar, he'd buy her one. Over the years he'd found ways to cut the evening short, but no real, true, red-blooded American father could completely escape the annual beg-a-thon. At this point in his life he wasn't sure how real, true, red-blooded or American he was. Fatherhood was probably his only remaining grip on any identity he was sure he could claim.

He was grateful for the role. The only time he ever wanted to bolt was when his little girl was down-in-the-mouth about something he couldn't fix. He'd negotiated with her on the costume, visited the dog pound "just to look," agreed to let her have the little black dog she'd liked best, even gritted his teeth and watched *The Wizard of Oz* with her for the umpteenth time—he hated that wizard a whole lot more than the witch—but he was looking at the one detail he couldn't fix.

It was time to hit the road, and his would-be Dorothy had only one traveling companion, and he was no fun. He didn't skip or sing or dress like a clown. All he did was carry a flashlight and slink along wishing he could really do magic. What was a guy supposed to do about his daughter's fickle friends? He couldn't very well hunt down a gaggle of little girls and twist their arms until they pleaded for the pleasure of Robin's company on their candy-picking expedition.

So here she sat in her blue-and-white dress, wearing the braids and the red shoes, the whole bit right down to the little black dog on her lap, and she was miserable.

So was he. Jesus, he could hardly wait for prom night.

"They're just jealous of your costume, honey. And your new puppy."

"It's going to be covered up by my jacket, anyway. I should just wear some silly mask, like everyone else. Why did you have to make Auntie sew this for me?"

Yeah, it was *his* fault.

"I'm sorry, baby. I don't know what I was thinking."

"You were thinking of the picture album, I guess."

"This is your best Halloween outfit yet." And his way of making the best of a dreaded chore. He could do without the door-to-door crap, but the dress-up part was fine. Like playing with dolls.

He sighed as he took a seat beside her on the sofa. "You're right, hon. The kids probably think you're showing off. But it's really me. I like showing you off." No use mentioning her original idea for the sparkly dress with the crown.

"I've got the best jingle dress in school, too."

"Sorry."

"Daddy?" She looked up dolefully. "They never saw my costume."

"But you told them about it."

"I told them about it, but not like I was bragging or anything. I just told them I'd changed my mind about the good witch and picked Dorothy."

"Maybe you got the time mixed up."

"Shelby said she'd call when she was ready, but she didn't. And nobody's home now. They just took off without us."

"You told them I was going?"

"I told them we had to let you go or else I couldn't."

"Unless one of the other parents was going, I said. Did you tell them it was okay if one of their parents was going?"

"No, but I said you wouldn't make us go home early this time."

"Early?" The dog was sniffing at his shirtsleeve. There was no going back now that he'd let the mutt into the house. He gave it a brief scratching behind its ear. "How late do those girls get to stay up on a school night, anyway?"

"Daddy, it's *Halloween*."

Birch heaved himself off the sofa and glanced out the front window. It was still light, and the sky was hanging so heavy and low that he imagined himself ducking once he got out there. Cold enough to snow, too. If they lived in the Cities, he could take Robin to the mall. She would be safe and warm, and her little red shoes wouldn't get ruined. She'd meet some new kids. And maybe he'd meet somebody.

What was that about?

Hell, Birch met people all the time. He was always meeting people, always doing the ol' Trueblood routine.

"Daddy?"

What would it hurt to meet somebody?

Birch cocked a speculative eyebrow. "How about if we go down to Little Falls and trick-or-treat?"

He wasn't sure where it had come from all of a sudden, but the idea sure turned on the light in Robin's eyes. Daddy was no dud after all. He shrugged, smiled. "They're probably giving out better candy down there."

The dog yip-yipped as Robin sprang into action, grabbing her coat. "Can we go to Miss Margaret's house?" She tossed her father a hoodie. "I want to show Rochelle that I look like her Dorothy doll."

"Sure thing."

A little meet and greet. He shrugged into an old denim jacket over the hoodie, still smiling. *Somebody sweet for his Halloween treat.*

It couldn't hurt.

They hit the road, heading southwest. It wasn't long before they passed the sign that told them they'd left home. Mille Lacs was a small reservation, even by modern standards, but if it hadn't been for a few "bad" Indians, there would have been no reservation on Lake Mille Lacs at all. Birch's Grandma Mary—his great-grandmother, if the family went by greats—had been one of the bad ones, even though she had married a white man several years after her first child was born and had two mixed-blood children by him. The bad ones wouldn't move. They refused to make way for the loggers. They figured they had as much right to a house on the lake as the European immigrants, whose descendants needed a city house *and* a lake house. Whether it was an RV, a trailer home or a winterized "cabin," the lake house qualified as a second home and a tax break.

But Birch wouldn't begrudge them their lake houses if they would stop looking for ways to deny his treaty rights. As he drove past the RV parks and the "resort" cabins that looked like oversize outhouses, he could feel the hot blood of the "bad" Indians coursing through his veins. His family had hung on. They were the last remnant of the band of people named for the lake, and the lake for them. They refused to be evicted or burned or starved out, and when they were down to too few to matter, they had finally been left alone. Except for the little bit left to Wadena and his stubborn, squatting relatives, the south shore had all been platted out for summer getaways. But to this day, the sport fishermen and the resort owners grumbled about that little piece of lakeshore and the people who would not be moved.

And to this day the summer getaways were, in the eyes of the Ojibwe, mostly eyesores. Thank God for the trees. They had, after a time, grown back. Pine, oak, maple, cottonwood, and the birch, whose useful white bark made it stand out from the rest. Sure, this was farm country. The cornfields and the herd of propane tanks corralled in the local gas company lot attested to the fact that farmers had supplanted loggers. But their habit of planting trees for windbreaks beat clear-cutting all to hell.

"Daddy, look at that flower bed." Robin pointed to a tractor tire in one of the roadside yards, its summer blooms blackened by frost. "Next year we could do that with those tires behind the house."

Okay, so the Trueblood place could use some sprucing up, too.

"I've been meaning to give those to your cousin John to use on his pickup."

"But we could plant stuff in them. I want a flower garden like Miss Margaret's. She has lots of them."

He was staring at a bumper sticker proclaiming *No Jesus, No peace.* They struck him as fightin' words, but he laughed. "Honey, I'm not having any tires in my *front* yard."

"What about big fat logs? We could make a square and plant flowers inside."

"Possibility," he allowed.

"And we could have two of those chairs beside it." She pointed to the samples in front of the Twist of Nature log furniture maker's place.

"Possibility."

"And one of those."

He glanced at the lot full of life-size metal cutouts somebody was selling for yard art. Elk, bear, dogs, deer, cowboys and golfers. "A scarecrow?" he teased.

"No, Daddy! I just think a garden would make our house look grander."

"Grander, huh?" He gave a chuckle. "Those clouds are looking pretty grand. We'll have more than frost on the pumpkins by tomorrow." Making for a short night, he thought with a smile. "How many houses should we hit?"

"I don't care," she said. "As long as we go to Miss Margaret's."

Big, fluffy snowflakes were falling by the time he chose a kid-friendly neighborhood. He could tell by the illuminated porch lights and the number of caped crusaders, clowns and queens plying the sidewalks. He parked the car, and off they went. But it wasn't long before Robin had to switch footwear from Land of Oz red shoes to North Country hikers. Still, she and her little dog were a hit at every door in the little town of Little Falls, Minnesota.

The sweet, self-assured sound of her voice reciting the Halloween greeting reminded Birch that he had good reason for standing outside at night in the damn cold, trying not to peer at the light flickering on the other side of some white guy's picture window to see what the family was watching on TV.

Had it not been for his daughter, Birch would have found a neon light, an open door, a drink and a smoke. He hated being on the outside looking in.

The steadily sifting snow was piling up quickly, and the jack-o'-lanterns' internal flames were getting snuffed. Rosewood would be their last stop. He wouldn't want to have to shovel *this* driveway, he told himself as they drove through the gate. Grandeur definitely had its downside.

"I wonder if they made a haunted house," Robin piped up from the back seat. "I told Rochelle I'd help her, but I forgot."

"I don't think she'd need much help hanging out the sign."

"You have to do a lot more than that, Daddy. The porch light is on at the white house. That must be where we go. If we lived here, you know what we could do? We could have a haunted house in the green one and a Halloween party in the white one. And everybody from school would come."

"For nine years' experience, you sure do come up with some big ideas, Tweety bird." He wanted to park near the front door, but the white ground cover made it hard to tell the driveway from the flower beds that lined it. Far be it from him to run over any angelic statuary. He allowed a few yards' distance. "Let's make this quick."

"I have to put my red shoes back on," she insisted when he opened the back door of the car.

Grateful for the hood on his sweatshirt, he tucked his chin into the neck and turned up the collar of his jacket. "I'm up to my shins in snow out here, Robin."

"I want them to see the whole costume. There." She reached for her dad. "Carry me."

"What about Blackie?"

"*Toto.* He can walk. He loves the snow."

The dog had never seen snow. He followed, bobbing up and down like a little black rabbit.

"See? Isn't it fun, Toto? We can go right up onto the porch, Daddy."

"Yes, ma'am." Birch trudged up the steps and through the glass door into the enclosed porch. Setting his chattering bundle down, he rapped the brass door knocker.

"With a porch like this, people don't get snowed on while they're waiting for someone to answer the door."

"I guess we're not in Kansas anymore, huh? What are you doing?"

"Taking my coat off so they can see—" The big door swung open, and the ever-friendly Ariel Sweet appeared. "Trick or treat!" Robin shouted gleefully.

"Oh, my!"

"Lions and tigers and bears," Robin chanted.

"Miss Margaret, come see who's here!" Ariel

shouted over her shoulder. "You two come right in. I was afraid Halloween was going to pass Rosewood by this year."

Out of sight, the wheelchair hummed an overture before Margaret Bruner appeared, dramatically backlit from the kitchen and striking Birch as a spirited force rather than an old woman. She operated her coach with one hand and gave her welcome with the other.

"Trick or treat, Miss Margaret!"

"Trick or treat, you say? Do I get to pick?" She buzzed across the floor like an injured bee—all determination, no more lift. But she had a smile for Robin. "I see you have a bag full of treats, Miss Dorothy. What's your trick?"

"No, you're supposed to give me a treat. I think it's if you like my costume, you give me a treat."

"I don't see any costume, Miss Dorothy. That's the same dress you always wear. Does your little dog do tricks?"

Birch snatched the dog up off the floor and stepped back onto the porch before Ariel could close the front door behind them.

"I haven't had time to teach him any. I just got him. His name is Toto."

"Of course it is. The whole world knows that, Miss Dorothy."

"We'll wait on the porch," Birch muttered to Ariel. "How are you doing, Miss Margaret? Robin will shake your hand for me. My job is to keep the dog from—"

"Miss Dorothy, you all better come inside before one of those witches gets Toto and that witless scarecrow of yours. They're out in full force tonight, you know." Margaret nodded to Ariel. "Pull him in here and close the door before we all freeze."

Ariel slipped between Birch and the door and pushed both in opposite directions. The lair was secure.

Birch laughed. "You asked for it. Straw and dog hair all over your floor."

"It's Halloween," Margaret said. "You think I worry about straw when there are green-faced witches about? And I hate those flying monkeys. They're worse than bats for tangling in a lady's hair. Now, about this trick you said you'd do for me, Dorothy."

"Miss Margaret, it's me. Robin Trueblood."

"Lord love her, the child's worried about you, Miss Margaret. She thinks you've gone batty," Ariel said.

"Batty my beak. It's Halloween, and I haven't seen one good trick all night."

"I can do this with my thumbs." Robin proudly displayed her double-jointed digits.

"Look what Dorothy can do, Ariel. For a trick like that, we fill 'er up."

"We've got a ton of candy left."

"Good." Shamelessly, Birch watched the candy bars tumble from Ariel's bowl into Robin's basket. "We can quit now and go home."

"Is Rochelle here?" Robin asked. "I want to show her my dress. Don't I look just like her Dorothy doll?"

Birch turned to the window in the door and pretended he could see something he hadn't seen before. "We've gotta get goin' honey. It's gettin'—"

"Hang the scarecrow on the coatrack, Ariel, and then go get Shelly."

Robin giggled.

"No kiddin', Miss Margaret, it's nasty out there." He chuckled. He had to say it. "Colder 'n a witch's teat."

"How would you know that, Mr. Trueblood?" The small, sweet voice prefaced the appearance of another silhouette in the kitchen doorway. These Bruner women had a flair for making an entry.

"Rochelle!"

"Oh, my goodness, is that Robin Trueblood?"

Rochelle glided in on soft soles, noiseless but for a single rubbing of floorboards, a brief catch that vibrated in his gut. It was a funny feeling. She was all eyes for Robin, only a twinkling glance for him. Funny as hell, because he was drinking her in.

"If they decide to remake *The Wizard of Oz*, you could be Dorothy," Rochelle cooed.

"I would, but I can't sing as good as she can. See my shoes? I had to change my shoes when it started snowing, but I put them back on when we came here, and Daddy carried me so I wouldn't be in snow."

"I hope you have some magic in those heels if we get stuck on the way home," he said, smiling as Rochelle approached him. Finally, he would get his due.

"What have you got there?" she asked, reaching for the wad of black fur tucked in the crook of his elbow.

"That's Toto," Robin supplied as she scratched around in her basket. "He's got some treats in here somewhere."

"New addition?" Rochelle's saucy glance accused him of weakness.

"Part of the outfit." He shrugged. "He still has to prove himself."

"We got him from those humane people." Robin offered a biscuit. "If you give him this, he'll like you right away. Maybe Miss Margaret wants to see him, too."

"Yes, indeed, bring him on over, Miss Dorothy. Let me check his teeth."

Birch relinquished control of the dog with a stern warning to his daughter in one fatherly glance.

"How are the roads?" Rochelle asked him.

"Passable."

"Were they predicting this? I haven't been paying attention."

"Me, neither." He was now. She had pretty eyes and a sweet mouth. "Have the spirits been bothering around since I was here last?"

"They haven't bothered me. Her smile teetered between sweet and coy. "But, then, they never did."

"No points for me, then."

"I didn't say that."

The bold look in her eyes said he had a few points on account, but still she blushed when he gave the slightest smile. Sweet heat. He liked that about her.

"Man, it's really piling up out there," Ariel reported from the next room. Birch hadn't noticed her drifting away.

"You're welcome to stay overnight," Rochelle offered quietly. "We have a fire going, and there's hot buttered rum."

"Tempting. Any occasion, besides Halloween?"

"We have guests."

But there's room at the inn.

"Daddy, can't we stay?"

You ask privately, not in front of other people, he reminded his daughter with a look.

And with a look, she continued to plead rather than give it up. Point not taken. Bad sign. She was acting like a spoiled white kid.

"My sister's here," Rochelle was saying. "And my nephew, along with—"

On cue, the sister strolled in smiling—a stretchier, slimmer, sleeker, slicker version of Rochelle. "Are the goblins holding you guys hostage out here?" she wanted to know.

"Crystal, this is Birch Trueblood," Rochelle said quickly. "And Robin, his—"

"It's a pleasure to meet you both." Crystal claimed a handshake from Birch and center stage from Robin as she dismissed her proffered hand with a pat on the cheek. "No Girl Wonder costume? It would make such a great introduction."

"I'm Dorothy from—"

"*The Wiz,* of course! And don't you look sweet enough to eat?" She turned to Birch. "I can't believe this. Major snow on Halloween. I hope you two don't run into any trouble on the way back to…"

"Mille Lacs, yeah, we're from the rez."

"And you came down here just to…"

"The sugar pickin's are a hell of a lot better down here."

"I hope you brought a carload," she said with a big, toothy smile. "More hands to push in case you get stuck."

"Daddy, can we stay?"

Robin was ignoring his message. On the other hand, most of Crystal's had gone right over her head.

"They're picked clean, honey. You got all the sweets. Time to hit the road."

"Birch," Rochelle said quietly, laying her hand on his arm. "There's plenty of room."

"More than we'd like, really." Crystal checked her watch. "We're supposed to have a wedding here tomorrow, but it's beginning to look questionable for some of the guests. My fiancé might be in the market for a best man."

"Better yet, Mr. Trueblood is an Ojibwe holy man," Ariel said.

"No kidding?" Crystal raised a shapely eyebrow. "I'd say I was an all-American virgin bride, but my sister would never keep her mouth shut. This is my second time around."

"No, I mean in case the minister can't make it, he could probably…" Ariel turned to him. "You could probably perform the ceremony, couldn't you?"

"Ojibwe, yes. All-American? Probably not. But I hope you get a break in the weather and—" he offered a parting handshake "—it all works out this time."

Before Ariel had the front door closed, Birch overheard an exchange between sisters.

"You look a little flushed, Shelly."

"I do?"

"Must have something to do with the chief. He's a hottie."

"If I'm flushed, maybe I'm the hottie."

Birch smiled as he scooped up his daughter and stepped out into the snow.

Standing at the front window, Rochelle was feeling pretty smug about her comeback. Crystal had returned to her guests in the living room, and Ariel had helped Aunt Meg down the steps so that she could join them. Rochelle let them all go. Her sister's intended was either painfully shy or fatally bored with his bride's family. The only comment he'd gotten in edgewise was, "Nice place you have here." His mother had dominated the conversation since the moment of their introduction, while the elderly aunt and uncle who had ridden with them began familiarizing themselves with their surroundings. They made no bones about their interest in the signatures on the paintings and the maker's marks on the knickknacks, which they noted aloud.

Rochelle had had her fill of talk. She was looking forward to being consumed by wedding hustle-bustle, when she could lose herself in the details and let the others do the socializing. In a couple of days they would all be gone, and she would have her life back.

She peered through the sheers, watching Birch's headlights turn tail in the twirling snow. She hadn't been outside since it had started snowing, hadn't listened to a weather report all day, but this was crazy. Not that snow on Halloween was unheard of in Minnesota, but seldom more than a flurry. She hated to see them go in this kind of weather.

She hated to see them go. Period.

Birch brushed the snow off the top of his head and turned the wipers on. Either the wind had picked up or the car had created a white maelstrom. Headlights weren't worth shit in weather like this.

"Are you buckled in back there?"

"Of course. Daddy, why can't we stay?"

"Robin, why can't you stop whining?" He leaned closer to the windshield, looking for a clue. "What is this shit? It's Halloween, for crissake."

"Daddy." Her tone had gone from whining to warning.

"Just close your eyes and plug your ears, Miss Prissy. I'll do what I gotta do to get us home." He turned up the heater fan. "You warm enough?"

"I can't hear you," she chanted. "My ears are plugged."

"And I can't see a damn thing." Turning a curve that wouldn't end, he steered into a skid and recovered. For the moment. "Nobody should have a driveway this long unless they live in the damn boonies."

He could just make out the ornate scrollwork on the metal gate at the end of the driveway. Using it as a guide, he steered left.

And nearly plowed into some iridescent idiot darting across the road.

He slammed on the brakes. The car fishtailed, but the front wheels grabbed a piece of something solid and hung on.

"What the holy hell, lady!"

Had to be a woman, the floaty way she moved, the flowing way she was dressed. Her hood blew back from her face as she drifted toward his side of the car. She was blue-white with cold, and her eyes were huge and haunting. Birch tried to curse her, but the words wouldn't come. He couldn't turn away from those eyes. His finite pain paled in the shadow of the eternity of hers. Across a cold void, they shared the nameless burden of a hundred years and more.

The wind took her away and filled her space with swirling snow.

"Robin?"

He wouldn't ask. She would tell him if she had seen what he saw.

"I'm okay, Daddy. It's worse that we thought, isn't it?"

"Guess I…" *Finally got religion or lost it, one of the two.* He put the car in reverse, gave it a little gas and went nowhere. "Guess I should have listened to you."

"Did somebody close the gate?"

"Damned if I know. I can't see the road for the gate for the…" He muttered the word *ghost* into the roar of his useless attempt to rock the car off its perch. Still, he tried a time or two past the certainty of failure. Getting involved in a family reunion was about the last thing he needed right now.

"Are we stuck, Daddy?"

"What do you think?" he said in disgust.

"I think I'd better put my other shoes on."

He could hear her rustling around in the back seat. The dog whined. Whining wouldn't do it for Birch. He wanted to howl.

"Can we take our candy?"

"And leave the dog?"

"No!"

"This packhorse can only carry so much Let's leave the candy here."

Feed the spirits.

He hoped this one had a sweet tooth.

Chapter Eight

Rochelle had escaped.

She'd made the crossing from house to house on the pretext of getting some old family pictures and called back to say that nobody was going anywhere on any kind of wheels. The snow was already that deep. Aunt Meg had promised to stay put, and Rochelle had done the same.

She had the new house to herself. *Ah, peace and quiet.* Nothing drained her energy faster than the chore of making small talk with bigheaded people. If Crystal was planning on producing a Tracy junior, she was in for some hard labor. His mother's hat size had to be one for the record books. Add his aunt and uncle to the mix, not to mention Crystal, and Rochelle—never one for winter sports—had happily hurled herself into the snowy night practically barefoot. But feet outdid wheels when winter came early, as the spinning of tires and the honk of a horn somewhere in the night attested. Halloween was over.

But Rochelle's evening was not. She'd just coaxed a stack of oak logs to catch flame when she heard the door knocker clatter. She groaned aloud. Anyone without a key wasn't welcome.

With one snow-covered exception.

"Figured we'd find you over here," Birch said, shedding snow on the porch as he stomped his feet. "Saw the light on."

"I'm glad you changed your mind." She stepped back and ushered the Trueblood family inside.

"No choice."

"Somebody closed the gate," Robin said from beneath the blanket bundle Birch carried. A black nose emerged from the folds.

"I don't think we could close those old gates even if we wanted to." Rochelle pushed the door closed against the cold. "My goodness, Birch, you look like a snowman."

"And I'm feeling abominable," he grumbled. He set Robin on her feet in the creaky foyer. "We didn't make it out of the driveway."

"But you made it to the gate?"

"Damn near rammed into it, thanks to your..." He glanced at her as he shrugged off his jacket. She was hanging on the bridge between his mishap and her fault. "Snow angel," he said with a wry smile.

"My what?"

He tossed his denim jacket on the foyer bench. "Guardian angel? Whoever she is, she's beginning to get on my nerves."

"Was there someone…?"

She caught his warning glance as he shifted it between her and Robin, who was busy with her shivering dog.

"It's not fit for snowman nor beast out there," Rochelle said cheerily. The look in her eyes asked what the hell he was talking about. "Come in the living room. I was just making a fire."

"I'm ready to melt at your feet." He rolled the snowy blanket around his hands. "Where—"

Toto shook his whole body the minute he hit the floor. Then he squatted for further relief.

"Hey! You're supposed to be housebroken!" Birch scooped up the dog and dropped the blanket over the puddle. "Sorry."

"Don't be silly. Poor baby. He's all discombobulated."

"I am, too, but my puddle is only snowmelt. Are you sure about that north gate?"

"That it's open? We never close the gates."

With a booted foot he swished the blanket over

the floor. Crude but effective. "Must have been the wind."

"They're chained," she insisted. "We haven't used them in years. You must have gotten turned around."

"Could be. Either that or my eyes are playing…" He glanced past her. "Are you alone over here?"

She nodded.

"Expecting anyone else?"

"I thought I was going to have to rig up some wings for that wheelchair, but Aunt Meg finally agreed to stay at the old house and take the room off the kitchen. She hasn't slept in that house in decades."

"Wonder why," he muttered as he opened the door and kicked the blanket-mop onto the porch.

"Can I see the dolls?" Robin pleaded.

"After we warm you up." Rochelle took her coat, tossed it on the bench and steered her up the six steps to the next landing. "Hot chocolate or apple cider?"

Birch followed with the dog. "What happened to that hot buttered rum?"

"Crystal's serving that in the drawing room," Rochelle said. "Shall we get all bundled up and make our way over there?"

"No, thanks."

"I think my clothes are all frozen on me," Robin complained as she reached for her shivering dog. Tucking him against her chest, she knelt on the ottoman facing the fire and whispered, "We're okay now, Toto."

"Damn that ol' Witch of the North." Birch took a seat on the warmer end of the sofa.

"Oh, no, she was one of the good ones," Rochelle said as she wrapped an afghan around Robin's shoulders. "The Witch of the West was the bad one."

"Oz is a different world from Indian Country. Our way, good things come from the west."

"I read that the author was no friend to Indians, so I guess that's not a surprise."

"The author of *The Wizard of Oz?*" He sounded surprised.

"L. Frank Baum." She shook the folds from a lamb's-wool blanket and dropped it over Birch's knees. "When he lived in the Dakota Territory he wrote vicious editorials about American Indians."

"The hell." He reached back over his shoulder, peeled his wet hoodie over his head and emerged wondering, "What did we ever do to him?"

Robin turned, wide-eyed with shock.

"But *The Wizard of Oz* is still a wonderful story," Rochelle quickly amended. "And Baum's mother-in-law was an early feminist."

"Good for her. Maybe *she* was the monkey that flew up his nose."

"*Monkey* up his *nose!*" Robin's raucous giggle prompted Rochelle to flash Birch an approving smile.

"Wonder if he knew your grandfather. The old lumberman."

"Martin Bruner." She saw that he was surveying the room. The earlier family photographs and paintings hung in the older house. In this room the sole likeness of the famous lumber baron showed an old man with his two granddaughters. "That would be *great*-grandfather, and I sincerely doubt it."

"*He* was no friend to Indians, either. But those guys are dead. Dorothy lives. Right, Toto?" The dog jumped from Robin's arms into Birch's lap. "You know that name already? I wonder how many little girls have believed in the Wiz man's story and named their dogs Toto."

"Not the man," Rochelle said quietly. "The dream. You seem to be doing a lot of wondering tonight."

He shrugged. "You wander in from the cold and it takes a few minutes to chase it out of your bones, you know? The wonder of it all."

"Is it as deep out there as it's getting in here?" She laughed. "Who's for a hot bath and some flannel jammies?"

"I'll take a shower and silk."

"Silk, is it?" Rochelle flashed him a twinkly glance.

"And I like my cider hard."

"You can either have it hard or hot. I can't do both."

"I can." He stood, putting himself between Robin and Rochelle, consuming all her breathing space. "You want me to show you how it's done?"

"I'm sure I could follow a recipe."

"Not without the necessary tools." His fingertips tracked her long knit sleeve to its hem, found the tender side of her wrist, the hollow of her palm, and finally the space between her fingers. "Which—I know for a fact—you don't have."

His words fanned the side of her neck. She stifled a foolish giggle. When she could meet his eyes tit for tat, she smiled. "This is a bad thing?"

"Not from where I stand."

"I think I might have a recipe for mulled wine."

"Mulling sounds like a good thing. Point Robin to a tub and me to the nearest shower. I'll leave you to your mulling." He gave her hand a quick squeeze. "Jammies are optional."

Robin never made it to the playroom to see the dolls. It was just as much fun to take a bath in Rochelle's bathroom, and use her liquid green soap and her big sponge that looked like shredded-wheat cereal. Hot bathwater had never felt so good. Rochelle let her wear one of her own soft nightshirts with little blue flowers all over it. With too-big fuzzy slippers flapping against her heels, she padded across the house to the living room and found Daddy poking at the fire with a metal stick and letting all the sparks fly up the chimney. She laughed and said they looked like lightning bugs flying up the chimney's nose.

When Daddy stood up, she *really* laughed. Rochelle had given him dry pants to put on and a farmer shirt that hung way down over them. He pinched her nose and called her a baby skunk in Ojibwe.

Then she cuddled with Toto as close as they could get to the hearth without getting a sweaty face, while her father tended the fire and Rochelle served hot drinks. The two of them kept on teasing each other, like they were talking on the phone just to each other and had forgotten she was there. She could tell they liked each other. If she kept quiet, maybe Daddy wouldn't notice that she was still up.

She thought about how her big Halloween adventure had started out being cruddy and then changed into a trip to Little Falls and a cozy curl-up on a snowy night. Wouldn't Shelby and Denise be surprised when they found out how perfect it all turned out? She was getting a sleepover at Rochelle's house, which was full of all kinds of wonderful things; she had her dog and her dad with her; and tomorrow she would get a snow day, even if everyone else had to go to school.

The fire was making her sleepy. She fought to stay awake, but she was lulled by her father's voice, which was the most comforting sound in the world. She liked hearing the two of them talk back and forth, liked it that they were sitting close together on the sofa, liked the easy feeling of having them near her. It didn't matter what they were doing or saying. It only mattered that Daddy didn't sound sad. He wasn't laughing, but he was making Rochelle laugh. It was a friendly, sparkling sound, like water trickling into a cup, and Robin could just tell that he liked hearing it. She could hear the smile in his voice.

The voice became a breeze in the grass. The fire was summer sunshine. Robin drifted on rising water as the voice whispered, "Same bed as before?"

And she snuggled into a soft, warm pocket. But where was her dog?

"I'll bring him right back, Tweety bird. Sleep now."

Birch could hardly wait to get back inside, but, no choice, the dog was picky about his every move.

Hands in his pockets, shoulders hunched against the wind, his own version of a familiar ditty whirling around in his head—*We're off to see the Wiz man whiz, man*—Birch tromped a path in the snow and followed the little son of a bitch from pillar to post until sufficient territory had been marked. He felt like a shivering fool, waiting on the whim of a pint-size animal who couldn't give a good whiz for the piss-poor fit of a man's borrowed clothes and the fact that the cold had shrunk his own necessary tools down to two peas and a pin.

But when the job was finally done, Shelly met him at the door with a cup of her warm, spicy brew. And then he felt fine.

"Your ears are beet-red." She pressed her hand over the left one, and when he smiled, she covered the right one. Through the window the yard light cast a pearlescent glow over her upturned face. "If you were in my class, you wouldn't go out for recess without a hat."

"What if I didn't own a hat?"

"Then you'd be stuck inside with me all winter."

"Ah, my chance to play teacher's pet." He smiled. "And do a little petting with the teacher. Let her toy with my ears and such."

"These icy flappers would crack if I played with them."

"We'll find something else to entertain us, then."

He took a sip of the fragrant wine, gave a sound of approval, then let her hold it for him while he shed his jacket. Then they traded jacket for cup, moving like players on the same team. Or like a couple who met each other at the door of the same house every evening. Were there couples who did that?

Maybe he shouldn't take this turn-on too far.

"What happens to the wedding tomorrow?" he asked, keeping an eye on the dog, who was sniffing around for traces of his own smell.

"Crystal was calling her guests." She opened a door and reached behind it for a coat hanger. "I think they were talking about waiting a couple of days. It sounds like the weather people don't know whether this system is coming or going."

He tried to take a peek inside the closet before she closed the door. Not that he expected anything to fly out, but in this place he was learning to expect the unexpected.

He smiled when she caught him. "I can tell you that it came, it's here and it ain't goin' nowhere for at least two days." He arched an eyebrow. "Mark my words."

She sketched a note on the palm of her hand with an imaginary pencil. "Consider them marked."

"Where did you find these pants?" He hitched them up and pulled the borrowed shirt away from his body. "In that barn out back?"

"You would not believe the truckloads of stuff I've given away since I started raking through the storage in this place." She gave him a once-over and giggled. "You remind me of Huck Finn in that outfit. Birch, the river rascal."

"You wanna see a rascal, you just take a light tug on these bloomers." At the top of the foyer steps, he looked both ways. "Where do you want me to sleep?"

"The room next to Robin's is Aunt Meg's, but down the hall—"

"Where will you be?"

"My room is upstairs on the other side of the house. Over the porch." She pointed up the staircase that bisected the house, waving her hand to indicate the directions up and over. "It gives me my privacy and a wonderful view of the river."

"Sounds nice."

"It's a little chilly because it's, you know, directly over the porch. But I prefer a cool bedroom, even in the winter." She nodded toward the living room. "And I love a nice fire."

"Especially in the winter," he agreed, slipping his arm around her as she led the way back to the hearth.

"It's not even winter yet. Fall is my favorite season, and we're obviously not going to get our share this year."

"Hey, the colors have peaked. What more do you want? It was spectacular up north. I did some work up at Red Lake and White Earth during those days when the yellow trees make the world around you glow, and you figure God's hangin' out in the woods."

She turned her face up to him again. She was all smiles, gleaming with approval, her neck and chin burnished by fire glow as she drew him down with her to sit at the hearth side. The cups of warm wine were set aside on a table, supplanted by fire and good feeling between two people. He thought about the cold and the unseasonable snow and how weird it was that he didn't mind being stuck right where he was, like a creature inside a cocoon. He didn't mind feeling deep-down good. He could be who he was, talk about anything he wanted, and it was all okay with this woman. She didn't expect him to make medicine, didn't ask him to bring purity into a world getting more impure by the minute. She had no fantasies about what magic he'd been born to make. To her, he was simply a man—cold, lonely and real.

Did she know how easily satisfied a simple man could be?

"Mille Lacs must have been utterly desolate back in the days when they clear-cut the trees," she mused.

"They?"

"My ancestors, yes. That *great* category makes Martin Bruner an ancestor."

"Fair enough. And the difference would be…"

"Time."

"Ah."

She questioned his sincerity with a dubious glance.

"No, that's interesting," he assured her. "You hear Indian people tell about what their family went through a hundred years ago, and it sounds like they're talking about yesterday. It's a story, you know? Something they heard from an uncle, maybe, but they shed tears when they talk about it." His turn to question with a look. "But you don't feel that way."

"Maybe it's part of the difference between Indian time and…"

"Real time?" He laughed. "No, you've got a point, and I think we're onto something. We're living in different zones here. We don't think too much about marking time. And when I say *mark my words,* I mean in your head. But you'd sooner mark them on paper and file them away so you can pull them out and use them on me later."

"Like I need more records." She crumpled an imaginary paper in her hands and tossed it over her shoulder. "There. Can't prove it by me."

"Like it matters."

"Exactly. In two days, it'll either be snowing or it won't." She wrapped her arms around her legs and rested her chin on her knees. "I'm interested in family history, too, but, like you say, after a while, not all of it matters."

"I said that?"

"I've been sorting through two attics full of old records and papers, trying to figure out what's worth keeping so we can get rid of what isn't. There are lots of historical bits, but no one would ever be able to find them for all the useless pieces."

"What kind of historical bits?"

"Personal and business both. It's like a window on the past. They talk about harvesting as though they'd planted the trees themselves on their own land. The way they talk about the removal of the Indian people as though…"

"*They* who?"

"A sheriff, a senator. In response to inquiries, demands. Bribes, maybe. Who knows?"

"I don't think any bribes were necessary in the face of—what was it called? Manifest destiny?" He did a passable Tony Soprano. "It's strictly business."

"I don't know what to say."

"There's a story," he began, as he turned his attention to the depths of the fire. "Or maybe it was a rumor turned folktale turned joke, but it goes like this. Martin Bruner used to visit the logging camps around Mille Lacs pretty regularly. By day he minded his business. By night he minded his pleasure. And the women he found pleasurable were Ojibwe." He glanced at her, knowing he would find her eyes wide with wonder even before he delivered the kicker. "My grandfather never knew who his father was, but the rumor was that it was Bruner."

Her eyes widened. "I've never heard…that particular…"

"Like I said, a folktale. Some tales never cross the tracks from our side to yours."

"What tracks?"

"Different tales for different folks." He reached for his cup and fortified himself with a deep, heady drink before tossing up the burning question. "So you haven't found anything in your papers about an Indian bastard?"

"Nothing about…an Indian bastard."

"Would you tell me if you did?"

She had to think that one over. "Do you think it might be true?"

"My grandfather's name was Trueblood. First,

last, that was his name. His stepfather never adopted him or anything. My father said that his blood was true Ojibwe. Not full or pure, but true." He lifted one shoulder. "That's what I believe. Nothing written on paper would change that."

"But you're curious."

"My dad used to say, if it's dirt you need, go dig around in the past."

"Was he a politician?"

"Far from it. He was a holy man, like me. A hell-raiser, too, from what I've heard." He chuckled. "More folktales, I guess, although Tiny Trueblood was more like legendary."

"Tiny?"

"His father was Trueblood, so the son was Tiny Trueblood, and don't ask me whether he had another name or why it was *tiny* instead of *junior.* Tiny is all I know."

"What does it say on your birth certificate?"

"I don't know if I have one. I know my father is listed as Tiny Trueblood on the tribal rolls." He sat up straight, stretched his back. "See, I don't have to worry about sorting through an attic full of papers. For one thing, I don't have an attic."

"You don't need one for folktales and legends."

"Good point. And since I'm a breed, I guess I'm not papered."

"What do you mean by *breed?* Didn't you say that both your parents were Indian?"

"But they weren't enrolled with the same tribe," he averred. "Can you think of another group of people that has to keep rolls to show who they are? By blood quantum, no less. And the funny part is that most of what's in those records is about as reliable as the stories people tell. I don't know how many times in the last hundred years they've changed the rules on blood quantum. One generation counts your Lakota blood and your Ojibwe, another says we only go by how much Ojibwe you are. Then along comes the casino, and everybody in the country starts digging around in the family album for a picture of a brown-skinned woman they can call Grandma."

She laughed.

"Yeah, it's pretty funny how one generation's dirt is another generation's gold mine."

"No kidding."

She went quiet for a moment. He could see her gathering up all those so-called historical bits she'd accumulated in her mind. *What does* this *mean? What does* that *mean? Who are you, and who am I?*

"Do you think we're somehow…related?"

He gave a nod. "I think we're all related."

"No, I mean…" She reached for the cup he'd just drained. "Would you like a refill?"

He shook his head. "That's some potent stuff."

Again she went quiet. Between his folktales and her bits of history, something had put a damper on the conversation. Maybe the fire, too. Maybe letting it all go cold was the best way out.

She was the first to move, putting him in mind of a host emptying the ashes from the pipe they'd shared as she rose and stretched. A glimpse of bare skin and belly button above the waistband of her pants drove pipe and ashes from his mind.

"I hope to have breakfast ready by eight," she said.

"I have a feeling I'll still be here this time."

"I don't know how soon I can get the service to come over and clean the driveway."

"I'm gonna need a tow."

"I'll ask if they can do that." She glanced away, exposing her uncertainty. But she recovered, touched his sleeve, then backed away. "Sleep well."

"You, too."

"We can't be relatives, Birch." She gave him a strangely innocent come-on look. "That just won't do."

She left him wondering what difference any of it made—related or not, innocent or not. He told himself to forget. He left the dog with Robin and went to bed alone.

And he couldn't sleep, neither well nor poorly. He had options, but forgetting wasn't among them. Chafing against a ticklish *can't be* and a fuzzy *won't do,* he pulled his own jeans back on. They were still damp and cold to the touch, but he wouldn't go to her in the old baggy pair she'd found for him. She'd been looking so fine in her soft, pink shirt and pants. Was that what they called jammies? All he knew was that, wearing Rochelle's grandfather's baggy pants, he wasn't going to get anywhere with the woman.

Jesus, could they have been her great-grandfather's pants?

He shuddered.

Rochelle had given him directions to her bedroom, made sure he wouldn't wander around the castle all night searching for her. Sweet Shelly. Had he ever called her Shelly? He liked *Rochelle.* Very pretty name, pretty sound, pretty pictures bobbing around in his otherwise set mind.

Rochelle and Birch, both alone now. And there was no need for that. *Can't be.* It would be a shame to sleep alone on a night like this. *Won't do.* Any hot-blooded man had the cure for this kind of cold. *Will do, sweet Shelly.*

Will do Rochelle.

He found the place she'd described, the door left

open, the woman with the pretty name sitting in near darkness on the far side of a long, narrow room lined on one side with bookcases packed with books. The other side was a breathtaking wall of snow-bright windows.

"Do you need something, Birch?"

"A warmer bed." He approached her cautiously, the cold floor creaking beneath his bare feet. "How 'bout you?"

Rochelle rose from the chair like a column of smoke, a curvaceous silhouette against the window, a face shielded in shadow. She wasn't rushing into his arms, but she hadn't told him to go away. Somewhere in the night below, the glow from a yard light spun snowy pinwheels beyond the glass behind her.

"A cool room feels nice when you're warm in bed," he whispered when he reached her side. "God, it's been so long since I've been warm in bed."

"I should tell you to skip the snow job, but I won't."

"I don't want to skip anything."

He unclipped her hair, pushed splayed fingers through it until he felt the weight of her head against his palm. Her lips parted, and he filled the void with a long, lush, lavish kiss.

"What do you say?" he asked, his lips a scant whisper above hers.

"It's too soon for *thank you*."

Too hungry for her to laugh, too delighted by her not to, he gave a guttural chuckle. "I was lookin' for a simple yes." He kissed her again and whispered, "Yes, Birch, come share my bed."

"Yes, Birch, come…" She slipped her arms around his neck and whispered in his ear. "I've been sitting here, just…"

He lifted her feet off the floor. "Wishing?"

"Wondering whether you needed an engraved invitation." She tipped her head back and laughed as he carried her across the room. "The Bruners have been known to send lovely invitations."

"Couldn't prove it by the Truebloods," he said as he lowered her to the bed. "Until now." Shucking his jeans, he joined her. "This is a lovely, lovely invitation."

"It's kind of small, but—"

"Give me a break, will ya? This place is damn cold." He pulled the puffy comforter over them and drew her hand to his groin as he settled in next to her. "Warm me up, and I'll grow on you."

"The bed!" she scolded. "The bed's small. All our beds are small here, but nobody…oh, my."

"You got room for all that?" She sucked in her belly to accommodate the hand he slipped into her pants. "Hmm? Somewhere?"

"I dearly hope so."

"You wanna find out?"

"I do." She stroked him tentatively and whispered in his ear. "But I'm a little embarrassed to be…unprepared."

"I'm not," he whispered, nuzzling. "Not embarrassed. Not unprepared."

Their lovemaking was by turns tender and torrid. His hunger touched and terrified her. Bearable emotions, but barely so. She had wanted him long and hard, and now—exalting in every naughty notion somersaulting through her head—she had him exactly that way. Long, hard, heating up inside her, just short of hurting. Scarcely controlled, almost overboard, repeatedly inching closer to a cataclysmic brink. He persisted in tipping her over, bidding her *come for me* even as he held himself back.

But he took her there again and again, jazzing her skin with wet kisses and warm breath, teeth and tongue razing her nipples until they buzzed like bees glassed within her breasts. He dazzled her with deliciously dirty talk, and delivered on outrageous promises with sensations surpassing heavenly and beyond profane. The simple act of removing her clothes made her dizzy. The knowledge of his all-over nakedness all over hers made her giddy. Dry torso turned damp. Eager tunnel turned dewy. His searching hands, lips and fingertips uncovered senses her body never knew it had. Blissful discovery, in his hands she became full and fine, all knowing, all feeling, all one with him.

Birch got his due. When he came, finally, his resistance had been fully tested, and his pleasure was fully warranted. Power on, full pressure, full release, just the way he liked it. A fucking fire hose. Nothing mattered but pouring everything he had into this fiery female. A screaming battering ram, booted smoke-jumper, free-falling parachutist, he was a goner.

But what a way to go.

He rolled off and sank down beside her. Too exhausted to make another sound, he covered her downy mons with a possessive, protective, appreciative hand. It was all good, and he told her so with a natural gesture.

And she felt good all over. She was all spread out, but weightless and worry-free. Life was wonderful. She was all woman, and she'd been had by a real man.

Thanks be to God.

Simple satisfaction kept them quiet for a good, long time. When he moved, it was only to find a nest for his nose between her breasts. When she moved, it was only to slide her fingers into his hair.

"Thank you," she whispered at last.

"Anytime," he said. "My pleasure."

"Ours."

"Mmm."

As the snow drifted over Rosewood, reality inevitably drifted over Rochelle's bed. And she began to feel its weight.

She closed her eyes. "I wish we could stay like this all night."

"As long as I don't fall asleep here, we won't get caught." He slipped away. She kept still, absorbing sounds and assurances. "I've got some business to take care of, but I'll be back in your arms very soon."

While he was gone, she availed herself of tissues and the glass of water she always kept on the nightstand. She glanced out the window as she pulled her long-sleeved top over her head. This was turning into a storm that would mark the year.

You call this a snowstorm? she would challenge her grandchildren someday. *Gather round and hear the tale of The Great Halloween Snowstorm. Now, that was a snowstorm. Wasn't it, Grandpa?*

"Incredible."

"Oh!" Rochelle nearly flew out the window.

"This snow," Birch said, laughing. "What? You forgot about me already?"

"I was lost in it. No, I'm glad…" She patted the bed, wanted him there with her for the duration.

She smiled, watching him lose the jeans. Until spring would suit her fine, she thought, but she said, "This is one for the books. I was just thinking that most people will remember this Halloween by the storm."

"And you?"

"I'm glad you're back."

"It feels like this is where I'm supposed to be," he said as he crawled under the covers beside her. "I've never thought of myself as one for the books, but this feels right. Was this the library?"

"Every room in the place is a library. Aunt Meg never met a book she didn't like. She's donated tons of them to the local library, but she likes being surrounded by books."

"They're comforting." He stretched out his arm, and she lifted her head to accept the cushion. "Do they improve your dream life?"

"Not that I've noticed. I don't often remember my dreams." But she would remember being surrounded by the warm feel and smell of his skin, the low timbre of his voice, the easy way he moved. "This room is a wonderful place to sleep in the summer, but the storm windows are old and drafty. Something else that needs work. Still, it's my favorite room. I hate to change."

"Definitely a woman's place." He helped himself to a drink from her glass and bumped a pair of costumed dolls off the nightstand. "What's with you and the dolls?"

"Everyone needs a hobby, and I've always liked dolls. Some of them were in tough shape, so I took a workshop, bought some books and started restoring them. They remind me of innocence and fun. They're toys, after all."

"You miss your teaching?"

"Yes. Well, I miss the kids. It's become such a difficult job. You get a child who's way behind in reading, say, and maybe he makes remarkable progress. I feel good about that, but if the tests show that he's still below grade level, he's just more proof that the public schools are failing. And I work for the public school system."

"Bummer."

"It can be, sometimes."

"You could just hole up here and play with your dolls and not worry about it."

"I'm trying to save the family farm, as it were."

"You're losing it?"

"Not yet, but we will if it doesn't start pulling its weight."

"As it were," he echoed. "So how's the innkeeping business?"

"Maybe a little bit too relaxing. But this wedding is going to be beautiful, and I'm going to use the pictures in the brochure I'm designing. We have to get the word out and bring in more small group events like weddings and retreats."

"Damn." He snaked his arm around her, drawing her close as though she needed sympathy. "I thought I was shaggin' a rich girl."

She stiffened. "Shagging?"

"What's wrong with that?"

"Shagging?" Her scowl was lost on him. "You mean you're *fucking* me because you thought I was rich?"

He sucked a breath through his teeth. "Harsh words. Can't believe they came from you."

"I can't, either." She made a halfhearted attempt to pull away, but his arms weren't budging. He thought it was funny, and maybe it would be, but only from the outside looking in.

"As long as the words are out there, hovering over us in the cold, let me ask you this…" He nuzzled her ear. "Was it a good fuck?"

"Yes. Very." She sighed. "Which makes me sorry I'm not rich."

"Me, too. That cuts the novelties down to the Halloween snowstorm and the haunted house."

"What about the good fuck?"

"That's the only kind you're gonna get from me, honey. Life's too short for anything else."

"Do you go around—"

"No," he said. "I don't go around. Not only is life too short, it's already too damn complicated."

"So you're not…seeing anyone else?"

"I see people all the time, but I don't go around with anybody. What goes around comes around, and I've got a kid to look after."

"I don't have many friends around here, either. And I'm not…"

"I know you're not. I don't have to ask."

"I'm sorry," she whispered.

"What for? You *should* ask. You should've asked an hour ago."

She sighed. "Would it surprise you to hear that I used to dream of being with you like this?"

"After you just told me you don't remember your dreams, yeah, that does surprise me."

"No, it doesn't."

"And it surprises you that I don't sleep around."

"It does not!"

"You don't like surprises, and I don't get many." He chuckled. "Except when I come here. This place is full of surprises."

"It's a big ol' drafty white elephant, but I don't want to lose it. Not as long as Aunt Meg is alive. It would kill her to lose her home."

"Long time ago my Lakota grandfather lost his

place out in South Dakota. They built a dam on the river and flooded it. My grandmother said they coulda just as well put a bullet through his heart."

"Who's *they?*"

"*They* ain't us." He chuckled again. "You got your Indians, and you got your non-Indians." He gave her an affectionate squeeze. "And here's an Indian who's got a non-Indian in a dark room, having a sweet time and thinkin'…"

That was a kiss, wasn't it? His lips brushing her temple, the place where she kept all her thoughts. Not *theirs,* but hers, and that was his kiss, and she felt safe in asking, "Thinking what?"

"Thinkin' on male and female and how, up this close and personal, that's the only difference. Except for the dolls."

"And the ghosts," she reminded him. "I'm glad your father's people…" Father's people? Maybe defining relationships was another difference. "I'm glad the Ojibwe and the Truebloods were able to stay on at Mille Lacs."

"The Truebloods," he echoed, as though the name itself were a hoax. "I don't know what that means. Trueblood. What's true about it?"

"You are," she said. "True *to* it. It's who you are. I don't know about—"

"You know what really surprises me? That this

feels right. Being here, now, lying beside you in this bed, it feels natural. I can think and do—" he braced himself up and leaned over her, touching her cheek with one careful finger "—and feel only what's true."

"Can you say it?"

"Not yet." His kiss was a gentle overture. "But I think I can show it to you."

Chapter Nine

The phone dragged Rochelle up from the cozy depths of a blue-water dream. It took a moment to get her bearings. She was alone in her bed, nearly naked, and numb in her nether parts. Blissfully numb. Pleasured beyond belief, but the languid sound of it in her voice was undeniable.

"Hello?"

"Do I have to go over there and drag you out of bed?"

Crystal.

"Shelly, have you looked outside yet this morning?"

"No." She had barely begun to breathe this morning. The white linens were scented with sex, their personal honey-and-cream blend. They should bottle it. From soft blue dreams to sexy white linens, what could be brighter? She closed her eyes and smiled. "Yes. It's snowing."

"What's with you? You were always the early riser. We're in crisis mode over here. I *hate* Minnesota!"

"Come on, Crystal, chill."

Rich, deep laughter came calling at the bedroom door.

"That sounded like a man," Crystal charged. "Do you have a man over there?"

"I have guests, yes."

"How in the hell did *you* get guests? I've had to call off my wedding because *my* guests are snowed in."

"So are mine."

"Are you decent in there?" Birch demanded. "We have a surprise for you."

"I'm always…" Not quite. Her top was clothed, but her bottom was bare. "Wait just a minute! Crystal, I'll call you back."

"No, Shelly, you wait—"

Rochelle dropped the black receiver into its fifty-year-old cradle, grabbed a pink fleece cover-up off the wicker chair nearby and zipped herself into it, all the while trying to make sense of the whispering that was going on outside the door.

Robin peeked in first. "Can we come in yet? School got called off today, and Daddy made us pancakes."

"Madam? Breakfast is served."

"Madam, is it?" Rochelle stepped aside to admit her gift-bearing guests. "This is so not me, sleeping in this late, but what a nice surprise. Pancakes and—" she watched the tray go by in Birch's familiar hands "—peanut butter and jelly?"

"We couldn't find any syrup."

"I like my pancakes with peanut butter and jelly," Robin reported as she made a beeline for the Sonja Henie doll on the bedside table.

"Hey, when you're snowed in, you make do." Birch assumed a post opposite his daughter. "Get back in bed, madam. We want to do this right."

"Breakfast in bed because we beat you to the kitchen," Robin proudly announced. "Are you surprised?"

"Very pleasantly."

Rochelle pulled the covers over her lap to make a tablecloth for the proffered tray. Toto thought she was making a space for him, but Birch's harsh hiss sent the dog directly into a U-turn, back to the floor.

"Was this doll broken, and did you already fix it?" Robin was trying to get her pinkie past Sonja's composition lips for a feel of the four authentic-looking teeth. "Is she old, like the other ones?"

"Her wig needed some attention." Rochelle winced at the thought of the doll's teeth getting knocked down her throat. In pristine condition—as she was for the moment—she had to be worth close to a thousand dollars.

"Easy on the lady's toys, Tweety bird. I'd hate to get a bill from the dolly dentist."

"Rochelle fixes her own dolls. They don't have to go to—"

The phone interrupted Robin's protest.

"I'll get it." But a mouthful of pancake and a slow reach nearly brought Rochelle's claim up short. She gestured frantically for Birch to grab the receiver over.

He held it away. "You're eating. I'll…"

"Let me handle her. She'll make a big deal out of…" She waved off his skeptical look, and he relented.

"Hello?"

"Are you going to tell me what's going on over there, or do I have to drag these antique galoshes on over my Pradas?"

"I'm having my breakfast."

"In bed!" Robin shouted. "There's no school, and we brought her breakfast in bed."

"Who was that?"

"You met her last night, Crystal. Remember Dorothy and Toto? They got caught in a blizzard this time instead of a tornado."

"I remember Chief True Love."

"Birch Trueblood and his daughter, Robin, that's right. Their car got stuck, and they had to walk all the way back to the house in this awful weather."

"Just to make you breakfast. How sweet. I'm coming over."

"Keep your Pradas dry, Crystal. We'll be there shortly. Give us half an hour. Have you seen a weather report this morning?"

"I did. They said, Surprise! You're socked in. Eighteen inches and counting."

"The wind makes it hard to deal with."

"Tell me about it. What are you eating?"

"Pancakes."

"We only got fruit and cereal over here. What are we going to do, Shelly?"

"Add milk."

"I mean about the snow," Crystal snapped.

"I can't help you there." Rochelle looked up at Birch. "My sister wants to know what we're going to do about the snow."

"How much does she want?"

"Well, well," Crystal chided. "Good looks *and* a sense of humor. It sounds to me like someone is having entirely too much fun over there while her sister teeters on the brink of a breakdown."

"Take a pill, sister. I'll be there soon." Rochelle flashed Birch a smile as she hung up the phone. "But I'm going to enjoy my breakfast first."

"Were you planning to keep us a secret?"

"Us?"

Eyebrow arched, Birch cut a glance at his daughter, who was busy with her inspection of the doll.

"Oh. No." Not *that* us. "As long as you don't mind the never-ending drama."

"We don't object to a little entertainment, especially on a day like this."

"Crystal says there's eighteen inches out there already."

"And it's still comin' down."

"I can promise you won't go hungry. We were planning dinner for thirty tonight." She winked at Robin. "And you'll have someone to play with. My nephew is just about your age."

"I can just play with Toto. Or I could help you fix your dolls."

"That's a good idea, too. We've got all kinds of great stuff around here. I remember being snowed in for two days once when I was in school, and I never ran out of things to do."

"We'll take that as a promise," Birch said. "Snow days are like found money to a kid."

"Teachers, too."

* * *

But the smiles of those who had gotten lucky were less than welcome at the main house. Birch had crashed some wedding parties in his time, but never one that could have passed for a funeral. For that matter, he'd attended cheerier funerals. Not that an air of disappointment was totally out of order, but hadn't anybody ever heard that snow happens? Everyone Shelly introduced him to was standing in front of a window. And every one of them asked him when or if it was ever going to stop snowing. Like he was the Native version of cable weather.

Beyond the burning question, the couple introduced as the groom's aunt and uncle were folks of few words. He was agitated, and she was either bored or medicated. The groom's mother was between phone calls, and the groom was getting ready to go outside for a smoke. Birch would have been tempted to join him if Robin hadn't given him the evil eye. She hadn't seen him smoke a cigarette in over a year, but she was a witch when it came to reading his mind.

They found Crystal hovering around Garth and his great-aunt Margaret, who were head-to-head over a chessboard perched on the corner of the dining-room table.

"I heard that you two had taken shelter from the

storm." Miss Margaret's was the only available smile for the new arrivals. "How far did you get last night?"

"Almost to the end of your driveway before the spirits called us back."

"It's good they stopped you before you got out on the road. There are reports of people stranded all over the state, and no one can get to them until this wind dies down. I can't even get back to my bedroom."

"Tell me where to find a shovel, and I'll clear you a path." Birch rubbed his cold hands together. It had been no easy trek from one house to the other, but he knew where to lay on the charm in the Bruner household.

"No hurry. I've got my hands full right here." She leveled a challenging stare across the game board. "It's your move, young man."

"Maybe Garth would like to move out of the hot seat for a while." Rochelle's teasing hand on the back of the boy's neck made him yelp, but he didn't take his eyes off the board. "She's a terror, isn't she, Garth?"

"Aunt Margaret is a good player, isn't she, Garth?" Crystal said.

The boy nodded obediently as he moved his bishop, exposing his king.

"I see how it is," Margaret grumbled. "Humor the

old woman until someone more interesting comes along, and then—" Her rooks, one behind the other, claimed the only open file on the board. "Throw the game to escape her gnarly hold."

"I didn't see that," her opponent muttered, staring, envisioning the inevitable sequence.

"My intelligence has been tested a time or two, but never by a more convincing pair of eyes than yours, young man. You might be kin, but you're still just as transparent as any other male. Thank you for the game."

The boy glanced at Birch, seeking an ally. Birch raised his eyebrows and mouthed one word, just between guys. *Whoa.*

Margaret angled her wheelchair away from the board. "Would you care to try me, holy man?"

"No, ma'am. My game is no match for yours."

"Something I've always appreciated about Indian men." She glanced at Rochelle. "They have a healthy respect for a woman's power. Garth, this is Mr. Trueblood."

The boy was given two ticks of the foyer clock.

"Well? Stand up and shake his hand. Let the young lady's father see your mettle right from the start." The old woman chuckled. "Don't look so shocked, boy. I know you're only ten, but a Bruner is never too young to display good breeding," she continued, presiding over the handshake. "Or good taste. This is Miss Robin Trueblood, who dances like a dream and paid your old aunt the honor of a lifetime right in the middle Main Street, Little Falls. I think you two will get on well in this bunker full of mightily inconvenienced grown-ups."

Garth glanced back at the chessboard, where he'd felt more comfortable, even in defeat.

"What grade are you in?" Robin asked.

"My school doesn't go by grades."

"Oh. Well, mine does. But I'm way above grade level in reading and language arts. What kind of costume did you wear for Halloween?"

"I'm not allowed to eat candy."

"Don't you dress up?"

Garth raised his chin and stepped away from the ladder-back chair. "I've dressed in costumes for two plays. I was Julius Caesar."

"Ah! Killed in the capitol, yes?" Miss Margaret poked the air with a finger she would never again straighten, thanks to arthritis. "Who killed you?"

"Brutus, of course, played by Thomas Theranopoulos, which looked ridiculous, because he's half my size." He gave Robin an imperious look. "I wore a toga. But it wasn't for Halloween."

"I had to leave my candy out in the car. I know how to play checkers."

"We have checkers, don't we, Shelly?" Meg said.

"We have all kinds of interesting stuff. Garth did a little exploring on his own last night. Did you find anything interesting after I left?"

"I wasn't comfortable looking around on my own," he said quietly.

"It's your house, too, Garth," his mother reminded him. "I mean, this is your ancestral home as much as it is Shelly's and mine. Isn't that right, Aunt Margaret?"

"Definitely. As much as it is any Bruner's. Why don't you show Robin some of the highlights from Auntie Rochelle's exhaustive tour?"

"If you like costumes, there's a ton of old clothes from, like, a hundred years ago." His eyes had brightened the instant he'd been designated a Bruner. "There's a top hat that's pretty cool. It's real beaver."

"A hat made out of a beaver?"

"And some old gargoyles up in the attic that used to be outside. They put them on the roof to scare demons away. They're like from the Middle Ages, but Great-great-*greatgreatgreat* Grandmother Rose's sister was scared of the dark, and she was from down South where they have all kinds of voodoo and stuff, so—"

"Maybe I'll just go along on the tour." Birch

wasn't quite as eager to follow the procession upstairs as Robin's puppy was, but circumstances behooved a father to supervise, possibly a holy man to summon some kind of protection, even though demons and voodoo smacked of a whole different spirit nation. He grabbed Rochelle's hand and dragged her along. "You can help fill in the gory details."

Crystal suddenly shot out of her chair and followed behind Birch. "It's been a while since I've seen what's up there besides bedrooms." Catching up with the procession at the foot of the portrait-lined stairs, she muttered, "And cranky faces." On the second-floor landing, she added, "And creaky floors."

"We'll start at the top," Rochelle said, directing Garth to take the lead.

"Yeah, there's cool stuff up there," he said.

"Closets full of cobwebs," Crystal whispered.

"Any skeletons?" Birch asked her over his shoulder.

"We're not quite that cool."

"Skeletons of a sort," Rochelle amended as she brought them to the final landing, where Birch had to duck to clear the doorway. "It's been so long since anyone has actually stayed up here, who knows what we might find?"

"A light, maybe?"

"Uh-oh."

"What?" Times four.

"Cold spot." Rochelle laughed as she turned on a table lamp. Even in daylight, the third floor was a dark and chilly place. The walls were paneled with the pine once milled directly across the river, but its rich scent had long since dried up, leaving only dust for a visitor's nose. Small beds and writing tables were tucked into dormers, and brown-bound books filled shelf after shelf. Where once a maid or a young cook's helper had slept, now cross-stitched pillowcases and the wisdom of Ben Franklin done up in crewel stood testament to someone's enjoyment of a little color.

"Are there names for these rooms, too?" Robin asked.

"Dingy and Dingier," Crystal said.

"They haven't been used in a very long time, except for storage," Shelly said. "Years ago guests' children sometimes stayed up here, but mostly the live-in staff."

Birch smiled to himself. She couldn't say *servants*. Or didn't. Maybe she didn't like the term, but he figured the "staff" had been servants. Butlers, chauffeurs, maids, all kinds of help. He'd seen his share of movies. And he remembered seeing Miss

Margaret's vintage limo pull up in front of the Tribal offices one day, and the driver hopping out to get the door for the rich college girl and her aunt. Oh, yeah, he'd noticed her back then. Few privileged women—privileged meaning *cashy*—had ever escaped his notice. On that day he had just been dumped by one woman, and he'd been on the prowl. Vengeance would be his.

Not much, as it had turned out. Right time, right place, wrong woman. He'd come close enough to recognize a lying sonuvabitch when he saw his face mirrored in the young woman's eyes. Which wouldn't have made much difference—he'd felt purely wicked to start off with—except that she'd been so damn sweet. He'd liked her then, and he liked her even more now.

Now that death had parted him from the "right" woman, the one who'd enjoyed his bed. But his home? Not so much.

Jesus. Once a sonuvabitch…

But he'd been good to her last night. Unholy as hell, but not so she'd noticed.

Her eyes had been playing cat-and-mouse with his all morning, and he didn't mind it at all. He was feeling a little giddy about the whole thing, in fact. Their hands brushed as she stepped around him to point out that there was, indeed, a door in the low ceiling, but it was only to an unfinished attic. They would not be going any farther than this.

He caught her hand before she could move away, planted his thumb in the hollow of her palm and watched her blush. He wanted to say a prayer, do a dance, sing a song.

Let it snow.

"I know what let's do," Rochelle interjected. "Let's make up stories for the clothes in the wardrobe room."

"Wardrobe room?" It was a reflexive echo on Birch's part. He figured that lilt in her voice was really to do with the clothes they were both thinking about taking off.

"I've been sorting through stuff, putting all the really interesting clothes in this room. I've put some things on display throughout the house, but there's so much more."

"Where are you putting the jewelry?" Crystal wanted to know. "I mean, I hope you're not…well, we'll talk about that later."

"There's lots of fabulous costume jewelry here." Rochelle sat her sister on a tapestry-covered bench and handed her a lacquered box. "We played dress-up with it once, remember?"

"One generation's costume jewelry can be…" Crystal was already raking through the box.

But Rochelle was all about the rack of old clothes. "My favorite thing to do was to get into Great-grand-mother Rose's closet and make up stories to go with the clothes. There was 'Rochelle Meets the Riverboat Gambler' for this dress," she recalled as she slapped hangers across the metal rod, switching red for blue for pink for green as though she were giving a slide show.

Birch pulled on a string that dangled next to his ear, and she thanked him with a smile for shedding more light on her display. He enjoyed her enjoyment. She didn't need to know that he was more interested in the crescent of pale skin between her pants and her hiked-up sweater than the ghost clothes she was pushing around.

"And this one inspired 'Picnic on the Lake,'" she was saying. "Oh, and one of my favorites was 'The Mystery of Cupid's Bench.' I found a silver bracelet under the bench once, and the story was about a stolen bracelet. It went with this gorgeous white flapper dress."

"Where's the bracelet?" Crystal asked.

"Somebody stole it," Rochelle repeated. Then she shrugged. "I lost it. It was all tarnished, but it had an *R* engraved on it, so I wanted it to stand for Rochelle."

"What did it really stand for?" Birch wondered.

"Probably Rose," Crystal said. "There's lots of stuff around here with the letter *R* on it."

"Her sister's name was Rebecca." Rochelle fingered the trim on a dress sleeve, musing. "I don't know a lot about Rebecca. She died young. But she lived here with Rose and Martin for a while."

She turned to the children, enthusiasm renewed. "We could make up a little play. Look at this, you guys. We're surrounded by costumes."

"The teacher emerges," Birch said.

"No, I'm afraid it's my little sister, reliving her childhood," Crystal averred. "I just got her into some stylish couture for the wedding, and she regresses to the ragbag."

Like the children, Rochelle had no interest in anything but who might fit into what.

"I could be an inspector from Scotland Yard." Garth tried on the tall beaver hat he'd fallen in love with at first sight. "Mom, look, it almost fits."

"That's because you have a mammoth head, and you're working on the trunk to go with it."

"Mom, you could play Rose," Garth suggested, his mother's put-down apparently sailing over his head, which—Birch felt a little tug on his heartstrings—didn't look any bigger than most white kids'. Forty-acre foreheads, the Indian kids used to say. "She was the lady of the house," the fair-haired boy persisted. "You could wear one of these fancy ladies' hats."

"I was going to wear a wedding dress. Ohh, my wedding," Crystal whined. "It's all in tatters."

"There's a nice one on a mannequin downstairs," Garth said in a small voice.

"I wouldn't wear that. Good God."

"It's just a play, Mom. I'll write you a great part."

"She doesn't want to wear the wedding dress, but I do," Robin volunteered. "Just before the thief steals something important, and we call in the detective." She turned to Garth. "If you're the detective, you have to get it back."

"Not a dumb old bracelet."

"Maybe a letter," Birch offered.

"Why a letter?" Rochelle pulled a hatbox off the shelf above the clothes rack.

"A story I read in high school."

"We read that, too. 'The Purloined Letter.'" Garth glanced at Robin. "*Purloined* means stolen."

"Why don't they just say *stolen?*"

"Because *purloined* sounds better, and kids get to learn a new word."

"This is going to be so much fun." Rochelle lifted a red feathered bonnet from its paper nest. "Can you think of a character for this, Garth? And I know just the costume for a thief." She smiled at Birch.

"A tall thief with broad shoulders and dark, dangerous eyes."

Birch slid her his signature wink.

"Can I be the bride?" Robin pleaded.

"My mom—"

"Your mom will not be playacting." Crystal pushed herself off the bench. "I should get back downstairs and see to my guests." On second thought, she retrieved the lacquer box. "I know there's a lot more jewelry, and it's real, and it better be around here somewhere."

"Crystal..."

"I just mean we have to be careful with all the outsiders coming and going. You know, this B&B thing you've got going, and Ariel..." She saw the protest coming and headed it off with a gesture. "It's a good thing you're overseeing the property, Shelly. Taking inventory and all. I'm glad you've gotten a start on that."

"Inventory?"

"The camcorder I brought along for the wedding might be handy for—"

"Oh, yes, we'll make a movie of our play." Rochelle pressed the hat on her sister. "Try this on."

"I don't think so. Care to join Tracy and me for another round of coffee, Birch?"

"Sure." But the creaky floorboards underfoot

gave him a quick chill, and he remembered that ghostly face peering at him through the car window. "On second thought, I'll stick with the tour."

Rochelle laughed. "We don't have a show yet, and already you're thinking about a tour."

"Have fun, kids," Crystal said as she made her escape.

Garth hung his head.

"We do need an audience," Rochelle reminded him, laying a tender hand on his shoulder.

"She doesn't like to watch, either." His top-hat-sporting reflection drew him to a mirror on the inside of a tall wardrobe door. "I could carry one of those walking sticks you have downstairs. Do any of them have a secret compartment? I could, like, unscrew the knob and pull out a stiletto."

"Not if I have to play the thief," Birch said.

"Maybe I'll be the thief."

"The good guy gets the hat." Birch was teasing as he reached for it.

"No way!" Garth grabbed both sides of the brim and held on. "I get to wear this. I saw it first."

"Let me tuck a little padding into the sweatband so it fits you better, sweetie," Rochelle offered. Garth relinquished his prize to his aunt. "What else do you want to wear? Something dapper, or something dastardly?" She glanced up from inspecting the hat's inner works. "What did you find over there, Robin?"

Robin lifted her find over her head. "Funny white boots."

"Those are high-button shoes, and they look like they might fit you. I know where there's a button-hook. We'll take those with us, and I'll show you how to put them on."

Garth swung a generous drape of heavy green wool around his shoulders. "Is this cape for a man or a woman? I want one that looks like Sherlock Holmes."

"I don't know that I've seen one just like…oh, my…" Rochelle's hands froze, one on the hat's brim, the other inside. She stared. Then, finally she looked up. "Birch?"

"What? Found a skeleton in the hat?"

"Something like that." Carefully she peeled a long, thin braid of black hair from its coil within the hat.

He leaned closer, held out his hand as she dangled her find in his direction, then let it curl into his palm, felt its once-living weight, ran it between his fingers and knew its texture, even its gender. "Whose hat was this?"

"It belonged to my great-grandfather."

"This braid didn't come from the head of your

great-grandmother. It didn't come from any of the women in any of the old pictures I've seen around here."

"Maybe it belonged to a man," she said quietly.

"Now, that would be one hell of a skeleton," he allowed, fully knowing beyond the need for reason that a woman had grown, plaited and cut it. "Whoever it was looked more like a Trueblood than a Bruner. It's bound at the ends with bits of sinew."

"What is it?" Garth wanted to know. "Is it like a scalp or something?"

Scalp?

Momentarily blinded by a fiery mental flashover, Birch brandished the black braid. "Does this look like a bloody scalp to you?"

Garth backed away quickly. "No, I guess not."

"You know what I think it is?"

Birch felt her hand on his arm, heard her calm voice, but it wasn't until his eyes found cool presence in hers that he recovered himself. From what, he couldn't say, but he found voice to ask, "What?"

"Back in the old days, women used to give men locks of their hair. They were made into watch fobs, or woven into hat ornaments, or some other keepsake." She massaged his arm, rubbing his fleece-lined sleeve against his skin. "Didn't the Ojibwe use human hair in decorative ways?"

"You got me. Horsetail, maybe, but…" His glance took in both hands—hers on his arm, his clutching another woman's hair. "I've never seen anything like this. Not coming out of a white man's hat. It wasn't exactly being used as decoration, either."

"Keepsake," she reiterated

"Folklore," he muttered.

"It's as long as my hair," Robin said. "Maybe it was his little girl's hair. It's a real mystery, isn't it?"

"She's right," Garth said. "And we found a real clue. Maybe we should make it part of our play. Hey, it could be like a reality show."

"I'm not a fan of reality shows," Rochelle said.

Birch smiled. Why didn't that surprise him?

"Maybe his little girl was like Rapunzel," Robin supposed. "Maybe he kept this piece of hair under his hat because she ran away with a prince. And her father traveled all over asking everyone he met, 'Have you seen a girl with hair like this?' And every time somebody shook their head no, the father got sadder and sadder."

"This one's a going to be real tearjerker," Birch said.

"But we can make him find her! And she wouldn't marry the prince unless her daddy was there, so now he's there, so now they have a wedding, and I get to wear the wedding dress."

"No way," Garth said. "Forget the fairy-tale stuff. We're doing a mystery, and I'm wearing the hat. But that hair is a clue to help me find…"

"The bride," Robin insisted. "The thief takes the bride."

"What for?" Garth demanded.

"The cheese stands alone," Robin sang. "The cheese stands alooone."

By this time Rochelle was cracking up, cradling her belly with both arms, breasts jiggling inside her blouse like some special dessert she was about to serve.

What were they doing playing dress-up with two kids?

Birch had to laugh. He glanced from his giggling daughter to Young Man Afraid of His Mother, who finally gave and offered a pursed smile. Everybody was getting into it, and again Birch's heart felt uncommonly light.

Yeah, man, just let it snow.

"I think, for now, we might want to keep that braid under *our* hats," Rochelle said. She refused Birch's attempt to return it to her. "No, I think it's probably in the right hands."

"We don't keep stuff like this around," he told her.

"What would you do with it?"

"Burn it."

"Are you serious?"

"Damn straight."

"But it really is a clue. It might…"

"Mean what? Change what?" He gave a directional chin jerk. "How old is that hat?"

"Couldn't we put it back just the way it was?" she whispered as she finally reclaimed the hair.

"You can do whatever you want with your clue, honey. Except put it back just the way it was."

"We'll give it a little more thought," she decided. "Meanwhile, we need a dramatic-looking cloak to go with the hat. Let's try that one, Garth."

"Cool." A tug on the black wool cape she'd pointed out in the wardrobe flopped it into his arms. He heaved it around his shoulders. "Whoa. It weighs a ton."

"It's a woman's, but it looks like Sherlock Holmes."

"Is that the one that was hanging on the coatrack in the room downstairs?" Birch asked.

"The room we gave you last time you…"

The bare lightbulb overhead dimmed, struggled and finally succumbed to extinction. Toto whimpered.

"Daddy?"

"Right here." It wasn't completely dark, but close enough. Instinctively they closed ranks. "How 'bout a flashlight, Rochelle?"

"I can lead the way without one. It's the storm. We should probably take our costumes with us and work on our story."

The light came back on.

"There. See? It's the storm, like I said," Rochelle assured them as she gathered the chosen items. "We should probably prepare ourselves for more of the same. We've got flashlights, candles, firewood— everything we might need for an emergency. As long as we're prepared, we can enjoy the challenge. You know, just like a camping trip. It's an adventure."

"Lead the way, scout."

At the top of the stairs, Robin suddenly put herself in reverse. "We forgot the shoes!"

"You don't need those." Birch grabbed for her.

But he missed. "Rochelle's going to show me how to button them up with a hook," she reminded him.

"I'll get them." He waved her back. "You guys go find the camping gear."

"Dad-deee!"

Toto whined again.

"Go on, now, get this dog outside."

Six feet and four paws quickly took to the steps. They missed Birch's cautious return to the shadowy dressing room of the departed, his grab for the shoes, his unwilling but irrepressible glance into the mirror. Nothing there. He backed away, backed into the door, backed the damn thing shut.

Oh, shit.

He spun around. There was just enough light from the small window to permit him to find the doorknob. Which, of course, wouldn't budge.

"What do you want?" he whispered. "Your shoes? Hey, no problem." He put them back on the floor where he'd found them. "How 'bout the hair? Is it yours? You want it back?"

Was she laughing at him? He was pretty sure the sound was only in his head, but it was enough to convince him that he was amusing somebody besides himself. He turned to find the door ajar.

"Rochelle?"

Damn, had she gotten him again?

This was going to be an adventure, all right.

Chapter Ten

Ariel had a bad feeling about the Taylors.

She didn't want to say anything to Shelly, but those people were definitely up to something besides matrimony. The groom hadn't said much. He hardly seemed like Crystal's type—not that Ariel knew Crystal very well—but Ariel had expected Tracy Taylor to be a glad-hander, a big talker, a fancy dresser, a whole bunch of somebody…else. But he seemed mainly interested in staying out of the way. The other three were lurkers, always close by, but never quite where you thought they were. Aunt Florence and Uncle Frank reminded her of two roadside crows. An unexpected encounter with them in any given room always seemed to cue some sequence of hissing, hopping and scuttling across the floor.

"Oh!"

"Scared me!"

"Didn't hear you coming."

"What are we having for dinner?"

Caw caaaw!

When Ariel ran into Vera in the butler's pantry, her feeling became fact. Vera was actually taking inventory of the china.

"I count eight patterns here," she reported as she slipped a small notepad into the kangaroo pocket of her droopy sweater. "This is magnificent. Minton, Spode, Staffordshire, Meissen, Limoges, not to mention Chinese porcelain. Are they all complete sets?"

"You tell me." Ariel greeted Vera's nose elevation with an innocent smile. "I mean, I know very little about this stuff, except that it's old."

"Speaking as one who appreciates *this stuff,* it's an incredible collection. I hope Margaret has good insurance." She closed one of several huge glass doors. "I came to the open house when Rochelle announced the opening of the bed-and-breakfast, but all I got was a quick glance. I'm not an expert, but as a Realtor, I get into a lot of homes, so I've taken a major interest in antiques and fine collectibles."

"We thought we'd use these for the wedding dinner." Ariel pointed to the last door. "Service for about thirty."

"Spode blue-and-white transfer-printed bone china. Complete service for thirty?"

"We counted the dinner plates. The rest, well, you can see that there's a lot of it. Anything you want to serve, there's a special serving piece for it."

"Do you have any idea how much this is worth?"

"Did Shelly ask you to make a list?"

"Crystal is curious about what's here in terms of family heirlooms. She mentioned that she'd never taken much interest in antiques herself, and I told her that there's a trove of treasure here. As long as we're snowed in, we thought it a good time for her to take advantage of my expertise and learn a bit about the furnishings."

"You said you weren't an expert."

"I'm not a certified appraiser, but I'm certainly willing to help my daughter-in-law in any way I can."

"Can you make a wedding cake? We've got all this food, but the cake is stranded at the bakery."

"I'm afraid I'm no good in the kitchen."

But she was one heck of a bully in the china closet.

Vera sighed. "Anyway, Crystal says that postponing even a day or two throws everything into question. Several important guests were unable to recommit."

"Commit what? All they have to do is get on the road once it's clear."

"Who knows when that'll be?" Without so much as a mother-may-I, Vera peeked into one of the drawers. "What's the silverware situation like?"

"It's like out of sight, out of reach. It would take more work than your elbows have grease to get it all ready."

"Really." Vera folded her arms, automatically clasping her elbows. "There's that much."

"There used to be a lot more. Fancy china is one thing, but silver is a horse you just have to keep leading to the water."

"Hi-ho," Vera said, head bobbing, mouth twitching as she wound up for her comeback like a googly-eyed nodder doll. "I hope the silver didn't gallop away."

"Nope." Ariel smiled. "Miss Margaret hired a truck. Gave it to a worthy cause. Shelly had to chase down a tax receipt. We won't make that mistake again." Ariel chuckled. "Thank the goddesses for Shelly, huh? She's not about to let anything fall between the floorboards. I'm about to do up some linens. Do you have any dirty laundry?"

"What? Dirty—"

"I don't mind. Like they say, it only takes a few pennies to throw in another pound," Ariel said cheerily as she headed for the basement stairs. Not that she wanted to wait on the woman, but she didn't want Vera tampering with the washing machine. It had a temperamental streak.

And besides, laundry was one of Ariel's favorite

chores. Deep in the privacy of the basement, Rosewood's spacious laundry room was well lighted and had grand acoustics. A person could sort and hum, fold and sing, iron and play keyboard, bop around in front of the mirror between loads and suffer no smirking from…

Shadows shifted in the mirror. Ariel's song and dance shifted to yelp and jump.

"Sorry," said a man's voice. "I was prepared to stay quiet and enjoy the show, but I guess the mirror gave away my position." A metal spring creaked as Tracy Taylor leaned across the seat of the old porch glider, shedding some light on the subject of his charming, if sheepish, smile.

He was "positioned" in storage. The far corner of the laundry room had been taken over by lawn furniture brought inside for repairs never done, and by machines like the mangle and the Ironrite, whose days had come and gone.

He slid over as she approached him with the caution anything of questionable purpose deserved. His elbows rested on his thighs, one hand secreting something behind one knee.

"How long have you been down here?"

"Through about six choruses. You don't run into too many people who know all the words to 'American Pie.' You have a fine voice."

"Oh, sure. I croak like a bulldog."

"From one croaker to another," he said with a friendly nod, "your style is music to my ears."

She sniffed. "I have a fine nose, too, and it's detecting smoke."

"I already put it out, but you busted me on two counts." He raised his covert flask in toast. "That's right. I'm bad."

"Drinking alone in the laundry room seems rather *sad*."

"Join me, then." He patted the free space on the glider. "I won't tell if you don't."

"I don't care if you tell, but your secret is safe with me." She decided to sit, smiling when she found the metal bench pleasantly preheated. "I don't blame you for being disappointed. Who'd have thought a blizzard would spoil a wedding on November first?"

"They should've listened to me. I had my heart set on Halloween." He sipped from the flask after she shook off his offer. "That way I'd never forget my anniversary."

His lips looked lush with drink. It shone, too, in his eyes.

"Crystal says you're in a band."

"I'm actually between bands. Between jobs, between wives and between apartments." He smiled, seeing her surprise. "Crystal didn't tell you?" Ariel shook her head, and he said, "Good for her. She's putting my best foot forward, then I'll have a new group soon."

"You're not between mothers, are you?"

"Hardly." He wagged his freshly-barbered head. "Vera Taylor isn't the first, but she's the last, for sure, and the only one of her particular kind."

"A wicked stepmother?"

He laughed. "Depends on your point of view."

"And Crystal?"

"Ask me in about six months. Like the song says, 'when the new wears off…'"

"Six months?" She winced. "That's so sad."

"Hell, it cuts both ways, but she knows that. She's been there before, too."

"If that's the way it is, why go through all the trouble?"

"Good point," he said with a conspiratorial smile. "Why buy the cow when you're gettin'…"

"When you can get the milk at the store? Exactly. It just doesn't make sense."

"That's not quite the way I've heard it, but…" He lifted one shoulder. "I like Crystal. We've had some good times. And Vera's determined to see me settle down." Staring at the flask, he shook his head. "Again."

"I sense a struggle here, Tracy. Your inner child is fighting with your outer man, and the sparks are flying all around you."

"You sure paint some funny pictures," he said with a laugh. "Adrienne, right?"

"Ariel."

"Ariel," he echoed. "Isn't that a circus act?"

"Ariel is Uranus's moon." He did a comical double take, and she gave his shoulder a playful shove. "The planet, Uranus, Mr. Smarty-Pants. She's also a character in one of Shakespeare's plays. Are you a theater buff?"

"Buff? No, not much."

"Ariel is kind of a mischievous spirit. I happen to like my name."

"I do, too. You're quite a kick, Ariel. Quite a kick."

"I'm sure you and Crystal will be able to build on those good times you've had."

"Sure we can. Make the inner kid settle down and the man straighten up, and then we'll say *I do*. Because, the thing is, neither one of them likes livin' alone anymore. Not the kid, and definitely not the man."

"Then why are you sitting in the basement nursing a bottle? It looks to me like you've fallen off the rocker."

"Man, you crack me up." He proved it with little more than a chuckle. "I have yet to climb on the *wagon,* Ariel, and I don't like to be nagged about it."

"Hey, all I do is read the signs, buddy. Nagging is for horses."

"Hay, too."

"Hey, *you.* I think it's time you got yourself back in the saddle if you've got your heart set on sleeping in the honeymoon suite instead of the doghouse."

Now he was laughing for real. "I'm gonna be as dizzy as you are pretty soon with all this horsin' around you've got in mind for me."

"We've gone to a lot of trouble getting this place ready for your wedding. But I guess it's normal for a groom to get last-minute jitters."

"Thank God, a sign of normalcy."

"But don't let it go to your head."

"Tracy!"

"Shit," he muttered as he capped the flask. He had it stashed beneath the glider by the time the encroaching footsteps switched from wood to cement.

"Ariel, have you seen…" Crystal appeared in the doorway. "There you are. What are you doing down here?"

"Checking on the facilities. Looks like I'll be doing my own laundry for a little while longer."

"You'll be doing your own laundry for the rest

of your life, my sweet. Just like Garth does." She clasped her hands behind her back and sauntered from laundry tub to ironing board, making a pretense of looking everything over. "So. What did you find down here? Anything interesting?"

"Relief from last-minute wedding jitters." He decided to receive his part of the inspection standing up. "And what did you find upstairs, my sweet? Anything interesting?"

"Have you been drinking?" Crystal eyed Ariel, who followed Tracy's lead and stood in preference to being looked down upon. "With the help?"

"I didn't need any help. I managed all by myself."

"Ariel, would you excuse us, please?"

"Certainly. I don't believe I called this meeting, but if you're ready to adjourn…" She gave a polite but pointed there's-the-door gesture. "You're excused."

Tracy cracked up.

"I *meant*—"

"Jesus, Crystal." Still chuckling, he slipped his arm around his bride-to-be and gave a cajoling squeeze. "Lighten up, huh? I'm coming." Tracy sneaked a parting glance past Crystal. "Ariel, please excuse us."

He winked at her. *Crystal's intended.*

The groom-to-be was a sad case indeed. Sad and sweet, Ariel's favorite mix. But he was following a path that would surely take his spirit from sweet to bittersweet, and the descent from bittersweet to bitter would leave *him* sad and bitter, whereupon his nimbus would darken, and sad would turn to mad. Without an intervention, what then? A sad man gone mad, a sweet man turned bitter, and another sour voice pitching itself against Earth's natural harmony.

A Halloween snowstorm was Earth's unpredictable but perfectly natural response, Ariel decided. She had a bad feeling about the Taylors, and here was the chance for getting to the root of that feeling.

Thanks be to Nature.

The world beyond the windows was almost entirely white. For all Rochelle could tell, the house had been trapped in a snow funnel, but the howling wind didn't ruffle afternoon tea. *Nothing like a roaring fire and hot tea to put body and mind at ease,* her aunt had said, and so the tea tables were set, and some of the wedding sweets were arranged on tiered serving plates.

"What has everyone found to keep them so busy today?" Aunt Meg asked.

Silence. Suddenly mouths were full. Furtive glances were flittering around the two small tables.

"We wrote a play," Robin volunteered around a mouthful of chocolate tart.

"I wrote most of it," Garth quickly supplied. "But Robin had some good ideas for the story, and Aunt Shelly helped us with costumes."

"A play!" Instantly charmed, honestly giddy, Aunt Meg clapped her hands. "How soon can we expect it to open? It's been ages since I've been to the theater."

"We'll probably have to put it on right here." Garth pointed to the spacious landing above the four steps, framed by a dramatic arch that afforded the living room its grand entrance. The back wall featured a lion's-head fountain, and a niche housed the pipes for the parlor organ. "We thought right up there could be the stage."

"That's exactly where my sister and I used to put on shows. Grandmother would provide the music for us."

"Our play is a mystery. It doesn't need music."

"Oh, but think how a bit of eerie music might add to the mood."

"On the organ?"

"The organ hasn't worked in years," Aunt Meg said sadly. Guilt pricked Rochelle, who had promised to hire someone to repair it. She had found someone but hadn't been willing to pay his price. "But the grand piano is all tuned up and ready to go," the old woman continued, exchanging glances with her niece. *Mind reader.* "Why don't you let me audition for you after tea? I'll show you what I can do, and you two decide."

"I'm the head writer and the director, so it's mostly up to me." But Garth turned to Robin, whom he had quietly invited to share his settee and tea table. "Should we let her try?"

"Of course we should. It's Miss Margaret's house, and her costumes and everything."

"Okay, but we're not telling anyone how it ends. That's a surprise."

"It's a mystery, and that means lots of secrets, like what's inside—"

"Shh!" Garth clapped his hand over Robin's mouth, toppling her teacup in the process. "Sorry."

"Garth, you made a mess. Now clean it up," Crystal chided.

"Sorry." Napkin in hand, he shot Robin a heated glance before ducking under the table. "You almost ruined it."

"I'll help you," the girl said, and she lifted the corner of the tablecloth to make her apology. "I forgot, Garth."

"That's easy to do, honey. Everybody's really excited about your play." Aunt Meg said. "Aren't we?"

"We sure are," Tracy put in softly. "With no wedding, we've got a big hole in the schedule."

"That's what our play is about," Robin said.

"Shh!" Garth popped out from under the table, white cloth draped across his head like a mantilla. He shot Robin another scowl. "Nobody's gonna watch it if you tell them everything."

"Oops." Robin zipped her lips. Briefly. "I know for sure my dad will watch."

"He's in charge of props and staging." Garth crawled out from under the table, looking for his prop man. "Right, Birch? Robin said you could make it look like there's an interior and an exterior and fix a cliff for the death scene."

"Now *you* told!"

Birch laughed. "I'll fix you up, but you've gotta let me start the show my way."

"Oh, yes, that would be wonderful," Ariel said. She was sharing a tea table with Aunt Meg, close to the fireplace. "We're due for a smudging."

"Overdue," said Aunt Meg.

"And so appropriate on All Saints' Day. One ceremony postponed, another takes its place. For whatever reason."

"Ours is not to reason why." Tracy raised his cup in tribute to the woman at his side, but Crystal's interest had turned to a snag in her manicure.

"Ours is but to laugh and cry," Ariel chimed in as she began folding her napkin. "Isn't that just the way life goes? If we're having the play tonight, dinner should be served after the theater. A nice candlelight supper, I think. I'll be in charge of that." She took up her own dishes and waved off anticipated offers of help before any came. "No, no, sit and visit. The weather brings you the gift of leisure. Enjoy it."

Rochelle smiled to herself, enchanted by the notion of an unseasonable blizzard of gifts. She could feel her gift brushing against her pants leg, suggesting that Ariel's plan was pure poetry. She slipped her hand under the table for a furtive feel of hard male thigh. But she ran into a handful of furry tail.

"Just Toto," Birch said casually as he grabbed her hand and tucked it into his lap. When she glanced up, he mouthed, *Wanna play footsie?*

"I really should help with…"

Oddly Tracy suddenly appeared at her elbow with the teapot in hand, pouring for the somewhat handicapped Rochelle. "Relax and finish this up. I'll play busboy."

Beneath the table, Birch slipped her shoe off at the heel with his stockinged toe. She giggled her thanks as that big, brash toe massaged her bare arch.

She sipped the tea. It was less than lukewarm, but, yes, she would linger over it a little longer.

* * *

Tracy Taylor was a quiet man most of the time, but that didn't mean he never talked. He was good one-on-one when the other one was willing to put up fifty-fifty. He could tell right away that Ariel wasn't the kind to cut a man down to single digits while she dumped way more than what was worth listening to. He had seen it in her before she'd seen him, down there in the basement. She didn't have to be entertained. She could entertain herself.

She'd thanked him for the first load of dishes he'd brought to the kitchen, and he could tell he'd surprised her by finishing that job, patiently making several trips, and then taking up the dish towel. She didn't say much at first, so he hummed a few bars of "American Pie" and got her to smile.

"The trouble with this fancy stuff is that you have to wash and dry by hand," she observed, standing hip to hip with him now at the sink.

"Maybe that's another one of those gifts. It takes time, and right now we seem to have plenty of that."

She looked askance as she took a swipe at a wisp of her hair with the back of her hand. "And maybe you should spend it with your bride-to-be and your future in-laws."

"The last I heard, Rochelle almost had Crystal

talked into going over to the other house to look at some old records. They got to climbing the family tree, and Rochelle says she's been finding all kinds of history stored away here." He added a dry plate to his growing stack. "I'm not interested."

"Your mother seems quite taken with the collection of—"

"I'm not interested," he repeated firmly.

"Apparently your Aunt Florence is an antique buff?"

"She's gettin' to be an antique, all right, but buff? We won't go there."

"You're not interested," she echoed with a smile.

"You got it." He surprised himself now by confiding, "I put the bottle away for now."

"It didn't go well with the tea?"

"I thought about sneaking it into my cup, but no. Straight tea and crumpets."

Again she smiled. "Before I came to work for Miss Margaret, I didn't know crumpet from dump it. She's taught me a lot about so many things."

"The finer things?"

"Absolutely. I've learned that it costs very little to appreciate some of the finest things, like music and art, books and ideas. But you take these dishes," she said as she handed him a clean, wet, gold-rimmed plate. "They're beautiful, but I certainly wouldn't want to *own* them. I'd have to take care of them without getting paid for it."

"Good point. My family is bewitched by the so-called finer things. Vera loves to tell people who she knows and how much they're worth."

"Why do you call her by her first name?"

"She's my stepmother. She raised me, but I've always called her Vera." He sighed. "And now my ex-wife and her new husband get to raise my two kids, and I get to try to be a father to Garth, who's already twice as smart as me and looks at me like I'm an unpleasant odor." She wasn't asking, which might have been the reason he was telling. "My wife and I split when the girls were hardly more than babies. They were so small and scary, and I was gone a lot, so they wouldn't come to me when I was around. I'm not very good with kids."

"Maybe you haven't given yourself a chance."

"Maybe I'm just not good with kids. Is that a bad thing? Can you smell it on me?"

She sniffed his shoulder. "You smell like cigarettes and something else." Another sniff and she had it. "Clove."

"That's to kill the smell of the Scotch." He dried a cup, slowly set it aside and studied it, comparing it in his mind to a little girl's hat. "Birch is good with kids."

"He's used to being around them. I think that's mainly what it takes."

"He doesn't know it, but we're distantly related. My dad was part Ojibwe."

"I think Crystal mentioned that."

"Did she? I'm surprised she knows. When I was a kid, I wasn't supposed to tell anybody. But Vera checked it all out after the casinos opened, and my dad wasn't enrolled. She tried to get him enrolled posthumously." He chortled. "Isn't that a kick? It didn't work, and I wouldn't have been enough Indian to qualify, anyway, but she still wasted a lot of time trying to prove that he accidentally got left off the Indian list and she was his legal heir. So she had this whole pedigree drawn up, and there were Truebloods on there."

"I'm sure he'd be interested," Ariel suggested. "You should tell him."

"Yeah, right, I'd sound like Vera. It's way back, and I don't even know how it fits. Christ, I don't even know why I'm telling *you*. Seriously, I'm not interested in any of that stuff. Not the history, not the connections, and especially not Aunt Flo's antique buff." He dropped his head back and laughed. "Oh, my God, is it rubbing off? Am I beginning to sound like you?"

"You wish!" Ariel stared at him for a moment.

She could not for the life of her see what was so funny. She was offering him much-needed encouragement. "Unlike you, I'm interested in everything around me. The world is my clam."

He kept grinning at her like a drunken sailor. Either he was lying about putting the bottle away, or the poor man was seriously hard up for a source of humor.

Birch had finally found a room in the old house that he really liked. It was a man's study. There were two bloodred leather chairs with footstools, an oak desk and a sideboard with a tray and empty glass decanters with heavy stoppers that still faintly smelled—unless it was wishful smelling on his part— of aged whiskey. The wood floors sported rugs that must have been drab from day one. The walls were lined with dusty books on dark wooden shelves, and the bulky drapes shut out what daylight might be had.

He punched an old-fashioned wall switch, and three lamps with green glass shades raised the level of light from dark to dusk. Maybe he would find a cache of manly man's books in these brown-on-brown surroundings.

"What are you doing, Daddy?"

He'd been followed. He'd said he would look at their work when they were ready, and here they were, ten minutes later.

"Looking for something to read," Birch said as he squatted on the balls of his feet to read the shelves.

"Garth's play is ready for you to read. We need to work on our clues."

"Cues," Garth corrected as he entered the study on Robin's cue.

"We've got clues in it, too. It's a mystery." She took her rightful position at her father's side and turned on her new friend, arms akimbo. "I'm not so dumb."

"I know you're not," Garth said. "I was just explaining about cues, so I thought that's what you meant. I never said you were dumb." He gave Birch a man-to-man look. "She's actually very smart for a fourth-grader."

"You're both smart." Birch pulled a book off the shelf, choosing it for no particular reason other than its leather spine. "You oughta tell your teachers about your snow-day project. I'll bet they'll be quite impressed that you put on a play."

"If we ever get it ready. We need more practice," Robin said.

"I know all my lines," Garth boasted. "My old teacher would have given me extra credit for writing a play, especially if we made a video. But this year I had to change schools, and I don't think my new teacher gives extra credit for special projects. Plus, we're doing stuff in math that I did a year ago already."

Birch's knees cracked as he stood. "Did you move?"

"No. Not yet, anyway, and we'd better not, because I'm going back to my old school as soon as we get some money. I go to private school—my *real* school—but my mom got behind on the payments, so I had to go to public school this year, and it sucks. I don't know anybody."

"It takes time to make new friends, especially when you're really missing the kids back at the old school. Did you have some solid bros?" The boy looked blank. "Buddies? Guys you hung out with all the time?"

"Derek Merkle. I'll never have another friend like Derek."

"Sure you will. There must be other smart kids in your new school," Birch said absently as he studied the worn gold print on the spine of the book. He could only make out some of the letters, but he was pretty sure of the title.

"The second- and third-smartest kids in my class are girls, and they stick together like pink Velcro."

"I see what you're sayin'. You'd be…" He'd started a thumb-through, but the book fell open in the middle, and something fell out. "What the…"

Robin got to it first. "What's this, Daddy?"

"Looks like an old postcard." Black script flowed and curled across the aged paper, clearly written by a feminine hand. "Come take a look, Garth. It only cost a penny to send it. All the way to New York, looks like."

Garth fairly jumped at the invitation. "The stamp is still good," he said. "No postmark. 'To Rose Analise Bruner in care of K. Richard, 59 West 35th Street, New York.' Before zip codes. And it says 'This side is exclusively for the address,' so how are you supposed to write a message?" He turned it over to discover a note scrawled in the white space around what looked like a hand-painted Native Madonna. "Oh," the boy said with a start. He quickly handed the card back to Birch. "That's a funny kind of picture for a postcard."

"It sure is. An Ojibwe mama nursing her baby." The exposed breast explained the boy's sudden hot-potato pass. "Can't tell whether it's a painting or an old photograph that's been colored. 'Warm meals at all hours,' according to the caption. Duh!" He turned the card twice as he read the message inscribed around the picture. "'May 10, 1909. Dear sister, Am feeling much better now that the weather has improved. In your absence I am tutoring at the Indian mission school. This woman's face tells all, poor thing.'" Birch spared the face a glance and wondered just what all it told. *What are you staring at? I'm feeding my kid here.* "'But the little ones—so sweet and gay! Regards to Mink's and the Astor. Your sister, R.'"

"Gay?"

"Happy," Birch translated. "Gay also means happy. The baby, see? Having himself a warm meal."

Garth grimaced.

"Why does she say *poor thing?*" Robin wanted to know.

"Would you want people sending this picture of you to their friends and relatives?"

"I wouldn't let them take the picture until I buttoned up my dress and put some clothes on my baby."

"That's my girl." Birch winked at her and chucked her under her chin.

"Regards to minks," Garth mused. "Pet minks?"

"You got me." Birch placed the card back into the book, which he tucked under his arm.

"What is it?" Garth asked. "The title of the book."

"Oh. *The Complete Tales and Poems of Edgar Allan Poe.* Thought we might read it later."

"Yo, cool!"

"Okay, let's check out the stage, and you can clue me in on the cues." He laid a hand on each child's shoulder. "Or the other way around. It's your show."

* * *

With the kids at work on homemade sets, Birch sought a private audience with Miss Margaret. He found her hiding out on the so-called River Porch with a book and a blanket. An ornate freestanding parlor stove warmed the port she'd chosen, and the surrounding windows provided a view of the storm.

"Could you use some company out here?"

"If you can talk about something besides the weather." Margaret pointed to a chair near the stove. "I could certainly use some interesting conversation."

"I might have just the stimulator. Have you seen this before?" He handed her the postcard as he settled in the chair. "I found it in this book."

She adjusted her glasses, read the address side first, then took a moment longer with the message. When she looked up, her eyes betrayed no hint of her thoughts. She glanced at the book and gave a dry chuckle. "Leave it to Mr. Poe to bring us a voice from the grave."

"Your grandmother?"

"That would be Rose Analise Bruner. It's from her younger sister, Rebecca." She reread the message, slowly shaking her head over it. "I've never heard about her volunteering at the mission school. I didn't think she got out much at all. This was written less than two years before she died."

"Written to your grandmother," he repeated.

"Who must have been in New York at the time." She settled back, relaxing in her wheelchair. "The first time I saw the city of New York, I went with Grandmother. She made the trip at least once a year. She and her cousin, Kate, would do the town and shop for the latest fashions. The women in our family have always had a thing for new clothes. Except for Shelly, who's more interested in old clothes. Old clothes, old toys, old furniture, old stories, and—thankfully—one very old woman." She gave a knowing smile. "She's a sweet girl, my niece."

"I've noticed."

"Yes, I can see that."

"Any objections?"

"Can't blame a guy for noticing," she allowed before being drawn back to the postcard. "Rebecca was a classic beauty, just like Shelly. I never saw her in person, of course, but we have pictures. The only time my grandmother ever talked about her was during that first trip to New York, when I had Grandmother all to myself on the train. I watched the countryside fly past us while she spoke of other times, other trips and another companion. She and her sister grew up in the South, but the family traveled a great deal. Ships and trains, exotic countries and exciting cities. New York was Rebecca's favorite."

"What happened to her?"

"From what I've been able to piece together, it seems that Rebecca suffered from what was called manic depression back in my day. Or 'spells,' that was a good catch-all term. Evidently she got much worse when she came here to live with my grandparents. It was about this time of year, I believe, when she fell into the river and drowned."

"Fell?"

"That's the way Grandmother Rose told it. Rebecca had become a recluse, she said. But this…" She tapped the card on her thumbnail. "'Regards to Mink's and the Astor.' It sounds rather cheerful, doesn't it? Why didn't she go along?"

"She was busy tutoring Indian kids," he reminded her. "Must be where you got your charitable blood."

"I didn't know Rebecca had ever been to Mille Lacs. That's interesting. Grandmother spoke of Rebecca as though she were the eternal child, a life unfulfilled. Except…"

"Except what?"

"Except that she was clearly not the frail and tragic girl Grandmother described, not when she wrote this. Another piece of the puzzle. I have a few more stored away. Occasionally I lay them out, and

I move them around, but I've yet to push them together. I get close, and then I back away."

"What's the point?"

"I don't know. Grandfather was who he was, and he was all we had left, my sister and I. He had no interest in showing us the world the way Grandmother did, but he let us indulge whatever passions she had instilled in us. I'm grateful for that, and for his...guardianship, I guess you could call it. How much more do I need to know?"

For lack of an answer, he shook his head.

"No postmark," she said. "Must not have been mailed. Where was the book?"

"In that office with the big oak desk."

"Grandfather's study," she mused, and they were both left to wonder who had kept the card from being posted. "Lately it's Rebecca I think about most when I toy with those puzzle pieces."

"Is there a picture of her?"

"There's a nice one of Rose and Rebecca on the way up the stairs. Rebecca has a flower in her hair. I haven't been up there in quite a long time. Have you noticed whether it's still there?"

"Haven't looked."

"Well, she was a looker." The old woman chuckled. "That Shelly, she's been digging around in the closets again. Couldn't keep her out of them when she was a girl. She used to make such a mess playing dress-up with the old clothes. She'd strut around in the hats and shoes, tie up the skirts so they didn't trail on the floor."

"She's got Robin hooked, but, hey, if you don't want the kids messin' in that stuff, you just say—"

"No, it's fine. Shelly can do whatever she wants to up there. Whatever she finds, sooner or later it's going to be her puzzle."

"I don't think much good ever comes of stirring up the spirits. They're past the deadline for do-overs, so let them take their secrets with them."

"Your daughter will want to know her mother, and you'll have to decide whether to answer her questions or plead ignorance and let her seek that part of herself from some other source."

He shook his head. "Robin knows I'm here for her, whatever she needs."

"My mother left my sister and me when we were still girls," she said, as though there was some kind of connection. "Our father had been killed in the war, and our mother started taking her trips. We were in school by then. Our mother was here less and less when we came home on holidays, but no matter what she did, there was never a question that we would come home to Rosewood."

"Boarding school?"

"Essentially."

"Me, too. Maybe we're not so different." He sighed. "Tell you what, education is important, but not important enough to send little kids away from home for months at a time. Not my kid, anyway." He cocked an eyebrow, "Did your grandparents plead ignorance about your mother?"

"We were Bruners. That was all we knew, and all we needed to know. But it's different with Shelly. She's her own person. As far as what's in our closets, she's drawn to the history, not the mystery."

"Oh, I don't know. She's pretty excited about—"

"She doesn't believe in ghosts," Margaret assured him, as though he'd suggested otherwise. "Do you?"

He couldn't bring himself to say.

"Do you believe in your ceremonies, Mr. True-blood?" she asked him gently. "Are you giving people their money's worth?"

"You know I can't take…" He stared at the post-card, now lying on the white blanket that covered the old woman's knees. His people stared back at him through the eyes of one young enough to suckle a baby, yet old enough to wear the cares of many lifetimes in her face. He released a breath he hadn't meant to hold, didn't really know whose it was or where it had come from. "I guess that's up to them."

"I believe in ghosts."

He looked at her warily. "Have you seen any?"

"No, but I know they're here, and so do you. There's a history of loneliness and loss here, and I think that's what they thrive on."

"*Thriving* isn't a word I'd use to describe her. She's beautiful. Young. Spirited, curious, likes to play games. But she's long past thriving…. What?" He bristled at the funny look she was giving him. He felt tricked. "I saw her twice, and I was clear-headed both times. I'm only telling you because…I don't know, because she's your ghost."

"Amazing," Margaret mused. "Ariel's right about you."

"Now *that's* a little scary."

"Ariel has good instincts, and she said you possess a degree of sensitivity that even you might underestimate. Does that sound scary?"

"Coming from anyone else, including me, it would sound like bullshit."

"Especially you," she said with a laugh. "But unlike you, Ariel doesn't bullshit. So you might as well make your peace with it, Mr. Trueblood."

"After all the people I've helped bury, I start seeing ghosts when I come to this place? It's not just scary, it's absurd."

"I don't pretend to know how this sort of thing might work, but I wonder whether Rachel's work at the mission school bears any connection." Tenderly she touched the writing on the card with a gnarled finger. "Maybe an ancestor of yours befriended her. She would have had precious few friends, and with Grandmother coming and going at will, she would have been alone here with the staff and my grandfather." She looked up. "But Grandmother was home when she fell. I asked Grandfather about it. They were both here. They searched for days before the body was discovered downriver. Like poor Ophelia, she had been pulled under by her heavy clothes."

"Did anyone see her fall?"

"In her state of mind, would it matter whether she fell or jumped? I always thought it a moot point. It was a tragedy either way." She smiled. "The play, you know. *Hamlet*. Ophelia was truly an innocent victim. Everyone else…"

"Maybe she was pushed."

"No. Oh, no, that's not the way it happened."

"Are we talking about your grandmother's sister or a character in a play?"

"We're talking about ancient history. A woman drowned." Her gaze drifted to the window. The storm obscured the view, but the mighty river was always there. "I believe it's quite possible that her spirit hovers near the banks of the river that took her breath away."

"Is it possible that your grandfather had something goin' with an Indian woman?"

"What do you mean?"

"Old rumors, I guess. They say he fathered an Indian child."

"Really?" She leaned closer, her interest piqued. "I've never heard that story."

"Some people think that's why you've done so much for Mille Lacs."

She chuckled. "I thought the story was that I've been trying to pay the debt the Bruners owe the Ojibwe."

"Most people like the other story better. You'd be helping your relations, which is something we understand and accept. The other way..." He shook his head. "You can't repay that debt. No amount of money can touch it."

"I know." A quiet moment passed, and then she said, "Some old rumors never die, do they? But maybe they should be allowed to fade away."

"Not if Rochelle has her way. She's going to straighten out all those old records and come up with some sort of truth."

"I suppose."

"Daddy?"

The little voice startled them both.

"Oh, Miss Margaret, guess what? We finished making up our play, and it's a really good mystery. Is it okay if I wear that wedding dress that's on the statue upstairs? I'll be very, very careful with it."

The old woman smiled. "I would love to see you in that dress, Miss Robin. And I do adore a good mystery."

Chapter Eleven

Crystal's interest in the Rosewood records flagged after a couple of files and a few questions, the most telling one being, "How soon do you think you'll get it all sorted out?"

"With your help?" Rochelle surveyed the cardboard file boxes she'd folded, fastened, labeled and filled herself. There they were, lined up on the credenza she'd appropriated for her new office in the new house, just waiting for Crystal to find fault.

"I can't handle this kind of thing, Shelly. It makes me crazy. I'd only mess up the system you've got going." To prove her point, she tossed a file into the wrong box. "Besides, I'm not interested in grandparents and great-grandparents. I just want to know what's left so that when the time comes…"

"Don't expect much, Crystal. If these houses were on Summit Avenue in Saint Paul, it would be different, but this isn't Saint Paul."

"Vera says that with just the land by itself, we're looking at a tidy sum." Crystal sat on the edge of the desk, arms tightly folded. "She suggests tearing the new house down, having some cosmetic work done on the old house, maybe even get it designated as some sort of historical landmark and offering it up that way. She says we'd be looking at a whole different market then."

"I don't think that's what Aunt Meg has in mind," Rochelle said quietly as she moved the file to its rightful place.

"What *does* she have in mind? Leaving it all to you? If that happens, I'll have to contest it, you know."

"Oh, Crystal, let's not go there." She turned, one hand raised in protest, the other reaching back, as though protecting her files. But she made a conscious effort to relax, smile, cajole. "Let's enjoy this reunion. Call your guests, let them know that there will be a wedding just as soon as weather permits, and let's celebrate the fact that Aunt Meg is here to be part of it all. There's plenty of time for—"

"You don't know what there is and isn't time for. I'm tired of not having any money."

"If it's money you're looking for, I'm telling you, you came to the wrong place."

"Sooner or later, this place will be turned into money, and I should be in for half. I know it sounds crass, but I'd like to get an idea of what that half amounts to. If you don't know, maybe I can find some subtle way of asking Aunt Margaret."

"Don't." It was not a plea. It was an order.

"Why not? Practical people plan for these things. It's not like I'm on a death watch. I have debts, Shelly. And I have a child to raise."

"If you're in some kind of financial trouble, maybe I can help. I have some savings, a small retirement fund and, of course, no children."

"That's nice. No, that's really nice of you." Crystal took Rochelle's arms in her hands. "No, we're fine. I didn't mean to sound… I know sometimes I come across as being a bit callous, but I'm really not like that. It's just that we're only here for a few days, and there are some things, some concerns that I wanted to…"

"You're my sister, Crystal. Does Tracy know about these debts?"

Crystal shook her head.

"Let me help."

"I told you, we'll be fine." She glanced at the window, which was curtained from the outside in white. "The best thing you could do for me right now is find a way to stop this blizzard. I've never seen anything like this."

"They're forecasting more of the same for tomorrow."

Crystal groaned. "I'd better get back to my guys. You coming?"

"In a little while."

Rochelle needed some downtime. The wind's voice was enough for now. *Over the river and through the woods, hanging a curtain of snow,* somebody tweedled in her head, while the wind whistled insolently whenever it found a crack in the office window casings. She smiled, suddenly, sweet-secretly, thinking of herself as someone to be whistled at, body and soul. Thought, word and deed. *Girl, you are something else.*

She rearranged the file boxes and went downstairs to the playroom, where she mentally tallied the value of the dolls she'd restored so far. Aunt Meg had already given her the doll collection. Was it fair to hold it in reserve for keeping Rosewood afloat when Crystal and Garth were sinking financially?

She scanned the shelves in the Whole World Cubby, where kids had always been allowed to look but not touch. Most of the collection stood in testimony to Rose and Rebecca's childhood travels, but there was a group of old American Indian dolls that piqued her curiosity now more than ever, thanks to the braid of hair she'd found in Martin Bruner's beaver hat. One of the leather dolls had similar braids, tied off with sinew. Seed beads formed her facial features, and she was decorated with pony beads, fringe and shells. Rochelle wondered who had brought her into the collection.

"You're missing all the fun."

Rochelle gasped, spinning awkwardly, like a child's tippy cup.

Birch grinned and nodded at the doll she now clutched to her breast. "Who's your friend? Looks like Sioux."

"Sue? Sioux!" She laughed. "Of course, yes. Probably. Well, you would know." She punched him in the chest, doll in fist. "You're so sneaky, you nearly scared me out of my socks, you!"

"Let me try that again." Laughing along, he enfolded her against his chest, trapping her arms between them. "This time I'll go for the shirt."

She nuzzled his chilled neck and cheek, inhaling the cold-air smell of him. "How's the play coming?"

"They're working out the kinks." He rubbed her back, the whole length of her spine. "It might be a good time for us to do the same."

"I'm *so* not kinky."

"But you'd *so* like to be. Tell you what. I'll work yours up, you work mine out."

"Kinks?"

"Any word that makes you comfortable. I'm your guest."

"I want you to say." She leaned back, looking into his eyes and thinking how odd it was that being there in his arms didn't feel odd at all. It felt natural, as though they'd been together for a long time. "You say," she murmured.

"I'm no good with words. Times like this, most women don't want to hear the kind of words that come to a man's mind."

"Times like this, a woman doesn't want a man comparing her to most women."

"See? Better off to keep my mouth shut."

"Don't you dare." She lifted herself to him for a kiss, and he obliged, openmouthed and warm inside. And when he went to turn his kiss in another direction, she chased after it with her own. "Mmm, open…open," she whispered. He delved for the deep, wet taste of her, and she of him.

"Let's go upstairs."

She nodded. He tucked her under one arm as though someone might be spying on them and he would not have her exposed. He understood her so well. He knew the way upstairs, and he took the steps, teasing and kissing her along, making her feel cherished as he took her to her room.

She started to undress, but he moved her hands away from her buttons and undid them himself—her sweater, slacks, bra—gently kissing every part he unveiled, cherishing her more and more. She felt like peeled fruit. Her bare body tingled; nerves whimpered; skin wept for his touch.

"I have a special kiss for you," he promised as he laid her across her bed. With his mouth, he turned her breast from flesh to glass, drawing it to a painfully perfect point until her own quivering shattered it completely.

"But that's not it," he said softly. She reached for him, but he kept her down as along her body he moved, dropping a kiss here, a kiss there, until he reached her belly. He tucked his chin into her panties, nuzzled, nudged her knees apart at the edge of the bed. "Open."

She made a small, wary sound.

"Worth a thousand words, I promise."

He massaged her mons with his chin until her legs liquefied in his hands and opened the way for a kiss that gave its lover no quarter. So sweet-sharp, generous, it made no exceptions in pursuit of pure pleasure, all for her. Liquefied became electrified, and she no longer whimpered. She wailed.

He came to her, tearing at his pants in the front while she reached around him and pulled at the back, found his bold, hard buttocks and clawed at him until he plunged into her. She was crazy for him. There would never be enough of this, never, and she said as much. Or sobbed it. Or howled it.

She was a wild woman, and he was just the man to make the most of the moment. He knew that when the clothes were back on, the sweetness would be back on, too, and he loved that sweetness. But no one else in the world knew this wild woman. No one. She was all his, and he liked it that way. He loved the way she raked her nails down his back and fastened them firmly on his ass. He loved her hot moves and her vigorous vocalizing.

He could live and die by the love they made, and he told her as much—not in words, but in other ways. High on a precipice, breath bated at the cusp between promise and fulfillment, he sought to deepen their coupling with a shift of hips, found his reward in the full feel of her excitement, and lifted his body, angling for even better contact and more response. He was doing her right. He threw his head back and sang out, all primal male exuberance, so strong and true that he clearly saw God watching him through the window.

And she was beautiful. If not organic, certainly orgasmic. A vision bound to disappear in the blink of an eye and a triumphant gush.

But he didn't come. And he couldn't blink her away.

"Tell me what you want."

The woman beneath him whispered his name.

The one in the window simply stared, her eyes glinting like ice crystals as snow swirled around her.

"Jesus Christ, what the fuck do you want from me?"

"Everything, every…last…bit of…heaven…"

"You've got it comin'," he growled, and he drove her ahead of him.

They lay quiet for a time, rolled in white bed sheets, wrapped in each other, languidly lingering in the hazy abeyance they'd created for themselves. She wondered if she'd done something wrong, but she wouldn't ask. She would hold him and wait and let him say what he would and show what he could. If he was trying to recover something he'd lost, so be it. Next time, she would try harder to help him.

Next time? God help her, she was already projecting a next time. From all indications, he was feeling put-upon by this one.

"I'm sorry if I hurt you," he said softly. "I didn't mean to hurt you. I wanted to get so far into you that…"

She wasn't about to let a surprising statement like that go unfinished. "That what?"

"That I could stay and never come out. Crazy, huh? Impossible. But don't worry. I'm back to normal now."

"You didn't hurt me, Birch. The more you do, the more I want." She loved the smooth feel of his chest as she stroked it. "You make me crazy, too. Like nothing I've ever experienced. A glimpse of heaven. Is that part of being a holy man?"

"Part of being a man. I don't know anything about the holy part. But holiness and craziness seem to go hand in hand."

Her hand strayed to his hip, and she smiled, remembering how desperate she'd been to get into his pants, how delighted to discover only one layer. She braced herself on her arm, head in hand. "Don't holy men wear underwear?

He chuckled. "Sometimes."

"What kind? Boxers or briefs?"

"You writing a book?" He nipped at her arm. "Tightie whities. Must be an omen, huh?"

"Meaning?"

He shook his head, all innocence.

"So you weren't angry before?"

"I was delusional, honey. Thought I could make my cock long enough to touch the bottom of your heart."

"Silly man. You touched off fireworks."

"We did, didn't we? Is that enough to make it

real?" He looked up at her, his dark gaze gone soft over some fresh vision in his head. "Isn't that what you want, Rochelle?"

"Fireworks? Isn't that just a noisy display?"

"Ah, that's what you gave me." Smiling wistfully, he watched his own finger trace a line from the heel of her hand to the crook of her elbow, tickling all her soft parts. "A noisy display."

"Too noisy?"

"Not for me. Tells me you're alive and well." His gaze met hers. "And real."

"Are you talking about real in the flesh, or real feeling? Because I'm all about both. Like you said, I want real."

"I hope you haven't come to the wrong man."

"Your demands back at you, Birch Trueblood, minus the expletives. What do *you* want from *me?*"

"Minus the expletives and the passion, not to mention the..." He laughed and shook his head. "Okay, minus the crazy man. I want you to be good to me and let me return the favor."

"Too easy," she quipped.

"How would you know?" He shook his head, laughing again at some private joke. "Oh, man, if I'd brought you home a hundred years ago, the people would be standing outside the door right now thinking I'd just killed you."

"Because I'm white?"

"Because of the noise, honey. Indian babies were taught not to cry, and the women—birth, death, orgasm—they kept it to themselves, going and coming."

"Be good to your man, but do it quietly," she mused. "Let him thump his chest and make all the mating noises. Male display is still *just display.* Believe it or not, women from all over the world are well aware of that. But a girl can dream."

"Dream that he'll return the favor?"

"Dream that behind a boy's bravado lies the real thing."

"A man?"

"A man who can give her the real thing."

"A *real* man," he said, laughing. "Ah, honey, I came down here to smoke out the spirits. What do I know about—"

"The real thing between us." She laid her hand on his chest, found his strong, solid heartbeat.

"Real between us." He stared at the ceiling. "Most people need you to know them for what they are. I'm used to letting people know me for what they want me to be. You want native? You want natural? How about supernatural? You want a New Age shaman, hey, I'm your man."

"I'm interested in Birch Trueblood."

"See, the Trueblood part, that's the part I have a little trouble living with. My grandfather was Trueblood, and his grandfather was…" He looked into her eyes. *You want real? Here comes real.* "Trueblood's gift came from his grandfather. He was a holy man, also a man of great courage and determination. He was killed when the local sheriff burned his house down. The old man couldn't get out, and Trueblood nearly went down in flames right along with him. The incident caused a little embarrassment at the state capitol. After a bad winter and near starvation, the white government finally let the few who were left have their little piece of Mille Lacs."

"What about Trueblood's father?"

"Unknown," he said with a shrug. "MIA. Like a lot of Indian kids, he grew up in boarding schools. I did my time in them, too."

"Catholic boarding school?" she asked as she reached for a folder she'd tucked in her bedside table drawer.

"Mission schools and government schools. Trueblood's mother ended up married to a white man, but her brother looked after—"

The conversation continued as they both sat up. Her activity drew his attention to the folder and its unfolding. She showed him a black-and-white photograph of Indian children, all slicked down, dressed up, arranged according to height and book-ended by stern-faced nuns. "Have you seen this?" she asked, and he shook his head. "Do you recognize anyone?"

"I see a familiar face, but I guess you already know that." He tapped the image of a particularly handsome, if unsmiling, young man. "Am I nailing the right head? I have a school picture of a kid who looks just like this one."

"Yourself?"

He acknowledged her guess with a dip of his head.

"The children in the picture aren't identified anywhere, but these letters mention Martin Bruner's donations to the school and report on the progress of one child in particular." She removed one of the pages and pointed out the words. "'Young Trueblood,' the Sister says. He was doing well in school."

He stared at the picture. "And his skin is one shade lighter than his classmates'."

"The keepsake Martin Bruner carried in his hat must have been—"

He shook his head slowly. "That would make him my great-grandfather."

"Quite possibly."

"No way." He shook his head in all seriousness, then suddenly laughed. "No way are we goin' there, honey. Let's just close this up and file it in the loony bin."

"You said yourself—"

"I said there was a story." He reached over and shut the folder. "Leave it that way—just a story."

"It was a long time ago." She gripped her find in both hands. "It's history, and it's always interesting to learn, to *know*, what really happened. Maybe you're an heir. Maybe you can claim—"

"Shut up!" He spun away from her, swinging his legs over the side of the bed. "I've got no claim here, and nothing here can claim me."

"What's wrong?" She touched his back. "What are you afraid of, Birch?"

"Nothing. I don't want anybody thinking…getting the wrong idea."

"That would not be me. I don't scare you. Who would be getting the wrong idea?" She scooted up behind him, but he moved away, searching out his jeans. "Really, Birch, would it make a difference in your life somehow? Would you be unholy? If Martin Bruner were your great—"

"Hell, no, it wouldn't mean a damn thing," he protested as he jammed a leg into his pants. "My name is Trueblood. That much I know. I know Indian ways. I know the songs and the way to use…" His hands stilled. Half in, half out of his jeans, he braced his hands on his knees and shook his head. "I never saw much point in history, Rochelle. That's the way white people tell their story. Names and dates and genealogies all set up to prove who's entitled to what, you think that's interesting? You think that shows what really happened?" He turned to her. "Or who we really are?"

"No, but it gives us a point of reference. Totally academic. I'm a teacher, remember."

"Yeah, well, you can keep your history, and you can keep your house." He had his jeans on now, zipping carefully. "And your ancestors."

"Fine."

"Fine."

Hands on hips, he stared down at her in silence.

From her bedsheet nest, folder covering her bare breasts, she returned the same look in the same silent way.

"Truth or dare?" he demanded finally, stony eyes going just slightly starry.

She smiled. "Truth. Can you make it stop snowing?"

"Do you want me to?"

She shook her head.

"Then I won't." He sat down on the bed. Now he was smiling. "Dare. What if I run out of condoms?"

"Well, let's see, there's Tracy. There's Uncle Frank."

"They don't use 'em. Already checked."

"You *what?* You didn't."

"I didn't. I won't ask, beg or borrow. So that leaves stealing." He took the folder from her and put it back in the drawer. Then he laid his head in her lap and looked up at her. "Gotta do something. I'm not giving you up."

"Do you believe in anything like destiny?"

"Nah, that stuff's for girls. The girls get corny, and the boys get horny. Or…what's that thing where the full moon causes some kind of spontaneous—"

"Generation? That would be the sun."

"More like combustion. It's pure science. I don't think we have a damn thing to say about it. I think God enjoys playing in our genes."

She stroked his thick hair. "Nice talk for a holy man."

"I'm sayin' genes with a *g*. You can pile on the pills and stuff the warrior into a Trojan, but whoever's up next in line for life is gonna get made and then born. God says, 'Time for Robin Trueblood. I've got the egg all lined up. Now, where'd I put that sperm?'"

"I love it! Is that the story you're going to tell her?"

"I already told her the big bird story. Before I figured out the truth—that, sheath or no sheath…" He turned his face into her lap and kissed her belly. "We're playing with a hot fire and a mighty sword."

"You are so—" she closed her eyes, cradled his head in her arms and whispered "—so full of it."

"Maybe so, but that just means I have plenty of it to give." He snaked his arms around her waist. "I'm not giving you up, Rochelle."

"What does that mean, exactly?"

"It means you'll be seeing more of me." And then, with less conviction, "If you think you can handle it."

"I have a feeling I don't know the half of it. But I'm curious to find out. How much of it would I be called upon to handle?"

"All of it. I'm not the kind to go spreadin' it around." He sat up, searching for something in her eyes. "Are you the kind who worries about what people think? Because the vast majority of the population think I'm a pagan priest or some kind of witch doctor."

"How do you know I'm not part of that camp?"

"I know you're in my camp. Not as a believer, maybe, but as my lover. I know you accept me. Otherwise you wouldn't be with me like this." He touched her cheek with sage-scented fingers. "But what will you say when they ask you what your man does? What's his occupation?"

"My man?"

"Yeah. What does he do?"

"Am I your woman?"

"It feels like it. Doesn't it?"

She nodded.

"Are you afraid? Beyond these walls, will this feeling be a burden to you?"

She shook her head.

"How do you know?"

"I've never had a man or been anyone's woman. Not like this. But the feeling I have for you isn't new. It's just…for the first time it's not impossible."

"I don't mind tellin' you, I'm a little scared. This isn't something I ever expected to find again. Definitely not here."

"Why not here?"

"Too much baggage, I guess. Too much Martin Bruner. Too much history. I'm all for staying in the moment."

"Especially this one," she said, and she defined *this one* with a kiss and a smile. "Would that we could, but any moment now I'm afraid we're going to be—"

The creaky hinges on the front door sang out.

Rochelle was momentarily paralyzed, all but her mouth. "Omigod, the moment has arrived."

Female voices echoed in the foyer—one decidedly younger than the other.

"My daughter has arrived," he whispered.

With my sister, Rochelle mouthed. She pointed

across the room, still forming words without sound. "Your boots."

"You'd better cover your own sweet little ass," he whispered as he tossed her slacks across the bed. He followed with her pink panties. "Sometimes it pays to go without."

"Shelly, are you down there playing with your dolls?"

Rochelle glanced at Birch as she touched finger to lips. She kicked her bra under the bed as she wiggled into her wool slacks. At least they were lined.

"Shelly? The kids are getting antsy. Shelly, are you decent?"

"I'm in here, Crystal, and, yes, I'm always decent." She had to do some fast thinking. She wasn't sure why except that the voice was getting closer, and there was a child, and here was her dad, and... Rochelle pulled her sweater over her head and grabbed the folder from the drawer just in time to greet the two curious faces with a guilty smile. "You guys made it through the drifts, huh? We were just marveling at the intensity. I mean, nonstop. Just amazing."

"Really," Crystal said, giving Birch a pointed glance as Robin and Garth appeared behind her in the hallway.

"Really." Rochelle tucked a wild chunk of hair

behind her ear. "I've never experienced anything like it. We were just comparing notes."

"Notes." The corners of her mouth twitched as Crystal glanced at Rochelle's folder. "You're keeping notes on the weather."

Birch cleared his throat. He was standing on the other side of the bed, behind Rochelle. She could hear him shifting his feet. *Boots.* He'd gotten his boots on.

Crystal laughed as she turned to the children. "See, you guys, I told you there wasn't any more fun to be had over here than we were having over there. Now we have to plow all the way back—"

Robin peered around the doorjamb and located her father. "I thought Rochelle might be showing you more of her cool stuff."

"She was alone over here, and I wanted to make sure she was all right. And she's fine." He gave a highbrow answer to the look she threw him. "And we got to talking and, you know…"

"She's been boring you with her musty, dusty files full of documents, hasn't she?" Crystal said, helping out.

"It hasn't been boring."

"No, this has to do with the logging up at Mille Lacs, where Birch's—" Rochelle brandished the folder, but she took the hint when he cleared his throat again. "Where Birch is a member. I wondered if he recognized any of the names."

"We're a small band, so like they say, it's all in the family." He clapped his hands and rubbed them together. "Hey! Enough with the history. How about that show?"

"Not a history, but a mystery," Robin said gleefully. "Mysteries are never boring, and that's what our play is. Because you don't know who—"

"Robin!"

She glanced at Garth. "I wasn't gonna tell."

"You *can't* tell, 'cause you don't know. I've decided to improvise the ending so you can't give it away." He folded his arms and cut an imperious little figure. "Right now, nobody knows how it's all going to end."

Chapter Twelve

Birch took his time smudging every inch of the makeshift stage with the freshest sage he had in his bag of…

Not tricks. His bag contained sacred items, whether he was wafting aromatic smoke at a gathering of Ojibwe at Mille Lacs or a gathering of Bruners at their estate. He did what his father had taught him—sang the song, said the prayers—in the firm belief that it was what he was supposed to do. It might help somebody—surely wouldn't hurt—and whether he was himself truly holy didn't matter so much as long as he was respectful. There was a God of many names, and there was power in ancient ceremony. That was all he knew and all he needed to know beyond the ways he'd been taught. So he made the cleansing smoke the way he had always done, spreading it over the cardboard props, the plants, the fountain and, finally, the audience.

But something was different this time. Whether it was in the house or all in his head, this time he was sure there was a ghost. He'd always believed, but he'd never been sure. This was the first time he'd seen it with his own eyes. First time he'd seen it for what it was. Crazy time. Crazy weather, crazy place. Maybe he was finally, truly a crazy man. Weren't holy men supposed to be a little crazy? He'd always fancied the holy without the crazy, but who was he to say? For once he really had no choice but to go with the flow, do what a Trueblood was born to do, and hope he wasn't offending Rosewood's restless spirit.

Or maybe he already had.

She'd had herself an eyeful this afternoon. He should have smudged Rochelle's room before he'd jumped her bones. If he'd learned anything about this ghost, it was that she could be damn rude.

He sang as he circled the big room, directing the smoke with an eagle feather. Not everyone was comfortable with it, but he ignored Vera's subtle attempt to wave him away from where she sat, looking appropriately sneaky behind the screen of a lady's flowered fan. Everyone had been given pieces of Victorian garb to wear—players, audience, stage manager, musician, photographer. Vera wore a black velvet hat and fingerless lace gloves. Birch wore a cutaway coat and a jaunty ascot over his T-shirt and jeans. Rochelle wore a blue dress that ended just short of her sexy ankles.

Sexy ankles? That was a new one.

Everyone sported a fancy hat, a shawl, gloves, a beaded bag, a bit of plumage. They had been encouraged to choose for themselves, but for those who dragged their feet, "Wardrobe" selected for them.

Garth came to the fore and insisted that everyone move closer to the stage. He directed Ariel to situate Miss Margaret's wheelchair at the grand piano and asked his great-aunt to start them off with a musical introduction. "We were thinking the theme from *Star Wars*."

"Unless you have the sheet music, I'm afraid you're out of luck. How about the theme from *Gone With the Wind?*"

"As long as it's a theme from something," he said as he began distributing typed sheets of paper. "Everybody sit down now. This play is going to have audience participation, and everyone has a part. These are your lines. Pay attention to cues, okay? It's like an audience chorus."

Rochelle got to run the camera. Aunt Meg protested when she turned it on her, but Rochelle would not be deterred. She knew she would treasure this

video from beginning to end. Following the piano
overture, she zoomed in on Birch's reading of the
introduction and then the action.

Robin entered slowly, wearing the ivory satin
wedding dress with the bottom of the skirt draped
over her arm. The story of a bride left at the altar began to unfold. Garth introduced himself to the dis-
traught bride as the detective called upon to find her
missing groom. But he soon revealed his secret
identity as the culprit who stole the note the groom
had left to explain that he had suddenly been called
to duty in a foreign war. The boy had stepped out of
his shell when he'd stepped into costume and character. He'd given Uncle Frank the note to read in the
voice of the groom. Crystal and Ariel chimed in on
cue as the voices of Caution and Wisdom, and Aunt
Flo spoke for Jealousy.

Behind the camcorder, Rochelle was able to
watch and wonder. She knew children, and she appreciated the level talent and imagination that was
on display. She wondered about Robin's contribu-
tion to the script—surely the soldier going off to
war—and whether her nephew had seen *Othello*
lately. Were they teaching Greek tragedy to ten-
year-olds these days? Or was this his idea of *The
Perils of Pauline* meets *Doctor Jekyll and Mr. Hyde?*

Whatever the answers, Garth was quite the little

actor, and everyone was having fun with his clever script until the final scene.

"Miss Bird, you are dressed for a wedding," said the two-faced detective.

"I will wear it until my fiancé returns."

"Then you'll wear it to your grave, Miss Bird, because he's dead. Killed by terrorists."

"Don't believe him. He's not who he says he is," Caution said.

"No!" cried the lovely bride. "I don't believe you!"

"Demand to see his badge," Wisdom said.

"Show me some proof."

"Here's the proof." The imposter took off his hat and revealed a handful of hair. "He was scalped by insurgents!"

"No!"

The bride reached for her intended's last remains, and a struggle ensued.

The plait of hair mesmerized everyone in the room except the children, whose show ended with a brief tussle at the edge of the steps serving as a cliff. They managed two staged falls, pushes, or jumps—neither the method nor the motive was quite clear. Given the actors' stage whispers about who was supposed to go first and about watching out for the dress, the drama was not altogether tragic. Garth achieved the proper dead man's sprawl. In her effort to preserve the wedding dress, Robin landed on her feet. She proceeded to droop like a dying swan, carefully draping herself and her precious white satin over several steps as her irrepressible giggle overturned the pitiful wail that had been scripted.

"Stop laughing," Garth whispered.

But she had stopped, and still there was sound. Rochelle stopped the camera, but the high-pitched hum continued. She turned to the piano. Aunt Meg's hands were folded in her lap, chin resting on her breastbone, eyes closed, face pallid. Rochelle rushed to her side.

"I'm all right," the old woman said. "Is it over? What's that sound?"

"Does the piano have some kind of—"

"I'm fine," Aunt Meg repeated, as though someone had doubted her first protest. Suddenly whiter than pale and shaking, she raised her hands and tried, unsuccessfully, to clap. "Applause, applause. You children were… Shelly, who's crying?"

"No one. It's some…"

"It's coming from the organ," Birch reported from the parlor.

"Impossible. Hasn't worked in…" Aunt Meg tried to brace herself on the arms of her chair. "These children deserve a standing ov—"

"Aunt Meg, don't." Rochelle laid heavy hands on her aunt's quivering shoulders. "You look terrible."

"Sweet. Dressed… I dressed in my theater best."

"You're hands are cold. Your face is…" Rochelle fussed over her like a mother discovering fever in a child. She looked for Ariel, but it was Birch who caught her attention on his return from the parlor.

The flustered old woman also saw Birch coming. "You stopped it? What did you do?"

"Nothing," he said, clearly baffled. "It stopped on its own."

"Impossible. It couldn't have been our organ."

"It sure as hell wasn't mine."

"All right, Mr. Trueblood, whatever you say. You're the stage manager." She gestured for the children, who approached her cautiously, as though she suddenly looked like the bearer of some contagion. "You two were wonderful. Now, where in the world did this lovely thing come from?" Her unsteady hand fluttered around Garth's fistful of hair.

"It was hidden inside the hat."

"Inside the hat. Fancy that," she chirped, glancing up at Rochelle.

"Aunt Meg, tell me what's wrong."

"I need a little rest. It was the best play I've seen in years, but now I need a little rest before dinner. Shelly, would you help me to lie down?"

Concerned, Birch followed them through the kitchen to the quiet little room where Rochelle was lining the wheelchair up with the edge of the daybed. "Could you ladies use some muscle?"

"Show me what you've got, Mr. Trueblood." A thin cackle dissolved into a dry cough.

"Oh, how you tempt me, Miss Margaret." He scooped her out of the chair and laid her on the bed. "Should we call a doctor?"

"Do we know one who has a snowplow?" Not without difficulty, she waved the notion away. "No, I'm just feeling a little weak and disoriented. Confused. That braid of black hair was hidden in Grandfather's top hat?"

"We found it when we were helping with the costumes. I told them not to say anything," Rochelle said, eyeing Birch. "Did you know that was coming?"

"It wasn't in there when they showed me the script. Guess it was just too good to pass up. You know kids."

"I should have taken charge of that particular surprise myself. I'm sorry, Aunt Meg."

"Don't be. It's time I faced my own doubts." She lay there like a talking rag doll, allowing Rochelle to lovingly prop her up with pillows and tuck two quilts around her thin body as she spoke. "It appears there was some truth to those stories about Grandfather's dalliances. I've been haunted by certain suspicions, but my plan was to let them die with me."

"*Dalliance* wasn't the word that went with the stories I heard," Birch murmured.

"Of course not. Forgive me," she said quietly. "If he kept a lock of her hair in his hat, there must have been more to it than that."

"That's what worries me."

"Did you know about his donations to the Indian Mission school, Aunt Meg? Your grandfather received regular progress reports on a boy named Trueblood. That boy was Birch's grandfather. I found—"

"Trueblood?" The old woman turned to Birch. "What was his mother's name?"

"Mary."

"Mary Trueblood?"

"No. *His* name was just Trueblood. I don't know why the nuns didn't give him another name—they usually did. Or maybe they did, and he dropped it. They say it was his grandfather who named him Trueblood when he was born. He gave him the medicine bundle. It was the boy who carried the bundle from the house when they burned the village."

Margaret nodded. She knew about the burning. "And his father?"

"He didn't have one. And that's the truth, the way it was told to me. There was a stepfather later on, but we don't count him. He was white, too." He gave a diffident shrug. "I mean, he *was white*. Not…" Unaccustomed to backpedaling, he had to laugh at himself. "Okay, the stepfather was a white man. He was a river pig. You know, a log driver. Man, can you imagine what that must have been like, riding those logs down the river and breaking up log jams?

"Anyway, he got killed on the job, so the story goes. I guess a lot of them did, but that's why the pay was good. He was either crushed or he drowned. Maybe both. But they had a daughter, Trueblood's half sister. She sort of, uh—" he gave an apologetic glance, another shrug "—what they call *went white*. You know, got married and melted into the pot."

"I love it." Rochelle surprised him with a quick laugh. "The flip side of the guy who *went native*. Of course, why wouldn't there be a flip side?"

But Miss Margaret was bemused. "Martin and Rose had a son, so the story goes," she said, echoing Birch's storytelling style. "I really don't think it matters whether Rose gave birth to him. He was raised as their natural son. Their only child."

"Your father was adopted?" Birch asked.

"Rebecca claimed to be his mother. She said so in a note she left for Rose."

"A note?"

"If she left a note, her death couldn't have been an accident," Birch said.

"She was frail of mind, as Grandmother put it. Grandmother never knew that I'd found the note. It was like reading a burning sign. I wanted to put it down, but I was spellbound, don't you know. I could see it all happening. The poor woman hadn't fallen. She had spread her wings and tried to fly. But she was neither fish nor fowl, and so the river took her down. Later I decided to put the whole matter aside." She glanced at Birch. "As for Grandfather, he never spoke of Rebecca at all."

"What was he like?" Birch wanted to know. "What kind of man?"

"He kept the house the way Grandmother left it, honoring her in his way. He was not an affectionate man, but he was dependable. Steadfast. He was all we had."

"What did the note say?"

With a sigh, the old woman gestured toward the door. "Shelly, look upstairs in the sewing machine cabinet. In the back of one of the drawers, there's a handkerchief pouch. That's where you'll find the note."

Rochelle seemed oddly hesitant.

"It's up to you, dear. I've taken you as far as I can. If you want to read between those sad old lines, you'll have to look at them for yourself."

"Not if it will upset you."

"Go ahead. Now is the time."

Rochelle promised to come right back. She glanced around as she left the room, as though she was afraid her aunt would be gone when she returned. There was a hurried exchange as Rochelle passed Ariel in the kitchen. Aunt Meg had asked for something from upstairs. Wasn't the play wonderful? Dinner would be served very soon, and Tracy had offered to play some music later to round out the evening.

"Can I get you anything?" Birch asked, as they waited for Rochelle to return.

Margaret shook her head. "Sit down." She nodded toward her motorized chair. "Try my wheels on for size."

"If I called a local doctor and told him that Miss Margaret was having some trouble, I'm sure he'd move heaven and hell to get here."

"You exaggerate, Mr. Trueblood, but you do so out of kindness. I like that."

"What will she find?" he asked as he claimed the chair she'd offered.

"Don't let it worry you. She'll puzzle over it. She'll find it very sad, but she'll continue searching for more answers. Because, of course, they're not all there—it's never that simple—and Shelly will never let it end on a note like that. She'll want more, and eventually she'll have herself an interesting story. Interesting history. Interesting herstory. So don't worry about it upsetting her. That's not Shelly."

"How about me? Will it upset me and my—" he chuckled "—precarious balance?"

"I don't see that in you, Mr. Trueblood, no matter what else Shelly discovers. I can tell you that the note has nothing to do with Mille Lacs, nothing about the Indian woman. It is Rebecca's note to her sister, and it says, *I leave the whelp in your capable hands, sister, for he is the child you were meant to have.*" She closed her eyes. "What do you think that means, Mr. Trueblood?"

"Sounds pretty cold, doesn't it? *Whelp?*"

"Rebecca was frail of mind. *Frail of mind,* Rose said, and Rose was my grandmother. Not Rebecca. I refuse to ask—but perhaps someone should—did Martin Bruner take advantage of that poor woman?"

"Your grandmother, or mine?"

"Perhaps both, but my question to you is, should we be more concerned about upsetting the spirits, or about giving ourselves unnecessary heartburn?"

"For what it's worth, my answer to that one is, you're too late asking. The lid's already open on that box."

"At least we know that none of it will upset our Shelly."

"Our Shelly?"

"*Our* Shelly, Mr. Trueblood."

"Birch," he offered.

"Perhaps you feel a bit off balance because you're clinging so fiercely to the Trueblood connection at the moment. But don't be afraid. You're a Trueblood, no matter what other relations might come to light."

"*The* Trueblood," he said with a sardonic chuckle that dissolved in a groan. "What about you? Do you want to know?"

"I was brought up much the way you were in that regard. I'm a Bruner. My grandparents would be horrified to know that I had questions about where Grandfather dipped his wick." Now it was her turn to laugh. "Ah, it sounds almost as bad as *the whelp*, doesn't it? The way we talk, the words we use, the ephemeral veil that is the euphemism. Grandmother was nothing if not proper, and yet all the silliness and eccentricity were said to have come from her side of the family. She said so herself. Oh, yes, she brought the beauty and grace and charm—not to mention the adventuring spirit, which I surely had—but we relied on the Bruner blood for dignity and ambition and, oh, I don't know what all. When I dug in my heels, I was Bruner stubborn. When I won the spelling bee, that was the Bruner in me."

"And when you supported the arts and the Indians?"

"Grandmother Rose was gone by then, and Grandfather grumbled a bit about the time I spent away from home with 'those Bohemians in New York.' But he never denied me anything. We discussed many things, but we had an understanding about what he could and could not countenance. It was the original 'don't ask, don't tell' policy. Quite Victorian."

"Can't be any Bruner in me," he said, assuring himself. "I can't spell worth a damn."

"You are who you are, Mr. Trueblood."

"And who is that, Miss Margaret? The mongrel holy man who gets paid to come here and do sacred ceremonies for a bunch of wannabes?"

"Wannabe holy? Or wannabe mongrel? Which, by the way, sounds suspiciously related to *whelp*."

"You got me there," he said jovially.

"And you're on thin ice if you're talking about Ariel, Mr. Trueblood, because she is—"

"Not a wannabe. I could almost believe Ariel

was Indian in another life, if such a thing really happens."

"That depends on your understanding of reality, I suppose. I should be finding out pretty soon. But for now…" She adjusted the quilt over her bosom. "My true ancestry in this life seems to be in serious doubt, and since this is something we both value, your ceremonies have brought me comfort. Thank you for bringing them here. I have no qualms about putting cash in the plate. That's the way I've always done."

"All I know is, I've gotta feed my…" He turned to the doorway, where Rochelle stood, paper in hand, tears glistening in her eyes. "Hey," he said softly.

"I found it."

"And you're making a liar of me, missy. I was just telling Mr. Trueblood that this would not upset you."

"I'm not upset, really. This is just so sad. The poor woman must have had terrible bouts with depression, and no one understood. Seasonal affective disorder, obviously, but that's probably only part of it. Look, Birch, it's so…"

Sad.

He'd read most of the note by the time the lights in the room started flickering. He glanced up at the lamp, chuckled and shook his head. His acquaintance with their ancestor was more personal than they could possibly imagine, and he knew what was coming.

It was no surprise to him, knowing his ghost's flair for the dramatic, that she would punctuate the reading of her suicide note with a final *lights out*.

Chapter Thirteen

"Ariel?"

"Candles and flashlights, coming right up!"

Rochelle was glad for the voice in the dark, and for the sounds of kitchen drawers rolling and cabinet doors banging. "This was bound to happen," Ariel was saying, "but don't worry. We're prepared. Here's one. I know we have…oh! Found another one."

"Would you check the fuse box?"

"That isn't the problem, Shelly."

"Just to make sure."

"While I'm making you sure, you make everyone else calm and explain power outage mode." A flashlight was pressed into Rochelle's hands as Ariel's voice-from-the-darkness promised, "You'll figure it out. Feel free to make it up as you go along."

Rochelle flicked the switch back and forth on the flashlight. Nothing happened.

"It needs batteries. Don't worry." More drawers, more rattling. "Here. No point in leaving them to go bad in the flashlight."

"Good thinking," Rochelle said, finding another bit of comfort in the coming of two fat batteries into her hand. By feel she unscrewed the top of the flashlight, ignoring the voices calling out for bearings and buttressing. All but one.

"Daddy?"

"He's right here, honey." She flipped the switch and found a little face with big, scared eyes. Redirecting the beam, she extended her free hand. "I'm sorry, sweetie. He's right—"

"Right here, Tweety bird," he called out. "Electricity's out. No biggie. We know all about this, don't we?"

"Yeah," she said tentatively, still dragging the voluminous dress.

"Should we take that thing off?"

"I'll be naked!"

"We'll do a little wrap and tie with the skirt, then. Old doll dresser's trick. Aunt Meg, we'll have to move you again," Rochelle announced as she knotted a handful of skirt. "It's going to get cold in here very quickly."

"To the River Porch," Aunt Meg decided. "I'm going to be selfish with the parlor stove. Power failure can bring out the best or the worst in people, and no matter which way this group goes, all I want right now is peace and solitude."

Birch groaned. "No shit."

"Ship, yes. Our floundering ship needs a captain, and our captain needs a strong first mate. That would be you, Mr. Trueblood. You have my blessing, regardless of any distant—"

"Hey, now, aren't you jumping the gun here, just a little?"

"I have no strength for jumping and no time for subtlety, Mr. Trueblood. It's a blessing, not a shotgun."

"Can't be running from a blessing, now, can I?" He lifted his daughter into his arms. "I'll start hauling firewood in from the front porch."

"When you return, please bring a blessing for me. I found the scent of sage to be very comforting this evening."

"It doesn't seem to be having much effect on the spirits."

"Seems to be working them up just fine," Rochelle muttered as she handed Birch the flashlight.

Aunt Meg chuckled. "You'll make a believer out of her yet, holy man."

It took some smooth talking and a roaring fire in the living room to calm the stranded wedding party.

The hard-won cheerful mood brought about by the children's play had quickly gone south, but Tracy was the only one who had been moved to actually *move*. Birch figured it for a move to get out of the way, but it turned out to be a soothing one. He'd claimed a chair near the window and set about tuning and softly plucking at a guitar he'd discovered in the basement. As a former garage band member without the garage, Birch knew a good picker when he heard one. Tracy was good. Birch would take his music over that of an aged pianist or a dead organist any night of the week. Especially this one.

"This is just great," Crystal grumbled as she positioned a wing-back chair for maximum heat. "The wind is building an igloo around us, and now we have no lights, no heat, no appliances. What else can happen?"

Ariel came through like an express train, announced, "Blankets," made a drop-off at the end of one of the sofas, and turned her flashlight beam in the direction of her next stop.

"City or well water here?" Birch called after her.

"City," Ariel said in passing.

"So you have running water and flushing toilets, Crystal."

"I should be grateful for small favors?"

"Where I come from, we'd call that no small favor in weather like this. Plus, you've got plenty of dry cordwood."

"And marshmallows," Rochelle offered, floating in from the dining room behind another light beam. "And popcorn. We have a fireplace popper."

"Oh joy."

"That sounds cool, Mom."

"Cool is not what we need. How's Aunt Margaret?"

"Snug as a bug in the chaise on the River Porch. That parlor stove will keep her nice and toasty."

"Flo and I wouldn't mind sitting with her," Vera offered.

"She'd mind," Rochelle said. "She needs rest. But Ariel had dinner under control before we lost power, so we'll have a nice—"

"Dinner is served." At the top of the steps came Ariel's flashlight signal. "Mind your shawls and gloves, ladies. They are about to come in quite handy."

"You mean, we won't be roasting wieners?" Birch complained.

"Ariel has candles on the table and everything, Daddy. We can roast wieners another time." With her father in tow, Robin caught up to Rochelle on the way to the dining room. "That's Daddy's favorite."

"I'm an easy keeper."

"Will you sit by me, Rochelle?" Robin asked.

Myriad candles, all shapes and sizes, cast a soft glow the length of the table. The role of cheerful hostess fell to Rochelle. Her seating suggestions were ignored by everyone except Robin and Birch. Did anyone notice how pretty the dining room looked by candlelight, all festooned for the wedding? Birch did. Weren't the costumes just perfect for the unexpected occasion? Robin thought so.

"Well, I know we're all going to enjoy Ariel's dinner," Rochelle promised. Maybe she sounded just a bit like Aunt Meg in her prime. *Must come with the station,* she thought. That imperious view from the head of the table. *Keep it up.* "There, now, *that's* an easy keeper." She pointed to Toto, who followed close behind Ariel's serving cart, cleaning up after a drippy soup tureen.

Birch took the conversational hint. "Yessir, we're becoming a team. Jack Sprat and his dog."

"Pass me your bowl, Jack," Ariel said, ladle at the ready. "This is the soup course, so I don't know how you two will separate the wheat from the chaff, but I'll bet I know who's going to lick the platter clean."

"It's the spirits we need to worry about. The way things are going, we'd best keep them well fed."

"How do we do that?"

"I'll take a dish out to them later," Birch promised. "If they like your cooking, maybe they'll leave the organ alone and stop messing with the electricity."

Rochelle laughed. Birch didn't.

"Does that mean your ceremonies aren't working?" Crystal asked as she passed her bowl for filling. "Maybe it's because this isn't your turf."

"If you say so."

"I'm not saying one way or the other, just wondering whether it makes a difference." She turned to her son. "So, Garth, what was that hairpiece all about?"

"It's a mystery. We found it inside the lining of the hat."

"And where do we think it came from?"

"We think somebody got himself a nice scalp lock," Birch said.

Rochelle scowled at him across the right-hand corner of the table.

"Daddy, that was just in the play. It's not a whole scalp lock, just a skinny piece of braid, like a keepsake." Robin received the hostess's nod of approval. Encouraged, she waxed romantic. "I think the man who wore that hat was keeping a bit of the lady's hair because she went away, and he missed her. I didn't get to keep my mama's hair, but it could help, maybe. You wouldn't feel like all of that person is gone."

"A person needs to take her hair with her when she goes," Birch said.

"Now that's just plain morbid," Crystal said over a spoonful of soup. "But I supposed that comes with the territory?"

Birch wouldn't bite.

"Maybe you'd like to tell us a bit more about your territory," Crystal continued. "The world of the twenty-first century Native American medicine man? It must be something like being in a time warp."

"That sounds like science fiction," Birch said. "Definitely not my realm. You came a lot closer with *plain* and *morbid*."

At opposite ends of the table, Rochelle's and Tracy's laughs were met with Crystal's heated two-way glare.

But she wasn't giving up.

"Has your work changed with the times? Modern medicine and all?"

"I don't call it medicine."

"What *do* you call it?"

"I don't call it anything. It calls me. See, if I called it something, the State would have something to call it, too, and they'd want to require a license or a permit or some kind of paperwork. Somebody needs me, they call me. 'Get Trueblood,' they say, and I'm on my way. If you don't understand what it is I do, you don't need me."

"Obviously my sister understands."

Silence ensued.

But not heavily enough.

"Not that the rest of us aren't enchanted, as well. You certainly do…how does the saying go? Speak with straight tongue?"

"Crystal—" Rochelle warned.

"No, I think it's refreshing to find such a direct approach," Crystal said.

"Straight shooter, that's me." Birch left his chair, taking his bowl with him. On his way past the serving cart, he dipped another helping of savory soup. "The spirits don't like to be kept waiting. What do you call this, Ariel?"

"Minnesota minestrone. You've got your veggies and your wild rice."

"Something for everybody. I'll be back for coffee."

"Daddy?"

"Gotta do my job, Tweety bird. You mind your manners, okay?"

He disappeared through the door to the River Porch.

"Crystal, how could you embarrass me like that?" Rochelle hissed.

Vera piped up with her version of coming to the rescue.

"I'm staying out of this, of course, but can't you see that…" She offered Robin a tight smile. "Well, he's just having fun with us, isn't he, dear? Trying to scare us into checking under our beds for goblins. But don't worry, ladies. With a house like this, the rumor of a haunting adds to the appeal."

"How much?" Crystal wondered. "And would it be in dollars, or merely more quirks?"

"Daddy's not trying to scare you. Right, Rochelle? He knows what to do so we don't have to be scared."

"Nobody's scared, honey. It's just the storm."

But Uncle Frank muttered something about strange weather bringing all kinds of things out of the woodwork, and Aunt Flo chimed in with, "What about that winter thunderstorm? It was a leap year, remember? Lightning in February. They say it caused a whole town to vanish from the map."

Garth glanced at Robin, who made an incredulous face.

"As if we don't have enough to worry about, now we're headed into the Twilight Zone."

"There's nothing mysterious about rude behavior, Crystal."

"Maybe you'd prefer the company of ghosts, too."

"I would *love* to meet a ghost," Rochelle enthused. "Wouldn't you, Garth? Robin? Think of all the interesting things we could learn about other places and other times. *But—*" she smiled at each of the children "—exciting as that would be, somehow I don't think it's going to happen."

"Not as long as you have your own personal medicine man," Crystal said, chuckling.

"Ah, here comes—" Rochelle took a deep breath as Ariel approached with a serving-cart presentation worthy of Goodfellow's or the Capital Grille "—our feast, and it smells heavenly. Ariel, please sit down with us and eat." *Please, don't you desert me, too.*

"I'm half tempted to taste the beef, but you know the saying, the enemy of my antonym is my friend. It doesn't seem right to eat him, no matter how delicious he smells."

"Now that would be the ultimate in rudeness, wouldn't it?" Crystal said, clearly not amused.

But her fiancé was.

"There's an empty chair at my end, Ariel. We can be like Birch and Toto. Play some Jack Sprat. I'll be the beef eater."

"Isn't that some sort of wine or something?"

"Something."

"There's wine in the sauce," Ariel said as she prepared his plate. "How would you like yours?"

"I'm takin' it easy on the sauce." A touch of merriment. "You inspired me."

"I did? I didn't mean to. I mean…" It was a rare moment of awkwardness for Ariel. "I have a bad habit of saying whatever comes to my head sometimes."

"You could've fooled me." He took the plate from her hands before she could set it down in front of him. "Thank you."

Crystal was on a roll. "That's probably not something you want to advertise, Tracy."

"What? That I'm easily fooled?"

"Easy is one thing, but must you beg for it?"

"I haven't been fooling with him at all," Ariel insisted. "I don't have time or the patience for fooling with anyone. You fool with them once, it's shame on them, and then you have to either undo it or keep on fooling, and all that is such a waste of good karma, and that makes it shame on me, and who needs it?"

Rochelle wanted to hug her. "You're an inspiration to us all, Ariel."

"Fooling is one thing," Crystal said. "Fooling *with* is quite another."

"How about *screwing* with?" Tracy muttered. "Or—"

"You two kids behave yourselves," Vera barked. "Your wedding jitters are going to spoil everyone else's dinner. I suggest we pick another subject and have some pleasant table talk. How is Miss Margaret doing, *really?* I just hope we can get her through this rough patch and get her some medical treatment soon."

"She has amazing stamina," Rochelle said.

"Well, she must. Now, when the time comes, you'll want to have some appraisals done. You'll want to get an idea of the market value of everything you have here, and I would be more than happy to help you with that."

"Thank you, Vera. Now, on to the next pleasant table-talk topic. Tracy, you can really make that old guitar sing."

"That old guitar is a Martin, probably 1940s model. It's a beautiful instrument."

"I could listen to you play it all night," said Ariel, who stood at his shoulder, serving platter in hand.

He glanced up at her smiling. "Mmm, Ariel, it's all absolutely delicious."

"Wish I could see what I was eating," Uncle Frank grumbled.

"As long as it tastes wonderful, who cares how it looks?" Rochelle asked. "Ever notice how everything seems so much more appealing by candle-light? I mean, daylight has no mercy, but candlelight has a gentle way with old clothes, faded colors, even tired faces."

"And if you're a little bit overweight, candlelight can be slenderizing," Ariel said.

"What a miracle," Crystal said. "Who knew that a simple candle could render a multitude of sins invisible?"

"And right before our very eyes!" Ariel enthused. "It's like I always say—you can't judge a book by the contents of its characters."

Chapter Fourteen

"What have you got there, Mr. Trueblood?" said a thready voice in the dark.

"Soup. Thought you might be hungry."

It didn't occur to him to question the voice. So the ghost of Rosewood had decided to speak to him. He was cool with that. He had spirits on the brain like never before. At this point he was cool with anything they did.

He'd almost forgotten about Miss Margaret.

"I told Ariel I didn't want anything, so I suppose they convinced you to come out here and coax me," she expounded. "Well, come on over and give it a try."

"I was gonna eat it myself." Chuckling, he balanced the bowl in one hand and used the other to pull up a chair next to her chaise. Candlelight from the adjacent dining room afforded him barely enough light to see. "It's the best I've tasted in a long time."

"Ah, reverse psychology. Oddly enough, I think it's working."

Her hand emerged from the blankets like a fragile creature from under a pile of leaves in the deepest woods. He gave her the spoon. It became a shaky extension. He held the bowl for her, taking the spoon and her wordless acceptance of his help on her terms. It was the kind of respect that was due any elder.

Whether they were related by blood or the Indian way, he reminded himself that it didn't matter. Certainty in such affairs was a white man's way of thinking. Proof of Indian blood quantum had been the white man's idea, not the Indian's. If you were born into an Indian family, you were part of the family. In the old days, if a white man fathered an Ojibwe child and chose to walk away, so be it. The child was Ojibwe.

And an elder was an elder.

"It's good, isn't it?" he asked quietly, and she nodded. He fed her until she greeted a spoonful with a shake of her head.

Obediently, he set the bowl aside. "Are you warm enough?"

"I'm as warm as I'll ever be," she said. "This is my favorite place in the house. I'd forgotten how much I loved the River Porch. Especially in the spring, when we change the windows from glass to screens. It's like opening the house up to the river, and the fresh smell of high water and mud and new green shoots. At night you have the parlor stove and the smell of wood burning."

"I grew up with a wood stove."

"Nothing like it, is there?" she said. "We kept this house closed for years. Grandfather always insisted that this was Rose's house, and that every stick of furniture and every doily would stay right where she'd left it. If something got moved, he knew it immediately. Not only did he put it back the way it was, but he went around making sure nothing else had been moved. It was almost like he was obsessed."

"Maybe he was." Birch braced his elbows on his knees and laced his fingers together. "Maybe it was his way of trying to keep her around. You lose your wife, you lose your bearings for a while. You do what you have to do, whether it's keep her stuff around or get rid of it all."

"It was more like he was afraid to change anything, and I guess the fear was contagious. I stopped coming over here altogether." She drew a steady breath. Her voice was thready, but taking nourishment had given her strength. "Rochelle insisted that we open it to the public. I went along with it, of course. Her little business seems important to her, and I'm just glad she's here. But it feels very strange to be back."

"What kind of strange?"

"Strangely comfortable. Unusually peaceful." She patted the blanket covering her bosom. "And yet, there's an edginess about it, a kind of Christmas-Eve anticipation, if you know what I mean."

"I've never been a fan of Christmas Eve, to tell you the truth."

"But that little girl of yours loves holidays."

"Like any kid does. And like any father, my biggest concern is putting food on the table. I buy it, cook it and serve it up." He chuckled as though she would question his skills. "Have since day one. I married a woman who couldn't cook and didn't even much like to shop. Except for birthdays and Christmas. She used to come home with so much stuff there was no place to put it all."

"Grandfather was like that, too."

"Christmas Eve, I'd be up all night putting together doll buggies and tricycles."

"Little girls are so much fun. My grandmother had a sister. I had a sister. My sister had two daughters. My father was the only…"

She had her Christmases; he had his. They drifted their separate ways for a moment, before the old woman reeled him back.

"Well, it's a good thing you have so many talents," she said, "because girls' toys tend to be a bit more complicated than boys'."

"Hell, all you need is instructions. 'Course if they're not written in plain English and the pictures don't match the parts, then you need enough booze to get a buzz on. Sometimes it helps to be cross-eyed." He laughed. "Her first little bicycle, I wasn't gonna pay ten dollars extra to have it put together. I can do this myself, right? Easy. It takes me four hours, and I end up with the handlebars on backward, and the damn pedals won't work because the chain's not on right." A chuckle. "Christmas morning, she didn't know the difference. She was too young to ride a bicycle."

"And you ended up paying the ten dollars to get it working."

"No way, man, I took it apart and put it back together myself. But not until that spring. I tried lubricating the bike instead of myself." He plastered a great grin against the darkness. "It worked."

"Sounds like you and your wife divided the Santa Claus chores according to your strong suits. Would you want more?"

"A guy can always use another strong suit."

"Children," she clarified.

"We never talked about it much. Didn't talk about

it the first time. If she'd had it to do over, I don't know if she'd..." He clucked his tongue. "She was a hell of a warrior, that woman."

"And you're a good father. Shelly would be—*will be*—a good mother. I know you haven't thought that far ahead, but you will."

"I've thought that far and then some, but you already gave me your blessing, Miss Margaret."

"And you promised me yours."

"I brought the pipe." He tucked into the deep pocket inside what had probably been Martin Bruner's jacket. "It's better outside, but a prayer's a prayer."

As he unwrapped the two pieces of pipe from their flannel bundle, he noticed that the voices in the dining room weren't sounding any friendlier than they had when he'd taken himself out of the mix. He'd been hoping to take the heat off Rochelle, who was trying so hard to keep the peace. Or create some.

"What's going on out there?" Miss Margaret asked.

"Who knows? Like you said, when the power goes, the true colors show."

He placed the bowl and stem on the quilt covering her lap and claimed her hand. It felt like newspaper, which seemed a little scary at first, but soon the scrap of flesh began to warm between his big hands.

"I try not to question too much, Miss Margaret. Some guys go looking for power. Some say they found it, and for the price of a book or a ticket to a show, they'll tell you the secret. Myself, I was born with brown skin, which is *my* true color, and with the name Trueblood. No secrets. What you see is what you get."

Slowly, gently, he rubbed the back of her hand. Her skin was loose, and her bones felt fragile, but he could feel a living continuity between her old hand and his younger one. She knew things he still hadn't learned. She could help him.

"So now I got this question knocking at the door," he confided, "and I don't know whether to leave it sitting there and hope it goes away or look for answers."

"Maybe you've got all you need. Robin. Rochelle. Food on the table and fire in your heart."

"If I'm related to…" He drew a slow, deep breath and blew it out quickly. "No, it can't be true. It's too fucked up to be real. Bruner and his kind took everything my people had and tore their lives apart. I'm not a Bruner."

"I am." He could barely hear her add, "My name is Margaret Bruner."

"But you're good."

"Like you, I've done what I had to do. Thought and studied and traveled and learned—did all that and came up with views on what I was supposed to do. Did some of it. A lot of it. I've also done a whole lot of what I *wanted* to do."

"That's like me, too."

"I know." She squeezed his hand. "That's how we're related. I don't know about the blood thing. My grandfather was all we had, my sister and me. In this life, I can only wrap my mind around so much."

"I know what you mean." He tucked her hand under the quilt and took up the pipe, a piece in each hand. "Can you wrap your mouth around a pipe stem?"

"That I can do, Mr. Trueblood." He could feel her watching as he fitted the pipestone bowl into the stem and filled its small cavity with sacred tobacco. "That much I can still do."

If the blizzard didn't end soon, Rochelle was going to wring her sister's skinny neck. Crystal was getting on everyone's nerves. Insulting Birch, bickering with Tracy, being snide and persnickety—

what was with her? She insisted on helping with the dishes and then complained at every turn. She didn't want to hear any more barroom music or any more bets on the snow accumulation, and how were they all going to sleep in the living room when there were only four sofas?

Off in a dim corner of the room, Tracy ignored her and continued to make soft music. Ariel stayed busy in the kitchen, and Vera was taking her time in the bathroom. Even Frank and Flo had had their fill. Rochelle helped them build a fire in the little bedroom fireplace upstairs and made sure they had plenty of blankets.

Then she turned her attention to the children. Making every effort to steer clear of his mother, Garth glued had himself to Robin and her dog, taking full advantage of the opportunity to be a kid on an adventure. And it was big. The snow, the house, the fire, the growing friendship, everything about it was almost as big as a kid's imagination. Rochelle brought out popcorn and showed the children how the popper worked.

"They'll burn themselves," Crystal grumbled.

"Not if we're careful."

Crystal crossed her legs at the knee and set her foot furiously a-jiggle.

"You know, I really don't like the smell of what's

going on out on the porch. How do we know what kind of medicine that man's making? I'm worried about Aunt Margaret." She flew from the chair as though she'd been bitten in the butt. "I'm going—"

Rochelle moved equally quickly to cut her off. "No. You're not."

"It smells like pot."

"Crystal, stop it. You don't know pot from snot."

"I beg your pardon, little sister," Crystal said as she glanced at Garth, who was shaking the popper over a pile of glowing embers and studiously ignoring her. She turned an elevated eyebrow Rochelle's way. "But I think I know a little more about snot than you do."

They had only an instant to glare at each other before they both laughed.

"Now, could we please just cool it?" Rochelle pleaded when the brief merriment regrettably faded. She reached for her sister's hand. "I know you're disappointed, but it isn't that difficult to revise a wedding plan when the innkeeper is family."

"That's not going to happen." Crystal raised her voice toward the far side of the room. "There isn't going to be a wedding."

Tracy looked up from his fingers on the guitar frets. "Why the hell not?"

"Do you think I haven't noticed your little flirtations? I know all too well what that means. Been there, done that, got the kid to prove it."

"Oh, Crystal," Rochelle said with a sigh. The things people said in front of their kids. How could she be related to this woman?

"And I've all but lost mine," Tracy returned, "but I'm not lettin' it happen again."

"Don't give it another thought. I'm not pregnant."

Leaning forward, he set the guitar aside. "Since when?"

"Since Garth was born."

Rochelle stepped back, getting off the tracks where two trains were about to collide. All she could do was put herself between two innocent children and two far-from-innocent adults.

"Are you being straight with me this time?" He was on his feet and edging closer.

"I thought I was. Or could be." Crystal folded her arms at her waist. "But I'm sure I'm not, and thank God for small favors."

Silence.

For a long moment Tracy just stood there as though he'd been hit in the gut and couldn't decide where to fall.

Then he grabbed his guitar and struck a strident chord. "Hot damn, I'm off the hook. What do we have to celebrate with? You got an extra marshmallow fork over there, Garth?" he said as he strode past Crystal and joined the children at the hearth.

"What do you mean by 'off the hook,' Tracy? You don't want to marry my mom?"

"She doesn't want to marry me, so we're gonna try something new. We're gonna pass up an opportunity to make a big mistake in favor of simply making fools of ourselves in front of all these good people." He played a jazzy chord progression, grinning like the Cheshire Cat. "Doesn't mean we can't be friends. Right, Crystal?"

"Whatever. All I know is that if this snow doesn't stop by tomorrow—" Crystal turned on her heel, running into Vera "—I'm going to shoot myself!"

Vera's mouth opened, but nothing intelligible came out. Thanks to her sojourn in the bathroom, she had missed out on the latest revelations. She stammered as she watched Crystal make a beeline for the john. The she turned a helpless gesture in Rochelle's direction, looking for enlightenment.

Rochelle shook her head. "We've got all kinds of stuff around here, but no guns."

"What's going on?"

"Another melodrama. I don't know why I worried about keeping you all entertained. We've got music, we've got marshmallows, and we've got my sister."

Vera stalked her stepson. "Tracy, did you do something to upset her?"

"Yeah, but she called in a small favor, and now everything's gonna be okay."

"What are you talking about? What kind of a favor?"

"Divine intervention. I think I'll write a song about it." At the moment he was intent on threading a handful of marshmallows onto a long-handled three-tined fork. "You kids like yours burned or toasted?"

"Burned."

"Toasted."

"Tracy, yours looks like a marshmallow man. You've got a head, arms, legs and two…oh, I guess you like yours burned, don't you?"

The small favors Rochelle most appreciated at a time like this were the children. Without Robin and Garth, she could see the party turning seriously ugly.

All Birch needed to make his wintry nap more comfortable was a warm blanket to wrap around himself and Rochelle. Pillows and cushions were optional, but they made a nest out of what was left of both in a dark nook flanked with bookcases. They'd moved the two sleeping children to one of the sofas flanking the fireplace. Crystal claimed the other. They moved a third closer to the heat for Vera and left Tracy to decide where he wanted the fourth one. He left it where it was—in a corner opposite the piano—and went to bed with the guitar. Ariel claimed the chair Birch had vacated on the River Porch. Crackling firewood and soft strains of guitar music harmonized with the whistling wind.

"Do we really need any more?" he asked her quietly.

"Not tonight."

"What about tomorrow? Is it really necessary to find out who fathered two boys who lived and died back in the dark ages?"

"I've been warned about it before. 'Dig around in the past, you'll just be turning over the dirt,'" she recited.

"Wise words."

"But how bad is dirt, really? It grows all kinds of things. A source of beauty and truth."

"Brave words. I'm for letting sleeping dogs lie." He shifted his shoulders and pulled her closer. "On top of the dirt."

She pointed to the kids' sofa. "There's one curled up over there on top of your baby's feet, keeping her warm."

"Easy keeper. Content to live in the moment." He nodded. "That's the only peaceful crew in the house. Maybe we should take the hint."

"Maybe we should." But she didn't. "Did you get any hints from Aunt Meg?"

"A few. She's a strong woman." He sighed. "I hope this wind quits soon. She needs a doctor."

"Birch?" She tucked her face against his neck and whispered. "I think I'm in love with you."

"I think you are, too." He chuckled. The scent of wood smoke in her hair reminded him of home. "And I'm pretty damn sure I'm in love with you."

Chapter Fifteen

Robin knew there was something different about this morning the instant she opened her eyes. It was so quiet that she could hear the tick-tock of the tall clock in the front entry. She lifted her head off the sofa pillow and connected with two more pairs of open eyes— Toto's and Garth's. Garth pressed his finger against his lips, and she nodded. The same finger invited her to get up and follow without making any noise.

The three of them crept past the bumps under blankets that stood for sleeping adults—didn't matter which was which—through the kitchen, into the quiet little sunroom and finally to the window. The blizzard was over, but the never-ending white world it had left behind was like nothing she had ever seen before, not even on TV. The snow was whiter than white, brighter than bright, and so piled up that it buried the bushes and made the trees look like little candles sticking out of a jumble of white cakes.

"Just look at it all," she whispered. "There's mountains of it."

"I wonder how deep it is. In places I bet it's…" He pointed. "Look at that one, Robin. It reaches halfway up the side of the garage."

"And nobody's even touched it."

"Nobody's touched any part of it," Garth marveled. "It's perfect. No wind, no noise, no cars."

She grabbed his arm with both hands. "Let's go outside."

"I don't have any boots with me."

"I don't either, but those ones upstairs fit me. Rochelle showed me how to button them. In all that stuff upstairs, I bet we can find great stuff to put on for snow." She tugged, using his arm for a bellpull. "Knock-knock, ding-dong, hel-lo. We can be explorers!"

"Arctic explorers." He smiled. "My mom won't like it."

"They're all asleep. They wouldn't want us to wake them up after last night. They're all tired out." A lamp caught her eye, and she remembered last night, wondered, tried the switch. "Look! The electricity's back on."

"The plows will be out soon."

Plows would ruin everything. People would get up and get out their shovels and snowblowers, and cut into the cakes and pull down the mountain, and pretty soon all the white snow would be icy and dirty. Robin looked out the window and tried to take it all in at once—the biggest backyard she'd ever seen in her life made into a wintertime Oz, and right this minute there were only two people who knew about it.

"Let's try it, Garth. If we don't ask, they can't say no." She tugged on his arm again. "Come on. It'll be so fun."

They looked at each other, both thinking the same thing. They were still wearing parts of their play costumes. They would have to put new outfits together. Arctic explorer outfits. Could they? Would they?

Garth nodded. Robin scooped up Toto and quietly led the way upstairs.

They were already familiar with the room that Rochelle had turned into a giant closet and the endless combinations they could make with the clothes. They'd been up there a few times, and, yes, they'd made a mess, but they knew what they were getting into now. They found pants and coats, hats and gloves. Robin took two pairs of pants behind the folding screen with the Chinese fans painted on it. She wasn't sure which pair she liked better. She'd learned that they didn't wear polyester snowpants back in the olden days. The pants she chose were scratchy, so she had to put some long white things on underneath.

"Hurry up, Robin," Garth whispered. She couldn't see him, but she knew he was standing next to the window, looking out and getting all antsy. "From up here you can see where the big dips are between the hills. Downstairs you can't. This is gonna be so cool. We can make a map, so when we get outside we can make a path around the drifts."

"Do you have paper? You could work on that while I get all these buttons buttoned."

"I'm working on it already, but I still don't have any boots."

She would have to help him get ready, just like she always did for her daddy. He was always missing something. Good thing Rochelle had showed her where she kept all the stuff that didn't fit into any of her other categories.

"Look at these, Garth. Rubber boots that can fit over your shoes. What did they used to call them? Big galoots?"

"Galoshes." He tried them on. "These will work."

"We're ready."

Garth carried the dog this time. Robin reached the foot of the narrow second-floor stairway, where they'd left the door slightly ajar. She turned and retraced her steps until she was one below Garth at the top. She gestured, he leaned down, and she whispered, "Somebody's up."

They slid around the corner just before the door below was opened.

"What's going on up there?"

"Uncle Frank," Garth whispered. "But I guess I don't have to call him 'uncle' anymore. I'm glad. I hardly know him."

"Somebody messin' around up there?"

"It's just Robin and me, Uncle Frank. We're putting the costumes away."

"Try to tiptoe, okay? Flo's still sleeping."

"We'll be quiet." It was Garth's turn to skip down, peek out and scoot back up again. "It's okay. He went back in the room. I'll go first and make sure it's all clear." He pointed to her high-top shoes. "Take those off and carry them. We'll put them on at the door."

"Oh, man! You know how hard it is to get these buttoned?"

"I'll help you."

Birch woke up with empty arms. It felt strange, not because they were empty, but because he was aware of the emptiness first thing. He'd gotten used to sleeping alone, but all it took was one night with

Rochelle to change his subconscious expectations. Okay, two nights, or one and a half. But he was impressed.

As usual, he was the last one up. The bathroom off the entryway was occupied. He would find another one soon, but first he followed the smell of coffee, which he found—along with a welcome armful of Rochelle—in the kitchen. "Good news!" She kissed him good morning and happy day. "We have power."

"Wind power?" Loath to let her go, he looked toward the window for a cursory observation of the obvious. "What do you know? Somebody finally turned off the fan."

"Haven't you looked outside yet?"

"I tend to move a little slow before coffee."

She grabbed him by the hand and dragged him across the house to the parlor window. About the only thing he could tell about the two vehicles parked outside was that one was bigger than the other and had a red roof.

"Can you believe this?" she marveled.

"After this little trick-or-treat trip, I can believe anything."

"No kidding." Crystal breezed into the parlor from the powder room. "One night without electricity, and the water's nearly cold. How long will it take these yokels to get the plows out?"

"I'm sure they're plowing the mayor out as we speak," Rochelle said. "And good morning to you, too."

"How long before they get to this end of town?" Crystal asked. "And where are the kids?"

"They're probably—"

"They're playing in those old clothes upstairs," Frank said as he rounded the newel post and joined them. "Flo's awake now, so let 'em stay up there. They're being nice and quiet, probably coming up with more playacting."

Birch mentally checked one concern off his list and turned to Rochelle with another. "You need to call and see if you can get Miss Margaret on the street-clearing priority list."

"Ariel says she's been resting comfortably."

"Don't tell them that. Tell them she needs to see a doctor as soon as possible."

She nodded and headed for the phone in the kitchen, where Birch heard Tracy's voice. "Just helping myself to coffee. Is there breakfast?"

"There will be. I'll help Ariel get it ready after I make this call."

"I'll help her," Tracy said. "Eggs and bacon are my specialty."

Birch glanced at Crystal, who was standing at the window. If the sound of her former fiancé's voice had any effect on her, she didn't show it. Rochelle had filled him in on the scene he'd missed last night. All he could say—and he knew it didn't help much—was that you can choose your friends, but not your relatives.

Not your in-laws, either.

Oh, yeah, he was thinking along those lines.

He smiled to himself. For Rochelle's sake he would forget about last night and give the woman the benefit of the doubt. There were any number of people who considered his stock to be worthless. Some were more polite about it than others, but when had he ever cared for anyone who flat out pretended otherwise?

"It's beautiful out there, isn't it?" he said.

"The cars are buried. It's going take all day just to dig them out," Crystal said.

"And probably tomorrow." He chuckled. "Halloween. The spirits really had fun with us this time, didn't they?"

"If you say so." She glanced toward the kitchen. "The least he could do is shovel my car out."

"Sorry to hear about the breakup."

"There's nothing to be sorry about. It was a harebrained idea that just sort of snowballed. Who's Shelly calling?"

"She's trying to get some medical attention for your aunt."

"Medical attention? Is she…not doing well?"

"About the same," he told her. "I can't believe her heart's failing. I've never met anybody with that much heart."

"Do you think she's dying?"

He questioned her with a look. Her benefit of his doubt was fast running out.

"Well, you're a medicine man, aren't you?"

"Which means what?"

"Who knows? I'm asking you what you think."

"I think she'll go when her time comes." He arched an eyebrow. "How's that? Soon enough for you?"

"I'm surprised. As busy as you've been getting in good with the Bruner women, this is the first opportunity you've passed up. Are you figuring two out of three is all you need?"

"For what?"

"She's my aunt, too."

"And that makes you important how?"

"We'll see. If they're going to get her any help, they'll have to bring in a helicopter." She shrugged. "Or an angel."

"Lady, you are somethin' else."

"Boy, this is hard going," Garth complained.

With his long, belted coat and the cane he was

using as his "depth finder," he reminded Robin of a shepherd in a Christmas show. The old clothes were fun to wear, but they were getting heavy. It was still worth it to be able to walk around outside and be surrounded by huge drifts that glistened like sugar. It was like a fairyland.

"It's not hard for Toto," she said. "He looks like a rabbit, bouncing along in the snow."

"I can't see anything but treetops and the roof of the garage."

"Let's check the map and see how much farther it is to the North Pole." She knew he liked taking out his map and fooling with the compass he'd found in the pocket of one of the jackets he'd tried on. She had to shade her eyes to see the trail he'd mapped out. She didn't really know where she was pointing—somewhere between the house and the river. "Are we here?"

"I think we went around this mountain already. I think we're right here." He squinted against the morning sun. "You know what? Since we're the first ones here, we get to name all the mountains. Explorers always get to do that."

"Don't we have to climb to the top and plant a flag?"

"That's only when you're claiming the land for queen and country. Or president or whatever."

"And taking it away from the people who already live there?"

"This is the Arctic Circle. Nobody lives here." He laid a gloved hand on her padded shoulder. "Anyway, we can't climb these mountains. We might cause an avalanche. That's when the snow comes down—"

"I know what an avalanche is, Garth."

"Okay, so we're right here." He pointed to the map again. "We have to get around the garage and down this hill. Then we'll be here." *Here* looked like an X between two blips in the trail. "I wonder what happens to a compass when you're actually standing on the North Pole."

She had to get her feet moving again so her toes wouldn't freeze. "Let's go find out."

Ariel felt much better about having Tracy help her in the kitchen now that the wedding was off. Crystal was right about the flirting, but it came too naturally to be anything but the reincarnation of a relationship from the past. It was the kind of harmony that some people took for love at first sight. But it wasn't that simple. It was more like second sight, or cosmic hindsight.

Wait. *Cosmic hindsight.* Had she read that somewhere, or had it just come to her? She would have to remember to Google the term the next time she got on the Internet.

"I'm sorry you folks had to witness that whole scene," he was saying as he lifted tongs full of crisp bacon from the frying pan and arranged it on brown paper to drain. "Great example for the kids, huh?"

"Sometimes it can't be helped," she said, just for something to say. It was all the encouragement he needed. That and the coffee she refilled for him.

"I felt like I was goin' along for the ride, you know? Vera hooked us up, all excited about her being part of all this, and I'm ready for something different. But I wasn't ready for last night. It was like going out on a stage in front of a full house and having your pants fall down around your ankles."

"That would be awful," she said. "But at least you didn't have to worry about any spotlights, since the power was off."

"Right."

"Makes it a little easier. Gives you a bit of privacy, anyway."

"I just sat there and took it, like I always do. Like it doesn't mean anything."

"Water on a dog's back."

He shrugged. "Or off a duck's back, either one."

"Water doesn't roll off dogs. It soaks into their hair, and it chills them right down to the bone." She lowered the gas flame under the pan. He was ready for the eggs. "It must have been hard, finding out that way." She knew he knew what she meant.

"I had kinda gotten used to the idea," he said softly.

"More than just used to it, I'd say."

"Maybe so. Anyway, it's over, and I'm a free man. Which is not all it's cracked up to be."

"Well, Tracy, you'll just have to pull your boots up by the ankle straps and dry yourself off. Because you know what they say." She gave a sympathetic smile. "Nothing smells worse than wet duck."

It was Robin's turn to complain.

"Toto's getting tired, and my feet hurt."

"Mine, too. The snow's getting into the tops of these galoshes." He stuffed his precious map into his coat pocket, put his hands on his hips and surveyed the terrain. "Mostly the snow's deeper than I thought."

"It's a long way back to the house, Garth." She pointed to a place that was much closer. "What's that building by the river?"

"It used to be a stable, but now I think it's for storing stuff. I'm not supposed to go in there."

"But we need a place to rest before we go back."

"We're not going back until we reach the North Pole. It's not that far now."

"But Toto has to rest."

He stared at the building's pitched roof and boarded windows. "I guess we could try. It's probably locked, though."

But it wasn't. It wasn't much warmer inside, but the place was full of interesting stuff. There was a bunch of old lawn mowers, some funny rakes with wooden prongs, all kinds of shovels, big metal tubs, and even some saddles. Everything was covered with dust, but at least it wasn't snow.

"Look at all this stuff for horses," Robin said. She liked horses, but she only got to ride them when Daddy took her to see their other relatives. "Grandpa Louis has a team of horses that can pull a wagon, and he has collars for them just like this. And all these straps. And Grandpa Glen and Grandpa Dallas have saddles like this. And Grandpa Phillip has a fence made out of this all around his yard."

"Boy, Robin, how many grandfathers do you have?"

"A lot. Daddy says Indian kids get more grandpas than white kids. Most of mine live in South Dakota. Hey, look." She pointed to a ladder that went up through a hole in the ceiling. "Let's see what's up there."

"I don't know if we should go up there."

"Why not? It's light up there. You can see the windows on the outside." He was such a chicken sometimes. "We're explorers, aren't we?"

"We should just keep on track for the North Pole. Look." He pulled out his map again. "We're here, and the Pole is here, and then it's only this far back to the house."

"I'll just take a peek, okay? There might be something really cool. Like treasure. Wouldn't your mom be surprised if we found treasure?"

"I don't know. She says Aunt Margaret has to be richer than Bill Gates, but she's keeping it a secret until she dies."

Robin was already halfway up the ladder. "Maybe the secret is up here."

Birch found Rochelle hovering over her aunt, who was steadfast in her refusal to be moved from the River Porch. She wanted the sun on her face, she said, and she was determined to watch for deer.

"I'll make her stop bothering you, Miss Margaret, but I doubt you'll be seeing any deer out there today."

"They'll be foraging. I've already seen something moving out there. Raccoon, maybe."

"How about you doing a little foraging, Aunt Meg?" Rochelle pulled and tucked her patient's blankets around her. "Did you get any rest out here last night?"

"As much as Ariel would let me. Stoking up the fire and checking to see if I'm still breathing every five minutes like they do in the hospital."

"We'll stop checking as soon as we can get you together with your doctor. One way or another, that's going to happen today."

The old woman closed her eyes and sighed. "How many messages have you left so far?"

"A few." Rochelle held an imaginary receiver to her ear. "'If this is an emergency, press one if you have health insurance, two if you're on Medicare, three if you own your own home.'"

"Zero if there's no pulse." Miss Margaret offered a wan smile. "It's turning into a nice day."

A voice called out from the kitchen. "Breakfast!"

"Better find the kids," Birch said.

"About the spirits, Mr. Trueblood." Margaret lifted her hand from the quilt, and Birch leaned close to her mouth. "Are they family? Will I know them when I see them?"

"I believe you will."

"There's a song you sing for the one who's on her way. When the time comes, will you do that for me?"

"I will."

"Garth, I think I found the treasure." Robin's face appeared in the ceiling hole where the ladder went through. "Come up and see. There's nothing scary up here."

All he could see around her tannish face was the old-fashioned white shoulder cape that was part of that fancy girl's coat she was wearing with a furry white hat. She looked almost like an angel. But she was acting devilish.

"I'm not scared. I just don't want to get in any trouble."

"We won't be in any more trouble than we already are. There's a big trunk up here with a curved top. I need help getting it open."

He put one hand on the ladder and scanned the progression of rungs, bottom to top. Ladders made him nervous. He'd fallen off one once.

"I don't know, Robin, maybe we shouldn't open it. It probably has mice and bats and everything else in it."

"You're scared, aren't you?"

"All right, I'm coming up. One quick look, and then we're getting out of here." A few steps up he heard a creaky sound under his foot. "Robin, I don't think this ladder is very safe."

"I got up here, didn't I?" More creaky sounds above his head. "Hey, I got it open!"

Garth tried to quicken his climb, thinking he'd better get up there in case she ran into something with teeth.

"What's in it?" he called up.

"I don't know yet. Some more boxes. One's metal, like a money box or something. Are you coming, or not?"

"Yeah."

Whomp! Something up there slammed. Toto started barking wildly at the bottom of the ladder.

"What was that?" Garth's hands were shaking, but he made his feet keep moving. "Robin?"

Knock knock knock.

"Okay, I'm almost there. It's kind of…"

Bang bang bang.

Ruff ruff ruffruffruff.

"Shut up, Toto, don't make me look down!"

Finally his head popped through the ceiling. He located the trunk and kept his eyes on it while he stepped around the top of the ladder and away from the hole. She was right about the window allowing enough light to see, but it smelled worse up here than it did on the bottom floor—so dusty you could almost choke—and the place was a jumble of junk.

"Where are you?"

"I'm in here. Help me, Garth!"

"You dumb kid." He headed for the talking trunk. "What did you get in there for?"

"I fell. Get me out, Garth!"

He tried lifting the lid, but it wouldn't budge. She kept banging around inside. He had to admit, he would have been bawling by now, but so far she was just mad.

He found two latches on the front of the trunk, and they were firmly fastened. But somehow she'd gotten the thing open and gotten herself locked in. He pounded against one of the latches with his gloved fist, but it wouldn't give.

"Can you push against the lid?"

"I tried."

"Try with your feet."

"There isn't much room. Okay, I've got my knees up."

He was looking for a hammer or some other kind of tool.

"Where are you, Garth. I'm…" Kicking against the lid. He could hear it. "Garth, what are you doing? You have to help me!"

He found a metal pole thing and tried hitting it against one of the latches.

"It's all rusty. I think it's locked, Robin." This was really bad. "I think it's locked!"

"Oh, noooooo. It's dark in here."

She was finally crying. "Who's scared now?"

"Me! I'm scared. Go get my daddy!"

"They're gonna blame me for this."

"I'll tell them it was my idea to come up here."

"Yeah, but I'm older than you."

"So what! Go get my daddy right now!"

"Robin?" On hands and knees he took a turn around the old hump-backed trunk, feeling the sides and the top for some way to get her out. He found nothing but bad news. "I can't even find any holes in this thing. Try not to breathe too much, okay?"

"Can you please go get my daddy?" she wailed.

"It might take a while, so try not to be too scared, okay? Be really calm. That's important. Okay?" She was sobbing. He felt sick and scared, but he had to stay calm, too. "Say okay, Robin."

"Okay. But, Garth? Would you try to hurry?"

Birch stuck his head into the kitchen. "I'm looking for the kids, but there's no one upstairs," he told Crystal, who was helping herself to a cup of coffee. "The dress Robin was wearing is there, but I searched every room above this one."

"Try the basement."

At the top of the basement stairs, he met Ariel on her way up. "I'm looking for the kids."

"If they're down there, they're awful quiet. Maybe it's a game." Ariel did an about-face and trotted down the step yodeling, "Ally ally out's in free!"

A thorough search of the house yielded nothing but abandoned costumes and half a bag of marshmallows.

Crystal was put out. Garth knew better.

Birch was frantic. They couldn't have gone outside. Put Robin on Garth's shoulders and the snowdrifts would still be over her head. But Birch started looking for tracks. There was nothing on the driveway side of the house. A U-turn on the kitchen steps evidenced small feet making their discovery of an impassable exit.

"How the hell did they get out?" Birch shouted as he tromped across the kitchen, no longer concerned about what he was tracking in.

He ran into Rochelle in the foyer.

"Birch, Aunt Meg isn't doing well, and I can't get through to…" She frowned. "How did who get out?"

"The kids are nowhere in this house. They have to be outside somewhere, but the back door's practically drifted over, and there are no tracks out that way."

"There's a door downstairs that goes out beneath the River Porch, but we never—"

He grabbed her arm. "Show me."

"I'll take care of Miss Margaret," Ariel offered. She set aside a stack of plates. "Tracy, go all the way upstairs and see if you can see anything from the window."

* * *

Garth was scared. He'd heard about kids getting stuck in toy boxes and old refrigerators, and he knew it wouldn't take long for Robin to run out of air. Backtracking uphill in the snow wasn't so easy, and he had to get back to the house faster than his legs wanted to carry him. He'd tried calling for help, but no one answered. A little way down the path he tried again. This time he had a lot less breath. He could either stand there and scream, or run for help, but he couldn't do both. This wasn't a yard. It was more like a city park.

He fell twice. The first time, he lost his gloves. The second time, Toto started barking. It sounded like *Up! Up! Up!* and made him try harder and suck in too much cold air. But he got up, pulled his earflaps down and trudged on.

"Garth!"

He looked up. The dazzling sun made his eyes ache, but something was moving in one of the upstairs windows, and the voice belonged to a man. Tracy? Garth couldn't speak, so he waved.

"You okay down there? Where's Robin?"

Garth couldn't get the answer past his burning throat.

"Birch!" the voice in the window boomed. "I see Garth!"

"I can hear the dog!"

"You're close! Maybe twenty yards away."

Garth was getting dizzy, but he kept going, trying to run. His tears felt warm on his face at first, but they soon turned cold. His legs were acting like mixing beaters, spinning but not taking him anywhere.

Up! Up! Up!

"Garth, we're coming!"

Up! Up! Up!

And up Garth was lifted. Strong hands pulled him out of the snow and onto his feet. He sobbed and sobbed and slobbered all over Aunt Shelly's blue jacket.

"Where's Robin?"

"Unh—uhnnn-uhnnn…"

"Take a breath, honey. Here." She pulled her scarf off and wrapped it around his nose and mouth. "Slow down. Now, deep breath."

"She's in the trunk!"

"Trunk? What trunk?"

Garth pointed toward the stable with a half-frozen red hand. "She got…locked in…a big…"

"Show us!"

Rochelle led the way. Birch was close on her heels, carrying the bawling boy.

Locked, locked… Rochelle was sure the stable had been locked. It was always locked. No one ever went in there anymore. She couldn't remember when she'd been in there last, but she had checked the door the last time she'd strolled the grounds. It was a habit she'd learned from Aunt Meg. *Make sure the outbuildings are locked up.*

Sure enough, the door stood open. Birch set Garth on the concrete floor. Before anyone could ask, the boy pointed to the ladder. "Up there!"

Birch climbed up, taking two or three rungs at a time. The first thing he saw when he poked his head through the ceiling was his daughter. She was sitting in an old steamer trunk. The lid was open. She looked up and smiled.

Birch released the breath he'd unintentionally been holding.

Garth came up the ladder behind him, followed by Rochelle, who, after a heartfelt Thank God! had the presence of mind to ask the child if she was all right.

Robin reached up as her father wordlessly lifted her into his arms.

"How did you get it open?" Garth demanded. "I tried. I really tried."

"Didn't you see the lady?" Robin asked.

Birch lowered one knee to the floor beside the trunk, holding Robin on his other knee, touching her face, hands, hair as though she were newly born. His hands were shaking. He glanced into the box, horrified by the thought that she might have suffocated.

"What lady?" Rochelle asked. "Where?"

"She was just here. I think I was sort of falling asleep in there, but she opened the top, and I woke up, and she smiled at me."

Birch cleared the gravel from his throat. He knew exactly what lady. "What did she say?"

"Nothing. I told her thank you, and she just nodded her head, and then she looked down at these boxes in here, so I picked up this one—I thought she wanted to see it or something—but then she was gone. And look." Clearly none the worse for wear, Robin slid off Birch's knee and took an open metal box from the trunk. "Her picture's in here."

"This is the lady?" Birch wasn't surprised to be looking at the image of his ghost. She was dressed in riding clothes, posing beside a high-headed black horse.

"It's Rebecca." Rochelle sounded amazed.

"You know her?" Robin asked. "Does she live around here?"

"She used to."

"There's some more pictures of her in here, and a man—I think it's her husband or boyfriend—and some other stuff. Do you think she might be looking for it?"

"I think she came to help you," Rochelle said softly.

"And I know I owe her, big-time." Birch stood. "We've gotta get you and Garth back to the house and get you warmed up."

"I'm not cold at all," Robin said.

"I am," said Garth. "I'm f-freezing. And I didn't s-see anyone else out here. And that l-latch was stuck. I tried and t-tried to…"

"It's okay, sweetie. It's not your fault."

"We have to take these boxes with us." Robin closed the metal lid and reached inside the trunk for what looked like a letter box. "The lady might come back for them. Is the lady a friend of yours, Rochelle?"

"She's a friend of *mine*," Birch said.

Rochelle didn't know how long they'd been gone. They entered the house through the basement, and Crystal met them at the top of the steps. There was no joyous greeting for Garth, but neither was there a scolding. Crystal had news for her sister, and Rochelle knew instantly that it wasn't something she wanted to hear. Her stomach turned over and backed its way into her throat. She felt dizzy. Crystal never called her Rochelle.

"Aunt Meg?"

Crystal nodded, took her hand and led her to the

River Porch, where Ariel sat waiting. Eyes closed, face ashen, Margaret Bruner had gone still.

"The light went out of her eyes, Shelly. It was as quick and peaceful as that," Ariel said.

"Was there…" Rochelle stumbled against a chair and sank into it. Her lips trembled over the word. "Pain?"

"I don't think she felt it coming. I didn't want to upset her, so I didn't say anything about the children, but I think she knew something was going on."

"What did she say?"

"She asked me what time it was. I leaned over to check the clock, but before I could say anything, she lifted her hand and said, *Good.* She said it twice. And then she was gone."

Birch stood at Miss Margaret's feet and sang a death song to let the spirits know who was coming.

Rochelle stretched her arm across the quilt, laid her head on her Aunt Meg's body, closed her eyes, and used the rhythm of her own beating heart to bring the dear woman's last words to life inside herself.

Good. Good.

Chapter Sixteen

The artifacts from the trunk had been set aside the day Aunt Meg died. Rochelle had looked at them once or twice, but each time she'd put them away for another day. She had more immediate cares and concerns through the course of the longest, snowiest winter in her thirty-year memory. She missed Aunt Meg. She missed Birch and Robin, even though they called often. They made plans that were canceled more often than not due to the dismal, tiresome weather. They spoke vaguely of a future together, dancing around their hopes as though speaking of them might call down some greater fear. It was all due to the weather, Rochelle told herself, especially the pressing, crushing, never-ending grayness.

Rochelle wondered aloud whether Rebecca had experienced a winter this bad. Ariel—who was getting her share of calls from Tracy—suggested they

"Google it," but Rochelle didn't have the heart to go digging around in old snowdrifts. She knew that she had it worse than Rebecca when the weatherman reported that the all-time record had just been buried under another six inches.

She had never been happier to welcome spring to Rosewood. And with it, an unexpected midweek visit from Birch, who joined her on Cupid's Bench with, he said, a proposition for her.

She held her breath.

"What are you doing next school year?" he asked mysteriously as they watched the nearby dam become a turbulent waterfall.

"I don't know. I'd like to get back into the classroom."

"We need a fourth-grade teacher at the Mille Lacs school. It's a lot closer than Minneapolis. I could set up an interview."

She said nothing. It wasn't the proposition she'd expected.

He shrugged and turned his attention back to the drama of the mighty Mississippi rushing through the floodgates. "It's something to think about."

"I have to make a decision about Rosewood."

"What are your options?"

"We could sell," she said quietly. It would be a huge project. "Start with a humongous yard sale.

Sell all the garden tools and the knickknacks. Then an estate sale to sell the furniture, then list the collectibles on eBay. I don't know about the antiques. Aunt Meg would have a contact for that, I'm sure. But she's not here." She scowled at him. "I'm keeping the dolls. I don't care what you say."

"I didn't say anything."

"Well, you asked. After that, we call somebody like our best old ex-future mother-in-law-*in-law*, Vera, and see about listing the property."

"Mother-in-law-in-law?"

"What do you call your sister's ex-future mother-in-law?"

"Bitch."

"Right. Okay, so option one, we could sell."

"Which you don't want to do."

"But Crystal does. Crystal gets a share from anything that's sold, but according to the will, it's my decision." She held up two fingers. "Option two, we keep the place and make a go of the business."

"Which takes time."

"And money, which is going to be in short supply after taxes. Either way, the big inheritance Crystal is looking for just isn't there."

"But those are your options?"

She stared at the opposite shore, squinting into the sun. "I'm not crazy about either one of them. I think about the first one, and I hear Aunt Meg playing 'Gone With the Wind.' And I don't know if I can afford the other one."

"I've got something to show you."

He took a piece of paper from his shirt pocket, unfolded it, and showed her a copy of a newspaper article. The headline read Log Jam Kills One, Injures Four.

"This is about my great-grandmother's husband, the river pig I told you about. I got to thinking his death in 1914 might have been news, so I searched some old newspapers and found this. Walter Krause. Says he emigrated from Germany in 1907 and worked as a stable hand for Martin Bruner before he went to work for the logging company."

"I thought we more or less agreed…" She cut herself off and read the article, which said little more, but no less than Birch's telling of it. It was a name, another connection. She returned the paper. "Those boxes are still sitting in the office. I've been walking around that metal one like it's a big hole. Don't want to step in it, can't bring myself to fill it in."

"Is this about you and me?"

"It's about Martin Bruner. It's about whether he was the father of Rebecca's son." There it was again, the possibility that had turned her aunt away from the search for answers and made Rochelle queasy, as well. Especially when she took the next step. "And Mary Krause's son."

"I've looked, Rochelle. Trueblood was born in 1902, but there's no record of who his father was. I don't want to believe it was Bruner any more than you do, but from what we know, I'd say the odds are pretty good that he was."

"I know."

The sat quietly, side by side, the river churning below them, eddying past the rocks.

Finally he took her hand. "Are you ready?"

She couldn't say.

"We have to lay her to rest, Rochelle."

She led him slowly back to the house and into her office. She wasn't sure Rebecca's restless spirit figured into her reluctance to open the lid on the mysterious box, but she didn't doubt Birch's sincerity. She was glad he was there to help her take the box down from the shelf and look inside. She knew it was time.

Among the photographs they found in the metal box, there was one of a man on a horse. *Walter Krause with Venture* was written on the back. Rebecca was shown on the same horse in a picture that was dated 12 September 1909 on the back. Another photograph showed a man straddling two floating logs. Written on the back: *From Walter—This is me walking on water, Spring, 1910.*

"Wasn't that when that postcard to her sister was written?—1910?" Birch recalled. "So she spent time up there that summer, and Walter was up there working. And she kept these pictures in a safe place, which means they meant something to her. What's in that letter box?"

The letters were from Rebecca to her sister. Together Rochelle and Birch concluded that the trunk in the stable loft had belonged to Rose, who had saved these bits and pieces, memories of Rebecca. The letters spanned a number of years and revealed the highs and the lows in Rebecca's personality. But there were no letters to Rose in New York during the summer of 1910.

"What do you think that was about?" Rochelle wondered. "No letters that summer."

"I think Martin intercepted that postcard and who knows what else. Or maybe they were keeping each other's secrets." Birch flicked at the photograph with his finger. "And I think this Krause was a busy man that summer. Trueblood's sister was a baby when the village was burned a year later."

"Maybe the marriage was arranged. The man worked for Bruner, after all. Maybe he wanted to make sure that Mary was taken care of." Rochelle took a white envelope from the bottom of the metal box and opened the flap.

"There are all kinds of possibilities here, but no proof of anything."

"Here's proof." She showed him the document from the envelope. "Baby boy, live birth, May 27, 1911, mother Rebecca Richard, father Walter Krause."

He stared at her. Finally one corner of his mouth began to twitch. "So your great-grandfather was actually the stable hand."

"The river pig," she said, grinning.

"You're not even related to Martin Bruner."

"Not blood kin, anyway. But aren't we all related?"

"Yeah." Birch looked at her great-grandfather's birth certificate again in disbelief. "Jesus, Rochelle, you're not related to him, and I am." He tipped his head back and laughed. "Martin Bruner was *my* great-grandfather."

"But only in the white man's way."

"Blood kin!"

They looked at each other, amazed. They could hardly believe, couldn't say why, and couldn't hold it in. They both burst out laughing.

Ariel found them sitting knee to knee, holding their sides and laughing like children.

"What the *h e* double toothbrushes is going on in here?"

Birch composed himself long enough to explain, "We're just comparing family trees."

Ariel looked at them like they were both crazy. For more proof, they laughed hysterically.

"I cannot tell a lie." Rochelle tried to get hold of herself with little success as she pointed at Birch. "It was *his* great-grandfather…who…who chopped them all down!"

"And hers…hers was just a river pig!"

Ariel tsked. "By the looks of it, you both have close relatives swinging from branch to branch."

"No, no, that's the beauty of it. We're not—" Rochelle covered her mouth, took her hand away and rolled the words on a wheeze *"—blood kin."*

"What's that supposed to mean?" Ariel demanded, loath to be left out. "Some kind of *yo mama* thing?"

"Good one, Ariel. It means…" Birch caught Rochelle's attention, straight face, serious look in his eyes. "It means she has to make a decision."

Rochelle cleared her throat and glanced from one to the other.

"Well, Ariel, we were just talking about the hard choice we have to make between the two options we have for Rosewood. Do we sell everything, or should we try to make a go of the business? Either way, we've got taxes, taxes everywhere and not a penny in cash. How funny is that?"

"I don't know about *we*, Shelly, but there's a third option for you," Ariel said. "You could follow Miss Margaret's example. You could give it away."

"Give it away," Rochelle echoed. Not that she hadn't thought of it, but how would such a thing work? "To the people of Mille Lacs? Would they want a white elephant in Little Falls?"

"We could turn it into a casino," Birch said.

"Oh." She looked at him. Was he kidding?

"Which is why it's not that easy to give land back to the Indians," he explained. "It would be taken out of the city tax base and put into federal trust. The city, the Ojibwe, the Bureau of Indian Affairs, they all have a say."

"It really ought to go to you, Birch," Rochelle said.

"That isn't the decision I'm looking for, woman."

"I'm not making this suggestion just dillydally," Ariel injected. "I've done some footwork. Is anyone interested in what I found out?"

"Absolutely." Rochelle sat up straight, straightened her skirt, got her face on straight.

Ariel took a seat on the corner of the desk and launched her report.

"My cousin Wheezy has been on the city council for years. She says they've actually talked about this, because they see Rosewood as part of the city's history. It's the best historic site we have, and the old house, with all the original furnishings, well, it's like taking a step back in time. Wheezy thinks they'd be open to some kind of an arrangement whereby Rosewood becomes city property but you own the business. You get the historical society in on it, and you've got tax breaks galore, plus city maintenance for the grounds, plus the bed-and-breakfast has a chance of paying off, plus you get to have—"

"Where do I sign?" Rochelle asked, jumping to her feet. "Crystal's going to be so furious, she'll probably come to the wedding just to torture me. And if she doesn't, she'd better send Garth."

"Wedding?" Delighted, Ariel switched gears. "What wedding?"

"Yeah, what wedding?" Birch said indolently. "I've been waiting to hear you say you'll marry me, but you jumped right over that part. A wedding takes time. We should have been married months ago."

"During which snowstorm?" Rochelle wanted to know.

Birch rose to the challenge. They stood nose-to-nose.

"Say it."

"I love you."

"And?"

Rochelle smiled. "And let's get married."

"Can you be ready in an hour? We'll pick Robin up at school and head over to—"

"I want a real wedding. If we don't have our wedding here, the spirits will never let you hear the end of it."

"Why don't they ever bother you? Or *you?*" he said, turning his demand on Ariel.

"I should probably leave you two alone. Will you let me know how this turns out?"

"I can tell you right now," Birch said. "The holy man takes a wife, the wife takes a child and the cheese gets eaten at the wedding." He took Rochelle's hands in his. "Traditional circle dance."

"Now that the gardens are in bloom, how about an outdoor wedding?" Ariel chattered. "The pictures will be gorgeous, and we'll use them in our advertising. We'll use the arbor so that we have a view of the river and the rose garden. It'll be splendid."

Rochelle nodded, but she only had eyes for Birch. "Weather permitting, of course."

When the sun defied the weatherman's forecast for afternoon showers, Birch had a hunch that it was the spirits permitting. In typical Minnesota fashion, the guests marveled at their good fortune, weatherwise. Crystal even teased him about "raising holy hell" with the rain gods. He laughed and allowed her to buss his cheek in that hoity-toity way of hers. Unfortunately, she was about to become family.

Fortunately, she didn't figure to be around much.

His bride wore an updated version of Rose Bruner's wedding dress that she'd had made at a local shop. Robin wore her jingle dress and performed with her dance troupe. But there would be no costume for this groom—no beaver hat, no funny-looking tie, no suffocating suit. Since the pictures meant a lot to Rochelle, he wore a plain black shirt, pants and boots to set off her white gown. And his understated smile. Later they would look at the pictures for the first time and come across one where he was flashing her that signature smile—it was all in the eyes—and there on his cheek would be a light bubble. Ariel would allay his sick feeling that it was Crystal's kiss of death when she proclaimed it a "spirit orb." Rochelle would be sure that it was effected by the camera flash. Unconvinced, Birch would simply smile. He was fine with being less certain about these things than either Ariel or Rochelle.

But he was sure of one thing. He knew how to

get to her, and by the look in her eyes when she saw him waiting for her beneath the vine-covered arbor, he knew he'd hit the mark.

And she took his breath away.

A string quartet provided music for her stroll down the garden path. The dappled shade caressed her satin-draped curves and played over the white flowers in her hair. She came to him unescorted, or seemed to be. In his mind's eye he saw a host of spirits leading the way. He wasn't actually seeing anyone but the woman he was about to marry, but he had a feel for them, a sense of their celebration. He felt more of them standing at his shoulder.

And they were all related.